Praise for

The Shiro Project

"An extremely talented writer."

— *Noir suspense*

"Suspense done to perfection."

—*Le Monde*

"A well-written, fast-paced, intelligent and well-documented thriller."

—TV host Gérard Collard

"Find of the year."

—*Ouest-France*

"Mossad, Japan, bacteriological weapons—all the ingredients of an impeccably written thriller."

—*Page Library Journal*

Praise for *The Bleiberg Project*

"A solid thriller."

—*Publishers Weekly*

"*The Bleiberg Project* is a fun, fast-paced thriller that is over all too quickly.'

—Jessica Howard, *Shelf Awareness*

"A unique, exceptional thriller... a phenomenon."

—TV host Gérard Collard

"Khara's thriller, with its pared-down prose, pell-mell pace, and extreme brevity, might remind some of Ian Fleming's Bond novels or Adam Hall's Quiller series.... A quick read to be savored."

—*Library Journal*

"An astounding thriller."

—*Tele7jours*

"The plot is inventive, intricate and moves at warp speed. The chapters dealing with the war are chilling & heart wrenching. The dialogue is a bit choppy in places but this may be due to translation... If you're a fan of Dan Brown, Steve Berry or Daniel Silva, you should enjoy this one."

—*Reader review*

"He was this amazing, scarred man who didn't allow himself to have anything other than the work he did and we find out why in The Bleiberg Project. That part of the story was riveting. The fight scenes were awesome and jumped off the page when you read them."

—*5-star GoodReads review*

"This book kept me completely involved from the first page. The suspense is incredible because all the events take place in a matter of days. And they are action-packed days. Khara did his research and used it to weave a tale so believable you'll find yourself shuddering because it could be happening right now."

—*Criminal Element*

"Khara has written a fast-paced race-against-time thriller with sympathetic characters. Everyone has a secret, it seems, and it is this vulnerability of each of the main characters that serves as a stark contrast to the power seekers for whom life is cheap.... This is a thriller that fans of John Grisham, Robert Ludlum or Ian Fleming will enjoy."

—*The Birch Bark*

The Shiro Project

A Consortium Thriller

David Khara

Translated from French by Sophie Weiner

LE FRENCH BOOK

All rights reserved: no part of this publication may be reproduced or transmitted by any means, electronic, mechanical, photocopying or otherwise, without the prior permission of the publisher.

First published in France as
Le Projet Shiro
by Editions Critic
©2011 Editions Critic

Published by special arrangement with Editions Critic in conjunction with their duly appointed agents L'Autre agence, Paris and 2 Seas Literary Agency

English translation ©2014 Sophie Weiner
First published in English in 2014
by Le French Book, Inc., New York

http://www.lefrenchbook.com

Translator: Sophie Weiner
English-language editor: Amy Richards
Proofreader: Chris Gage
Cover designer: David Zampa

ISBNs:
Trade paperback: 9781939474247
Hardback: 9781939474254
E-book: 9781939474230

This is a work of fiction. Any resemblance to actual persons, living or dead, is purely coincidental. For the purposes of the story, the author took authorial license with references to historical events, places, facts and people.

The power of man has grown in every sphere,
except over himself.
—Winston Churchill

PROLOGUE

Men lie.
Women lie.
Guns always tell the truth.
More or less…

PROLOGUE

CHAPTER 1

US Army Base Fort Detrick, Maryland, 1957

The loudspeakers were past their prime and certainly never intended for blasting rock 'n' roll. They gave off some static, but Elvis Presley's seductive voice filled the entire laboratory and most likely all seven floors of the building. The use of military equipment for these purposes wouldn't have been tolerated during regular hours. But late at night, when higher-ups and other old fogeys from the med school weren't around, such diversions were standard practice—especially since Dr. Philip Neville had joined the staff. The talented English chemist loved the fifties rhythms, which just begged for hip shaking and pelvis thrusting. And he never missed a chance to show off his dance moves.

At any rate, "Jailhouse Rock" enlivened the monotonous atmosphere of the research center and didn't really bother the few people present at this late hour.

Professor Jane Woodridge tolerated the rule-bending, as long as it didn't interfere with their work. The biochemist even succumbed to the music on occasion, tapping her foot to the beat when no one was looking. Away from the watchful eyes of colleagues, she could slough off some of the professional veneer and relax a bit.

4   DAVID KHARA

For the moment, she was allowing herself to be amused by Neville, who was rocking to Elvis while leafing through the reports on experiments conducted by that day's team.

What we're dealing with here is serious enough, she said to herself. We shouldn't let it get the better of us.

Neville seemed to read her mind. He picked up a jar of pencils—his improvised microphone—held it to his mouth, and began belting out the lyrics.

The magic moment was over. The Elvis impersonation had gone far enough. Sure, Neville had the moves, but his resemblance to the King stopped there.

Jane glared at her colleague. Under the heat of her stare, Neville lowered his voice and then settled for mouthing the words without making any noise at all.

"Phil, could you please bring me the registration receipt for the new pathogens?"

Neville sauntered toward the tall metal filing cabinets, opened a drawer, and set about searching through the suspended folders.

"Sorry, I can't find it. It must be in the general's office."

Jane got up with a heavy sigh. She walked over to Neville and gave the contents of the drawer a weary look. She pulled out a manila folder and waved it under his nose with a condescending smile.

"If you're more interested in dancing than scientific research, send your résumé to Hollywood," she said, returning to her desk. "Who knows, maybe some producer out there is looking for the next Donald O'Connor."

The music ended.

"I'll think about it," her colleague replied as he dropped into his chair. "Life is short, and I don't see myself rotting away here. How can you stand working

THE SHIRO PROJECT   5

in this stronghold four nights a week, especially with a kid at home?"

"That's none of your business," Jane responded. The familiarity offended her. "I love my son, if you must know. I do the best I can to balance my career and family life. Luckily, my husband is remarkable, extraordinary even."

"He must be, seeing that he puts up with sleeping alone half the week."

"You're being rude, and I don't appreciate it. Like it or not, I care deeply about my job."

Neville raised an eyebrow. "Ah yes, we're working for the glory of Uncle Sam. Concocting antidotes for our soldiers and citizens in the event of biological warfare—quite a noble task."

"Do I sense a hint of sarcasm?"

"That's not my style. Hey, if the soviets are capable of using that kind of weapon, what makes you think we wouldn't do the same?"

"Democracy, communism. The differences seem obvious to me," Jane answered, her lips pursed.

"Of course, the nation of liberty and justice for all would never dirty its hands with methods so vile and contradictory to the Geneva Protocol, which we haven't ratified, may I remind you."

The young man leaned back in his chair, visibly satisfied with the correctness of his viewpoint. But Jane refused to let him have the upper hand.

"What are you trying to tell me? That we're not developing treatments, but weapons instead? That's absurd! Leave the politics to the professionals, and concentrate on your dancing or, better yet, on your work."

"Tell me, Jane, don't you wonder why access to certain sections of the two lower levels are off-limits to us?"

The woman gave herself a few seconds to reflect, adjusting the bun at the nape of her neck. She reinserted two pins in her blond hair and then spoke solemnly.

"We're studying the reactions of test subjects injected with agents and creating the proper countermeasures. I don't see how access to storage units with viral strains concerns us."

"The company line, as usual. I'm convinced there's a hidden agenda."

"Then go complain to the authorities. I'm not stopping you. While you're concocting your dark theories, I'll be in the lab," she said as she glanced at the clock on the wall. "Time for the daily log. The office is all yours."

"Say hi to the guinea pigs for me."

Jane left the room and headed toward the elevators. She waved to the two military police officers patrolling the hallway. They always looked so creepy, more the punch-in-your-face sort than the type inclined to give a respectful salute. The elevator doors slid open, and she scurried inside.

Neville's skeptical nature was borderline eccentric. But he was right about life being too short. And working at the US Army Medical Research Institute for Infectious Diseases had been weighing on her since her son Sean's birth. Her husband supported her career and did his part at home. She felt privileged. Most other women were stuck being housewives, not because they had chosen the life, but because it was expected, and there were few alternatives. Jane hoped that she could serve as a role model for other women who yearned for more independence and opportunity. But she missed her son, and she could not wait for the workweek to end so that she could go home and enjoy those three days with her boy and her man.

THE SHIRO PROJECT   7

As the elevator sank into the depths of the building, she pondered what to do about Neville. If he continued to carelessly speculate about their work, she would have to notify her superiors, because the base wasn't just conducting research; it was involved in the production of biological weapons. For now, Neville's security clearance denied him access to such sensitive information. In light of his comments, she would recommend that he be denied that access permanently and be put under heightened surveillance.

The elevator finally stopped, and the doors opened onto a long room whose walls were lined with cages. A musky smell saturated the air, and shrill screams rose from the pens, where monkeys were jumping wildly against the sides of their cages. Practically every night, she would come down to the lower levels to check on the primates and see if any were dying.

The shrieking from the cages intensified as she walked toward them.

"Don't worry, my sweethearts. I'm not coming for you this time, but for your friend," she said as she continued past the animals.

At the end of the room, there was a reinforced metal door equipped with a large handle. Jane opened a small hatch in the wall to reveal a lock. She inserted the key that she jealously guarded in her pocket.

With a loud mechanical click, the door opened. Behind it was a large room with sad green walls. Two carts holding the instruments Jane used in her experiments were waiting beside a small bed.

A man in his twenties—the reason for her visit tonight—lay there, covered in a blue sheet. He moaned faintly. The sedatives were wearing off. From the pocket of her lab coat, Jane pulled out a small notebook and a pencil. She examined the patient's face.

Pus trickled from blisters around his discolored lips. Along the sides of his inflamed nostrils were clusters of ready-to-burst boils. The exposed part of his chest was similarly disfigured.

Jane was pleased to note the normal progression of symptoms and scribbled her observations in her notebook.

"Hang in there a little longer," she said. "Two or three days from now, we'll initiate treatment."

The only response was an agonized groan.

After injecting the young man with more sedative, Jane headed back. She had what she needed. She wished her monkey sweethearts a pleasant night and found her way to the exit. Just two more hours with Professor Neville, and then her shift would be over.

Jane stepped into the elevator, eager to wrap things up. But when she arrived at her floor, the doors refused to budge. Jane cursed the incompetence of the maintenance crew. Breakdowns occurred often, too often for her liking. She was about to pick up the elevator's black telephone to tell off the orderly, when the base loudspeakers started blasting an ear-splitting siren.

Jane pressed her hands over her ears to muffle the excruciating noise. Then the wailing stopped. It was replaced by a man's voice, which Jane identified as that of the duty officer.

"Attention, all personnel. Due to a security breach in sector four, we ask that you calmly make your way toward the emergency exits."

Jane's eyes widened with surprise. She felt her heartbeat speed up and her scalp tingle with sweat. "This is no time to panic," she said to herself. "Think fast."

She took a deep breath and held it. Jane frantically pushed the button for one floor up, where her designated exit was located. The elevator didn't move, but the doors finally opened.

Then she saw the guards sprawled on the floor. Their dogs were lying all around them, vomiting and shaking. The virus was already spreading throughout the facility. The alert had been broadcast too late. There was not a moment to lose.

You breathe, you die, she told herself as she rushed toward an open door on her right. She entered the stairwell and heaved herself up the steps two at a time. An object was rolling toward her. A jar of pencils. She stepped over Phil Neville, who lay dying on the steps. He stretched out a hand in her direction but was unable to grab her ankle. Jane thought of her husband, her son, her flaming lungs and repeated over and over, "You breathe, you die."

She found the corridor. A little more effort and she'd be out of this hellhole. Jane grabbed the metal door handle and pushed. It didn't open. She thrust with both hands, using all the strength she had. Nothing happened. She couldn't hold out for more than a few seconds. With tears streaming down her cheeks, she pounded and kicked.

Those bastards had locked the exits shut! As soon as the sector had lost its airtight seal, the virus had spread, and then it was lockdown. Now the brick-and-steel building was one big tomb.

Jane Woodridge leaned against the door and slid to the floor. She closed her eyes, visualized Sean's sweet chubby face, and filled her lungs a final time.

CHAPTER 2

The outskirts of Pardubice, Czech Republic, 2011

The radio was playing a cover of a Four Seasons tune from the sixties, "Beggin'." It was a pretty decent version by Madcon, a Norwegian hip-hop duo. Branislav Poborsky pounded along on his car's steering wheel as he sang the English words—at least the ones he recognized. The catchy beat gave him a shot of much-needed energy.

He was heading into familiar territory as he drove along the narrow road that snaked through the forest—so lush and dense at this time of year. Each mile racked up on the dash took him that much farther away from Prague. This was all he needed to feel relieved. There was nothing better than a week of vacation with his parents in Pardubice.

True to form, his mother would pamper him with homemade goodies.

"With your demanding job, plus all the stress of living in a big city, I'm sure you're not eating properly," she had said to him time and again. "You're so pale and stick thin. To think you had such chubby red cheeks, like apples, when you were little."

Just for fun, he would argue a bit, but he didn't want to get into a full-fledged fight. He would never change her set-in-stone Polish opinions.

THE SHIRO PROJECT   11

His dad, in turn, would subject him to an all-out interrogation. He would want to know everything about his pride and joy's career. It was the workaholic's way of staying connected to the demanding world he had left three years earlier. As production director at the Paramo factory, Branislav's father had provided his family with a more than comfortable lifestyle in communist Czechoslovakia. The Velvet Revolution hadn't hurt their finances at all—just the opposite. With democracy came unbridled economic liberalism, and foreign investors rushed to a new market that offered excellent growth prospects. Vladek Poborsky had left Paramo and become a consultant for big companies that wanted to locate in the Pardubice region. It was a profitable career change. Vladek was able to buy a luxurious home for his family on the shores of Sec Dam, and because his new line of work was much more leisurely than his old one, he could relax and call himself semiretired.

Branislav couldn't dream of a better place to forget his distress. His marriage was foundering, and divorce seemed inevitable. Maybe he should have spent less time at his job and more time with his wife, who was herself caught up in a career as a television makeup artist. But in the end, what did it matter? It was obviously too late to dwell on what had gone wrong. He needed to focus on the future. Thank God they didn't have any kids. That would have made the legal proceedings and emotional recovery a whole lot messier.

Branislav glanced at himself in the rearview mirror. His thick chestnut-brown hair complemented his gray-brown eyes. At the moment, however, he looked much older than his thirty years. His eyelids were drooping, and the five o'clock shadow on his pasty white cheeks was growing darker by the mile. He sighed.

12   DAVID KHARA

Just as Branislav was fixing his eyes on the road again, something flashed in the mirror. A headlight was looming up from behind. A motorcycle. It came within inches of his bumper before swerving over to pass. Mr. Hot Wheels slowed down a bit and then shot off without any concern for safety.

"Jackass," Branislav shouted. "You think you're invincible? You could've killed us both. Motocross season hasn't started yet, dickhead."

Branislav glanced at the dashboard clock. Another twenty minutes, and he would be at the family manse. In half an hour, he would be enjoying a nice glass of wine, lounging in a comfortable deck chair, and admiring the rippling reflection of the trees on the crystal-clear lake.

A jarring noise from above shook him out of his daydream. He leaned against the steering wheel and stared at the sky through the windshield. Two low-flying helicopters. They were large carriers displaying the Czech Republic colors: white, red, and blue. A smaller aircraft was close behind. It bore the NATO insignia.

Branislav's journalist instincts kicked in. Something was going on. He had been so intent on getting to his haven, he hadn't realized that his car was the only one on the road. Sure, he wasn't driving on a major highway, but to be so completely isolated—with the exception of that crazy motorcyclist—for such a long distance? And what about that biker? Where was he racing off to? Where were those helicopters going? Branislav slowed down and parked on the side of the road. He got out of the car, lit a cigarette, and took out his cell phone. He entered his parents' number.

The phone rang three times. Then an automated voice responded, "Your call cannot be completed as dialed. Please hang up and try again." He tried calling

the newsroom. Again, three rings and the same re-
corded message. He entered a bunch of other numbers,
all yielding the same result.

No other wheels in sight, three military choppers,
no way of making calls. Branislav needed to find out
what was happening and somehow get hold of his ed-
itors. He slid behind the wheel of his car and started
driving again.

A mile later, he came to a bend in the road and
found himself face-to-face with three police cars.
Branislav slammed on his brakes to avoid driving
over the spiked traffic strips. Six officers brandished
machine guns. Two of them started walking toward
him. He got out, grabbed his old light-blue jacket, and
went to meet them.

"Hello, officers. What's going on here?"

He flashed a friendly grin but got no smiles in return.

"This road is closed, sir," one of them said. "Please
turn your car around and leave."

Branislav glanced over the officers' shoulders.

"Yes, I can see the road is closed, but could you tell
me why?"

"Sorry, sir, we can't tell you anything. Please return
to your vehicle and leave."

The officers' all-business demeanor dissuaded him
from pulling out his press pass. Branislav figured they
were holdovers from the communist days and wouldn't
honor it anyway. And even though they were polite,
they were wielding their machine guns a little too
nervously for his comfort. No point in sticking around
with these guys. He knew other ways to get to his
destination.

Branislav nodded and gave them the peace sign
as he headed back to his car. He got in and made a
U-turn under high surveillance.

As soon as he was out of sight, he parked his car and grabbed his camera. He hung it around his neck and walked into the forest, which he knew better than his mother's poppy seed cake.

He figured he was three miles from the nearest village. Taking into account the hilly terrain, he estimated that his hike would take a good hour, maybe an hour and a half, considering he had more baggage around the waist than when he was a kid running around these hills. It was late afternoon, but his run-in with the police had piqued his curiosity, and anyway, he knew he could use a little exercise.

The trek was rougher than he had expected and he cursed his leather loafers, whose smooth soles kept slipping on the roots of hundred-year-old oak trees and mossy stones.

When he finally reached the edge of the forest, he shoved aside the branches blocking his view. About a hundred feet below, a village of pink-and-white houses shimmered in the sun. Their flower-adorned balconies would have been the final touch on any postcard image. But the scene before him was no wish-you-were-here greeting.

The sidewalks were littered with bodies. Men and women were sprawled on the ground in awkward positions. Dotting the landscape were shopping carts filled with produce purchased at markets on the square. Branislav spotted motionless cars on the main street. Drivers and passengers lay lifeless in their metal coffins.

Branislav threw up. He wiped his mouth and steadied himself enough to resume his assessment. Military tanks surrounded the village. Branislav spotted the three helicopters in the middle of a meadow. He forced himself to take another look at the bodies.

Two men in white suits were working their way around the corpses. Carrying large suitcases, they were taking long, slow strides, like astronauts on the moon.

What the hell was going on here? Energized, Branislav removed the lens cap from his camera. This was a story, and he was going to cover it. He focused his camera and began shooting.

"Put down the camera, and slowly put your hands in the air."

The voice was almost robotic.

"Now!"

The tone didn't inspire disobedience. Branislav complied, careful of his every move.

"Turn around."

Branislav did as told, his hands to the sky. In front of him were three men wearing dark uniforms and gas masks. They were pointing machine guns equipped with silencers and laser beams. Nothing close to average military gear.

One of the men approached him and conducted a brusque search of his pockets. He took out Branislav's wallet and handed it to one of the others, presumably his superior. The latter examined the contents carefully.

"Look, gentlemen, I'm a reporter. What you're doing is a clear violation of—"

"Shut up, and turn around!"

Branislav complied again.

"I need to know what your end game is here. Believe me, you'll be in big trouble when my editor reports this to the government."

Sometimes bluffing worked, Branislav said to himself.

"Shoot him."

Sometimes it didn't.

16   DAVID KHARA

He closed his eyes, steeling himself for what would follow. Surprisingly, his thoughts veered to his soon-to-be ex-wife. Maybe there was still hope for them. Damn it, this was supposed to be a vacation, not his execution at the hands of a special-forces team. He was hoping for a quick bullet in the middle of his skull. A rush of fear-induced adrenaline swept over him. He was burning up, and his legs were like jelly. Why the hell were those bastards taking so long to kill him?

"Your biceps are gonna cramp up if you stay like that, buddy."

Someone was talking to him...in English?

Branislav turned around and risked opening an eye. He saw the three men lying on the ground. Two of them had slit throats. The third was writhing with a knife in his neck. He spat up blood before stopping dead-cold in an absurd position at the feet of a bald superhuman-sized man. The giant, who was wearing jeans and a green army jacket, leaned over and pulled the impressive serrated blade from his victim's neck. The stranger was clean-shaven, extremely clean-shaven, no eyebrows even.

"Who... Who are you? What's this shit mess? Did you kill all three of them? What the hell is going on?" Branislav grilled him in a muddled mix of Czech and English.

"Is that all you want to know?" the giant asked, grinning. He took out a cigar and stuck it between his teeth, then pulled out matches and lit it. "Will you be really pissed off if I don't answer your questions in order?"

Branislav shook his head and lowered his arms.

"All right. Yeah, I killed those assholes. It was them or you. As for what's going on here, I want to know as

THE SHIRO PROJECT   17

much as you do. And I'm afraid this shit mess is just the first in a long series of shit storms."

The reporter started to pick up his camera, which had fallen to the ground with the first soldier.

"Sorry, buddy," Baldy said as he took the camera. "That's the one thing my services are going to cost you. I need those pics."

Branislav was about to complain but changed his mind. No news story was worth more than his life. If this dude wanted the photos, they were all his.

Then he remembered his parents.

"My mother and father. They live nearby."

"Only this village was affected," the giant answered. "If they were here, they're dead. If they live somewhere else, especially if they were inside, you've got nothing to worry about."

"They live about two and a half miles northeast of here, but the only road that goes by—"

"Then relax. They're fine. Thanks for the cam. I'll send it back to your paper. Grab your stuff and scoot before any more goons show up. I don't plan on destroying the entire Czech special forces. I'm going to get my bike and peace out, like you. There's nothing more either of us can do here."

"That was you who passed by me earlier, wasn't it?"

"Yep. An important piece of info, right? You'll sleep better tonight, I'm sure," he said with the hint of a smirk. "I slipped into the forest ahead of you. I followed you. Then I followed them as they were following you. Pretty lucky, right? Now hurry up. Oh, and if you want to stay alive, don't say a word about what you saw here. Got it?"

"Got it," Branislav responded as he headed back into the forest. After a few steps, he stopped and turned around.

18   DAVID KHARA

"You didn't answer one of my questions."

"Which one?"

"Who are you? I'd like to put a name on the face of the man who saved my neck."

The stranger took a drag of his cigar and exhaled a puff of smoke.

"Call me Eytan. Oh, you forgot something," he said, tossing Branislav his wallet.

The bald man grinned, the cigar clamped between his teeth. Branislav returned a hesitant smile and continued walking into the forest.

Eytan watched him disappear and then positioned himself in the spot where the journalist had been taking pictures of the village. He spent a long time observing the scene. In the name of what madness had these people been sacrificed?

The men in protective white suits had multiplied. He squatted and picked up a handful of dirt, then let it slip through his fingers in a thin stream.

"The first in a long series of shit storms."

CHAPTER 3

THE ISRAELI EMBASSY, BRUSSELS, FIVE DAYS EARLIER

The quiet that permeated the room was exactly what Ehud Amar needed, even if it was the calm before the storm. His problems would not be limited to today's events. He was sure of that. As nightfall came, his notion of time became fuzzier. At least the phone had stopped ringing.

He got up from the couch, where he had hoped to get some shut-eye. Despite his fatigue, he had too much adrenaline coursing through him. He decided to open a bottle of Italian wine—a present from his counterpart in Rome. Perhaps that, along with a cigarette—just one—would do the trick. Ehud had been saving the wine for a special occasion and hadn't had a smoke in a year, but drastic times called for drastic measures.

He jumped when the door to his large office swung open. A man sauntered in—as though he owned the place, Ehud thought. He sat down on the couch where Ehud had been just minutes earlier and leaned back. His olive-colored face was lined with deep wrinkles, and his balding head was covered with liver spots. But his blue eyes were piercing, despite his age.

"Where is he?" the man asked without even a greeting.

20   DAVID KHARA

"It's nice to make your acquaintance, Mr. Karman," Ehud replied.

"There'll be time for pleasantries once I see him. I'll repeat the question. Where is he?"

"In the basement of the embassy. We are equipped with a medical unit in the event of an emergency or if one of our agents needs immediate, and let's say discreet, attention. Follow me. I'll take you to them."

"Them?" the visitor asked.

Ehud grinned. Maybe he was just a military attaché, but he had thrown this hotshot from Mossad for a loop. Secret agents thought they were gods. They had no respect for laws and regulations. The superheroes stirred up the shit, and the worker bees—diligent diplomats and other government workers like him—had to clean up after them.

In silence, the two men headed toward the elevator. Ehud took out a key and slid it into a small lock next to a button that was missing a floor number.

"Need I remind you that you are about to enter a top-secret zone?"

Karman shot him a look that eliminated any further impulse to joke around.

"I guess not."

About twenty seconds later, the elevator opened onto a long hallway lit dimly by flickering fluorescent lights. Large pipes ran along the concrete walls. They made a loud clunking noise that sounded like a sputtering truck. The two men walked about a hundred feet to a gray door that had no handle. Ehud took out a magnetic card and swiped it across a sensor on the right-hand side.

The door slid open silently to reveal a state-of-the-art operating room. Ehud was well aware that it was on par with those of the most reputable hospitals in the world. In the center of the room, a young woman with long legs and short red hair was strapped to a surgical table. Two electrodes connected to her temples were transferring her cerebral activity to a monitor screen. The infrequent spikes on the display left little to the imagination. She was in a deep coma.

Karman walked over to study her face. It was hard and angular, as if sculpted from marble. Her skin was milky white, tarnished only by a purplish bruise on the left side of her forehead and strangulation marks that formed a chilling necklace around her throat. But aside from those small traces of violence, Sleeping Beauty was quite peaceful, her lips fixed in a half smile. Ehud surmised that Karman had never before seen an attractive woman in such a cold and disturbing condition.

"I came for him, not her," Karman blurted out as he accidentally brushed his fingers against the woman's hollow cheek. He quickly pulled his hand back, seemingly afraid of waking her up.

"We rescued both of them, sir. I assumed she was part of your team. But judging by your reaction, I was wrong."

"Precisely. She's not with us. For the last time, I don't have a moment to spare. Where is he?"

"Your agent's in the next room. We have abided by your instructions, but I won't lie. Our surgeon needed a lot of convincing. And it was quite difficult to find a tub of that size."

Karman headed toward the door to his right and opened it.

"I'd appreciate it if you waited here, Colonel Amar."

All right. Ehud was definitely going to break down and light up that cigarette. And he was going to enjoy every last drag. As soon as the nutcases cleared out.

22   DAVID KHARA

Karman closed the door behind him. He had prepared for the worst, even the possibility of recovering a body. But not for what he saw.

In the middle of this drab storage room, lined with shelves holding boxes of gauze pads, medicine bottles, and surgical gloves, was a tub filled with water. And in the tub, a man whom Eli Karman—keeper of Mossad's archives—feared he'd never see alive again was happily splashing.

"Eytan Morg, I think I hate you!" he announced with a burst of laughter.

The giant gave him a huge smile while he kicked his feet like a playful child learning to swim.

"I was expecting to find you on the verge of death, Eytan. You could have let me know you were okay."

"Yeah, but if I had done that, you wouldn't have come. Plus, you've seen me make it through too many cliffhangers with no bites or bruises. I needed to remind you that I'm not actually invincible," Eytan said with a wink.

"You think I really need a refresher course? Does it seem like I'm taking your condition lightly?"

"Of course not, Eli, but my last mission was a close call, and I had to see you. I almost didn't make it. To be honest, I didn't want to at one point."

Eli looked at the floor. He had worried that the agent's determination would wane, and, in fact, he had feared that they would lose him altogether.

"I'm anxious to see your report, but not here," he said, breaking the awkward silence. "We've already caused a great deal of trouble for the embassy staff. And playing the part of an evil, secretive character is tiring. Do you feel well enough to get out of here?"

"Yep. My shoulder wound is no big deal. I'll be a bit of a gimp until the hole in my thigh heals, but things

THE SHIRO PROJECT   23

could be worse. I'm assuming it was your call to put me in this freezing bathtub?"

"I've gotten to know you over the years, Eytan. Thank God you were injected with the serum in time. One of these days you're going to give me a heart attack, for Christ's sake. I'm not twenty anymore. Get dressed. I haven't been working with you all these years just for the opportunity to check out your perfectly sculpted body."

Eli looked away as his friend stepped out of the tub.

"We'll go over the details of the case back at the military attaché's office. The poor guy must be blowing a gasket on the other side of the wall. We might as well fill him in. He did a good job, and given the mess you left behind, I doubt that his troubles are over—especially since the ambassador isn't here in Brussels. He'll have to handle everything on his own."

Eli Karman left the room to return to the unlucky Ehud, who was most likely worrying up a storm over what was to be done with the tall athletically built woman strapped to the table.

"He'll be joining us," Eli informed Ehud in a surprisingly friendly tone. "He's going to share his report with us in your office, if that's okay with you."

"Uh, I believe so. But when you say us, you mean that I will be present for the debriefing?"

"Yes, Colonel Amar. You deserve to know more, since we're responsible for your troubles, and we could use your services in the future. Plus, you never know—you might be in for a surprise or two."

A few moments later, the two were seated across from one another in the ambassador's drawing room. There was no harm in borrowing the diplomat's lair, given his absence and the exceptional circumstances, Ehud told himself. The friendliness of the Mossad top gun persuaded Ehud to dig into the embassy's reserve of fine liquor. He wasn't hiding his desire to get hammered.

Eli was now brimming from ear to ear—a complete reversal from his churlish attitude just twenty minutes earlier.

"You did good work, Colonel, and I am extremely grateful."

"I'm happy to comply with your orders, sir."

"Please, call me Eli."

"All right, Eli," Ehud replied. He was beginning to relax, thanks to the visitor's newly calm demeanor and the effects of the cognac.

"What I am about to share with you is strictly classified information, Colonel."

"Yes, I know the song and dance, Eli. I've worked on cases with Mossad."

"Ehud—may I call you Ehud?"

The military attaché nodded.

"Nothing you have ever seen or heard before is anything like the story of Eytan Morg."

CHAPTER 4

Ehud Amar stared at the amber liquid he was swirling in his glass.

His skepticism was playing against his compassion. The story was so incredible, how could even a shred of it be true? But Eli's unflinching and candid response to his questions were those of a man being honest.

"You're telling me in all seriousness that within the Kidon, Mossad's terrorist-abduction and execution unit, there's a man who was genetically modified by SS medics in the nineteen forties? And in order for him to stay alive, he needs a top-secret serum that blocks cancerous cell necrosis?"

"Yes."

"That this man does not age as we do, and his physical capabilities are extremely superior to those of a normal human being?"

"Yes."

"And that this is the same guy we rescued today in the Sonian Forest, near what was an underground factory but is now a pile of scrap in a crater-sized pit? This is the man we placed in a tub of ice water?"

"Yes."

"Do you mind if I pour myself another drink?"

"Not at all."

Ehud poured himself a double and offered the bottle to Eli, who declined with a wave of his hand.

26   DAVID KHARA

"You'd be surprised by the amount of alcohol consumed by the few people who've learned exactly what I've just told you," Eli said.

"You don't say. But to get back to the more mundane matter at hand—with all due respect, sir, your superagent has landed us in a pretty big pile of shit. I'd like to know exactly what happened to him, if only so I can feed a story to the media. I'm sure they're ready to pounce on this."

"I don't know any more than you do at this point. Now that he's dressed, Eytan will be delighting both of us with his account."

Eli directed Ehud's attention to the doorway. The bald giant filled the entire frame.

The colonel couldn't decide whether he should readjust his uniform or offer to shake hands with the miracle man. The latter took a seat on the couch and swung his injured leg up on the coffee table.

"Eytan, this is the man to whom you owe your life, Colonel Ehud Amar."

"Well, thank you, Colonel Ehud Amar," Eytan replied, giving a two-finger military salute.

"Agent Morg, it is an honor to—"

"At ease, soldier. Call me Eytan, and let's drop all that military mumbo jumbo. I would like to get myself a drink, but…" He pointed to the leg that had taken the bullet, and he was wearing the same pants that he had been shot in.

Ehud eagerly saw to the drink. He handed the glass to Eytan and joined him on the couch. Eli Karman turned to Eytan and started the conversation again.

"Great, now that we've taken care of introductions and refreshments, I think you have some explaining to do. How did your mission to recover the lost MI6 files from the World War II bring you here?"

"I don't think you're going to like this," Eytan said. "I'll give you the short version, so we're not here all night. I found a lead on the guy who bought the documents. A French dude living in the US who belonged to a secret organization that helped fund Hitler's rise to power. The group went by the name of Consortium and had the mission of advancing the human race, regardless of cost or ethics. You can guess what its idea of advancement was. This secret organization—or society, if you prefer to call it that—survived the Hitler regime and continued its quest to produce the master race. It caused the cholera epidemic in Mexico. The plan was to wait until it became a pandemic and then offer a vaccine."

"But why go to all that trouble?" Ehud asked, unable to take his eyes off Eytan.

"The head honchos planned to administer a mutagen developed by the mad scientist to whom I owe my very existence."

"Bleiberg," Eli whispered. "So he didn't die in the explosion at the Stutthof concentration camp when you escaped."

"I don't understand," the military attaché said. "Why did they want to administer this mutagen?"

"To transform the human race into their version of a superior species—all at the cost of millions, even billions of lives. The doses of vaccine were being stored in a plant in the Sonian Forest. That's why I blew it up."

Eytan pointed to his shoes in all seriousness.

"In my line of work, thugs usually don't make you take off your shoes before beating you bloody. The best place to conceal explosives is in the soles. I always carry some. The facility needed to be blown up, and I saw to it."

"Okay, what about the woman in the basement?" Eli asked. "She's strapped to the table and out like a light, so I'm guessing she's an enemy."

"Yes, she takes care of their dirty work. She's the one who caused my injuries. Her name's Elena, and she's my closest tie to the Consortium. But I had another reason for keeping her alive."

"It must be a doozy. Taking prisoners usually isn't your thing."

"Elena was a guinea pig for Bleiberg's mutagen. She's an even more advanced version of myself."

Eytan turned to Ehud, who was soaking up every word of the story.

"Welcome to my world, Colonel!"

"How do you suggest that we proceed?" Eli asked Eytan.

"I'll type up a report so that you can lead the investigations from Tel Aviv. I'd like the colonel to use his connections with the Belgian government to look into BCI, the company run by the Consortium. The rest of the plans will be between you and me, Eli. No offense, Ehud."

"Well then, I'll leave you to it," the attaché responded as he got up from the couch. "It'll take me weeks to get this day sorted out, so I'd better start now. If you need me, I'll be having a smoke in the courtyard."

Ehud Amar picked up his glass and the bottle, searched the desk for a pack of cigarettes, and left the room.

Now Eytan could say what was really on his mind.

"Eli, I've been tracking Nazi goons for decades, and that work is pretty much done," he said. "The only ones left are bedridden shut-ins. I'm not saying these people should get away with what they've done, but

THE SHIRO PROJECT   29

after discovering the Consortium and its connection with the Nazi ascension to power and the Bleiberg project, I'd rather focus on taking them down."

Eli crossed his arms.

"So you need a new enemy," he said after a few moments. "Is that it? A new reason to continue the fight?"

Eytan was silent.

"Neither of us knows how much time you have left. And like a stubborn mule, you're keeping our specialists from conducting tests to better understand your condition. Can't you stand down on this one and enjoy a well-deserved rest for once? Let others take over the reins."

"Eli, do you really think there's someone else out there who can deal with this problem? I refuse to sit by and let the world wind up at the mercy of bloodthirsty maniacs yet again. The economy is swirling down the drain. The middle class is suffering, and the rich are increasingly out of touch with reality. Doesn't this story sound familiar? If these conditions worsen, they'll be ripe for some obscure and sinister force to swoop in. I've realized over the years that I can make a difference. I have to make a difference."

"That's exactly what terrifies me, Eytan. You're chasing the pipe dream of a perfect world. And we both know that will never happen. Meanwhile, you're hurting, and I know why."

"Please, enlighten me."

"You're scared that doing nothing will force you to confront your inner demons. You're the most dogged man I know, so I'm not going to tell you what to do. But I am asking: picture the possibility of living for yourself instead of for everyone else, of making peace with the world, of finally making peace with yourself."

"Eli, let me finish this final mission."

Eli sighed.

"My daughter in Boston will be having her baby soon. I'm leaving at the end of the week to be with her. There's nothing in this world that would keep me from seeing the birth of my grandson. So here's the deal, and it's non-negotiable: take a break to recover. Go home, and at least pretend to relax. When I come back, we'll tackle this problem head-on. Until then, you're Agent Couch Potato."

Grimacing, Eytan stood up and hobbled over to him.

"You've sold me on the R and R. Give Rose a big hug for me. Tell her I'll visit one of these days."

"You've been making that promise for the past two years. I doubt she still believes it."

The teasing remark hit Eytan hard. He had made countless sacrifices for the sake of his missions. And Rose was one of them.

"I swear I won't wait another two years."

"Perfect. We're counting on you, then. Ah, I almost forgot. What are you going to do with the notorious Elena?"

"I had her placed in an artificially induced coma to keep her nice and quiet. Believe me, she's dangerous—and smart. Underestimating her would have disastrous consequences. Have her transferred to a secure facility, then wake her up. I'll question her after my vacation."

"Message received. I'll take care of her transport to Tel Aviv."

"Well, we've covered everything here," Eytan said. "I believe this is where our paths part once again."

"I believe so."

Eli extended his hand to Eytan, who gripped it and looked at him without wavering. The giant was the first to let go. He headed toward the door, then paused and turned around.

"Hey," he said to the expectant grandfather. "Give me a call when the baby's born."

CHAPTER 5

SOMEWHERE OFF THE COAST OF IRELAND

The bow of the boat was cutting through rough waters. As the waves crashed on the deck, the four other passengers took refuge in a cabin at the back of the fishing trawler. The vessel served as a link between civilization on the mainland and the piece of land that they called their own, an island mostly overlooked by the rest of the world.

The captain, a stocky fellow with short hair and a bushy black beard, was maneuvering his skiff with the heart and diligence of someone who had seen his share of hardships at sea. Indeed, he had lost two young sailors about a decade earlier, when his boat capsized. By some miracle, he had managed to survive. Blame for that deadly outing could only be placed on the weather gods, and he was well aware of that. Still, a mountain of regret weighed on his shoulders.

Captain James O'Barr had taken a short break after the accident. But he soon yearned to be at the helm of a boat again. He asked the town council to approve two daily shuttles between the mainland, which was little more than a fishing harbor, and the island.

James was navigating toward the small island, inhabited by a scant number of year-round residents, daring tourists, wealthy eccentrics, and a handful of trekkers devoted to peace and quiet. Only a dozen houses towered atop the Big Rock, as the villagers liked to call it.

It was early afternoon, and the clouds that filled the sky were heaving a cold drizzle. The waves and the rain were enough to keep the few passengers in the cabin—everybody but one person. He was on deck, sitting on a coil of ropes, with a large khaki military bag at his feet. He was stroking the captain's German shepherd, Bart, and both seemed completely at ease with the weather and the crossing.

James didn't know much about the man. He never saw him more than once or twice a year. According to rumors—the primary source of information for these people—he owned an old abode hidden in the middle of the heath. Some surmised that he was a movie actor seeking solitude. Others suspected he was a criminal on the run. The stranger's extraordinary physique only exacerbated the speculation. Old Kelly Cahill thought he might be a secret agent. But the poor old man was already losing his marbles. The one thing that all the island residents agreed on was that the giant would make an excellent recruit for their rugby team. He would surely deliver regular ass-kickings in their matches with nearby towns.

After an hour or so, the towering shoreline appeared on the horizon. The rugged coastline, along with the winds and lack of vegetation, served as a natural barrier to development. One almost needed to be a masochist to live in this place.

At last, the boat pulled up to the dock. The sound of the slowing motor alerted the passengers in the cabin. They absentmindedly nodded to the captain as they disembarked, their arms loaded with boxes of supplies. They took the path leading to the heart of the island.

Awaiting them were the little electric golf carts they used to stow their purchases and drive home.

The giant, trailed by the panting dog, was the only one to shake James's hand. The stranger gave the animal a final pat on the side and exited the skiff, his bag flung over his shoulder.

Eytan arrived at the base of the steep path that snaked between the high gray rocks. He grunted a little louder with each step. Over the years, he had racked up a great many combat wounds, and at this very moment, he suspected that his body was finally paying the price. He felt ancient, crushed by the weight of his bygone years. What Eli had said seemed more like a prediction than a warning. His fight against the Consortium would be his last. Then he would retire to this island, which protected him from the world's brutalities. He'd turn in his weapons and spend his final days painting as he awaited death and the respite it would bring. At last. On the other hand, he'd been thinking this way for years.

He had known his whole life that nothing could make up for what that man Bleiberg had done to him. So he fought for others: his parents, his brother, and countless strangers who hadn't even heard of him. He had never expected a thank you or even any acknowledgment.

Eli was right. Eytan was afraid—not of what was outside, but of what was inside.

After half an hour of trudging across the heath, he spotted the large stone structure. This house was the only place on earth that could assuage the doubts and dejection that sometimes overtook him. It was the only place that he could call home.

Eytan paused in front of the building, with its four large windows and blue shutters. He looked up and saw white smoke coming from the chimney. He picked up his step, a smile plastered on his face. He entered the living room, which was furnished with the bare minimum: a round table, four wooden chairs (two of which had never been used), and a brown couch. The ensemble was left over from the previous owners. Instinctively, Eytan flipped on the light switch. As expected, the generator was already up and running, undoubtedly thanks to the same person who had cared enough to put two large logs in the fireplace.

Eytan threw his bag on the floor and opened the shutters to enjoy the last few moments of sunlight. His eyes were drawn to the paintings on the stone walls, and he lingered on a portrait of a child wearing short pants, a jacket, and an oversized cap. The gray hues and the boy's distant eyes gave the work a profound sadness. Without thinking, Eytan reached out and touched the child. Then he pulled his hand back and shook off the surge of melancholy.

He headed toward the kitchen to inspect the fridge. It was full of food that had been aligned with almost military precision. His neighbor Ann—he knew only her first name—had been living as a recluse since her husband's death. At one point, she had made Eytan promise to let her know whenever he'd be visiting. That way, she could make sure he'd return to a functioning home with a well-stocked pantry.

The seventy-year-old woman shared his passion for painting. Sometimes, they'd set up their easels together and indulge in their mutual interest without exchanging a word, only glancing sporadically at each other's work. Ann would stay until just before nightfall and then drive home.

The prospect of seeing her the following afternoon dispelled the nostalgia hovering along the edges of his mind.

Eytan decided to dedicate the first few days of his vacation to making much-needed repairs. The strong winds that were always eroding the coastline had damaged his house.

The tasks that needed to be done, which ranged from reattaching loose shutters to adding thatch to the roof, were daunting for someone unaccustomed to this kind of work. But he could always count on the shrewd guidance offered by Ann, who had slipped a box of adhesive strips into his medicine cabinet as a welcoming gift.

It was his third night at the house, and he was massaging his aching shoulders when the outside world intruded. Eytan glared at his phone. He hesitated a few seconds but couldn't ignore the call.

"Eytan?"

It was a familiar voice, and it was trembling.

"Rose? What's wrong?"

Eli Karman's daughter burst into sobs.

"Eytan, it's Dad."

CHAPTER 6

Meanwhile, in a suburb of Tel Aviv

Avi Lafner hated working nights, and after a couple of beers with his coworkers, he would quickly confess his equal hatred for working days. His job—the title notwithstanding—was just shitty by nature. Those who didn't know what he actually did would have easily imagined that he led the exhilarating life of a hero in a big-budget action-thriller. Far from it.

Avi's primary task as a Mossad medical supervisor consisted of performing quarterly checkups on special agents who were devoid of all charm and pizzazz. Patient-physician dialogue was limited to "hello, doctor" and "good-bye, doctor." That's how he spent most of his night shifts at the private clinic.

Avi had never thought that he'd wind up employed as a company physician for the secret service. His dream was to be a medical superstar à la Dr. House. And he had all the prerequisites: a handsome face, a devilish smile, a distinguished physique, an exceptional IQ, and skills bestowed upon him by the very best professors. What a waste.

Tonight, hoping to plow through as much boring paperwork as possible before heading off on vacation, he hunkered down at his desk, threw on a mix of his favorite jazz classics, and sorted through the pending

38   DAVID KHARA

medical files. After two hours, he was tempted to write "unfit, denied" on one recruit's file. It was just a prankish notion, though, as the agent's health was excellent.

So that's where he was—dreaming up mischief just to stay awake. If he continued down this slippery slope, it wouldn't be long before he'd be putting a whoopee cushion under the base captain's fat butt or itching powder in his clothes. At least it beat giving into depression.

When he wasn't meeting and greeting secret agents or going over reports, Avi spent much of his shift in the small break room off the main lobby. There, he could hit on his female colleagues at the vending machine. The dispensed espressos were mostly water, depriving the drink of all flavor, along with any hope of a caffeinated energy spike. Avi had made a huge stink about getting the machine replaced, to no avail. Ever since then, he'd been looking for a way to break the piece of shit, forcing the purchasing department to cough up for a new one. He didn't consider this vandalism. He thought of it as a humanitarian act.

It was about midnight, and the doctor was up for a little excitement. Sure, the pharmacy had an endless supply of more or less legal pick-me-ups, but he had encountered one or two dope fiends while doing his physical exams, and that was enough to dissuade him. Instead, he headed toward the break room, whistling as he went. If his scheme unfolded according to plan, no one else would be around. He would have the abominable vending machine all to himself. He'd be in and out. Unseen, unheard.

As he was going down the stairwell, the doctor felt the cell phone in his shirt pocket vibrate. Who the hell would be contacting him at this hour? As a bachelor

THE SHIRO PROJECT   39

whose parents had left the scene long ago, he couldn't think of a single soul who'd want to contact him. He pulled out the device and read the message.

"Internee arriving. Needs preliminary exam before incarceration. Meet at reception ASAP." It wasn't just the sender's number but his terse style that told Avi with certainty that the text was from the colonel at the military base about two miles away. The colonel had a short fuse and no sense of humor. He lived for two things: work and regulations. Because of this, people considered him either exceptional or obnoxious. Avi fell into the latter group. He loathed the man.

Five minutes later, or the time it took to go down three flights of stairs to the ground floor and make a detour to the secretary's office for the oh-so-important admission forms, Avi was walking down the long dimly lit hallway that led to the clinic's lobby.

That's when he heard the first gunshots. Instinctively, he crouched and continued forward, hugging the wall. Once he arrived at the entrance, he glanced at the ceiling. Successive gunshots were knocking out the fluorescent light fixtures, one after another. Now all that remained was the red glow of the emergency exit sign. The doctor struggled to adapt his vision to the near-darkness.

To the left, four blue benches bolted to the floor faced the loathsome coffee machine. To the right was the receptionist's counter, where the security guard was usually stationed at night. The gray linoleum flooring had been chosen to complement the mottled acoustic tiles and give the place a cold and medicinal aesthetic. On any other night—or day—the lobby resembled a soulless cube.

Avi fought to still his breathing. An empty gurney was careening toward him. The sound of metal

40   DAVID KHARA

sliding across tile attracted his attention farther down the hall—somebody had lost a gun. And nearby, on the floor, the security guard was writhing in pain. He cried out, holding his knee tight to his chest. Seeing the quickly growing puddle of blood, Avi feared that a bullet had hit his tibial artery. Having done his surgical training in a theater of operations—a fancy way of saying under a deluge of bullets—he felt compelled to give the wounded man emergency care. But the scene playing out before him held him back.

In the middle of three soldiers, an athletically built woman wearing nothing but her underwear was spinning around, throwing kicks and punches left and right. The men looked helpless and pathetic, compared with the fury that whirled before them. If one blow wasn't enough to knock out each soldier, her frequent thrusts would soon get the job done.

Why the hell didn't they pull out their guns? Avi was bewitched by the short-haired Amazon's moves. The soldiers' sloppy counterattacks were almost pitiful. And yet, by pure luck, one of the men took advantage of a simultaneous offensive, throwing a jab at the attacker's face and making a deep cut in her lower lip. She lost her balance under the blow. The soldiers closed in on their target.

"Don't forget the orders," one of them barked. "We need her alive!"

Far from calming the woman down, the prospect of being subdued seemed to fuel her strength. And her rage. When the man on her right moved in to grab her, she struck him with a swift uppercut to the chin, which wiped him out cold. Avi shuddered at the sound of bones breaking. The soldier facing her quickly launched two nervous right hooks. This guy definitely knew how to box. But he wouldn't be stepping into another ring anytime soon. Instead of blocking and dodging, the woman retaliated with two similar punches. Her fists collided with his knuckles. The man's wrists could not withstand the impact. Stripped of protection, he was rushed by a flash of pounding right and left jabs. A final kick to the middle of his throat sent him flying against the vending machine, demolishing the all-but-worthless fixture.

Avi couldn't believe it. The woman was getting faster and more powerful as the fight continued, and she hadn't even broken a sweat! She was barely even trying.

The last man standing had drawn the same conclusion. With his confidence waning, he shot a bunch of fake punches to test his opponent's nerves. The woman remained steady as a rock, carefully following his every move with her eyes. Then, with a wicked smile on her face, she bluffed an attack, causing the soldier to jump back in fright.

"Don't be scared, kid," she whispered, clearly delighted by the effect she produced. "Answer my questions, and you'll get out of here alive. I promise."

The soldier scanned his bloody companions strewn on the lobby floor. His will was hanging by a thread.

"To hell with the orders!" he shouted. "I'm going to shred you from head to toe, you bitch!"

He pulled his Uzi pistol from its holster. But before he could even take aim, the bitch in question had sprung on him, her fingers clasped around his neck. He never even had the chance to look into her cruel eyes before his windpipe was crushed. Gurgling noises rose from his throat as the woman's relentless grip finished off the job.

"What an idiot," she spat, half scornful, half stoic.

42   DAVID KHARA

The lifeless body fell to the floor. The woman bent down to pick up the gun and played with it for a few minutes. Avi, unable to think, continued to observe the scene. She slowly approached one of the injured men, looked at him carefully, and pulled the trigger. She executed each one in the same fashion: a single bullet to the head.

The doctor, now plastered against the wall with his eyes closed, covered his mouth to keep from crying out in horror. He managed to remain silent, but he could no longer keep track of his thoughts. He was too confused and panicked.

Who was this woman? Why was she here? What should he do? Could he make it out and get help without being seen?

He decided that opening his eyes would be a first constructive step. Then he slowly stood up, despite the risk of being spotted. He felt a wave of hopelessness. Surrounded by quickly expanding pools of blood, the four dead men were sprawled on the linoleum floor. The empty gurney had crashed into a wall. Sparks were spurting from the shattered light fixtures. Avi looked at the smashed vending machine and wondered if he'd ever have the chance to meet its replacement. The raging madwoman responsible for this massacre was nowhere to be seen. Considering the labyrinth that was this clinic, he knew she could come down on him at any moment.

Avi was no longer of any use to those poor bastards. He decided to seek shelter in his office and call for help. He retraced his steps in the hallway and headed as discreetly as possible toward the stairwell.

"One more step, and you're dead. I'm not afraid to shoot, as you can imagine."

Avi froze and instinctively raised his hands.

"I love obedient men. Turn around. Slowly."

He complied. The woman glided up to him. Considering the gravity of the situation, Avi thought she was supremely cool. She stationed herself three feet in front of him and stared him in the eye. Then she grabbed his chin and turned his head from one side to the other, as though he were a strange animal she was seeing for the first time. She let go and fingered the badge pinned to his white button-down shirt.

"Well, Dr. Lafner. I'm Elena. Pleasure to meet you," she said before falling to the floor, unconscious.

CHAPTER 7

THE BIG ROCK

Eytan felt a bottomless hole open up in his stomach. While hunting down war criminals around the globe, he hadn't realized just how old and fragile Eli had become. At his age, Eli certainly had to be experiencing some health problems. Eytan wondered if he had turned a blind eye, if he had been too afraid to face the reality of losing a close friend yet again. Nonetheless, a man with his past couldn't keep his head buried in the sand for long. In his heart, Eytan knew the dreaded phone call would come sooner or later.

"Our own death is nothing," he said to himself over and over. "It's the death of others that is unbearable."

"Calm down, Rose. What's going on with your father?"

The young woman took a deep breath.

"Dad called us from Tel Aviv. He gave Steve his flight number and his arrival time for Boston. Steve left to pick him up at the airport, but Dad never got off the plane. Steve went to the airline desk, and the staff checked the passenger list. Dad wasn't on it. I was so mad. I thought some new top-secret situation had come up, and he hadn't even bothered to tell me he wasn't coming. I tried calling him several times but just got his voice mail. And then, ten minutes ago, I got a call from his cell phone.

"And?" asked Eytan. He could hear Rose choking back the tears.

"It wasn't him on the line. It was a man who claimed to be holding him hostage. He asked me to give you a phone number and have you call it, or else he'd take Dad out. I don't understand why they didn't call you directly, since they have his phone."

"My number isn't saved on Eli's phone," Eytan told her as he pulled out a pen. "All right, I've got something to write with."

Rose dictated the phone number, which Eytan scribbled on the back of an envelope lying on the coffee table.

"Can you tell me anything about the call or the caller? Any detail that might help?"

"No… Well, maybe. I don't know if this is important, but the person was very polite."

"I'll call him immediately. Please, try not to worry. If someone kidnapped your dad in hopes of getting in contact with me, then you have nothing to fear for now."

"Eytan, I'm scared," the young woman whispered. "I've come to terms with the risks both of you face, and I've even managed to put them out of my mind for the most part. But now…"

"Rose, do you trust me?"

"More than anyone."

"I'm going to bring him home unharmed. I promise. Do you hear me?"

"Yes."

"I'll get back to you as soon as I learn something. Just take care of yourself. I'll take care of everything else."

46 DAVID KHARA

Eytan called the number. The abnormally long sequence corresponded with an encrypted communication system. It meant that Eytan had no means of tracing the call. After a few rings, with each tone more unusual than the last, Eytan heard a smooth, deep voice on the other end.

"Mr. Morg, thank you for returning our call so promptly."

"Considering the way you worded your request, how could I refuse? What do you want?"

"I see you're skipping the formalities and getting straight to the point. I'm happy to oblige, as I am also pressed for time. You'll be going to Prague, Mr. Morg. Make sure you get there by tomorrow afternoon. Call this number at five thirty, local time."

"Then what?"

"Then we'll reveal the location of our meeting, where we will discuss Mr. Karman's fate and the terms of the agreement that we wish to make with you. Do you accept the plan?"

"Do I have a choice?"

"You have free will, Mr. Morg. You can accept my offer or decline it. You're welcome to turn your back on your loved ones and your responsibilities and go your merry way. Of course, you can consider this option only by liberating yourself from the useless things that, in reality, keep you from reaching your full potential: your emotions and, more important, your principles. So basically, if you want total control, you'll have to renounce what you are." Eytan didn't have to see the man to visualize the little smirk on his face. "We know you well enough to assume you won't embrace such an attitude."

One more narcissist who enjoyed deluding himself with the sound of his own voice. Eytan was unfazed.

He refrained from saying anything. Before the silence could sink in, his phone partner started up again.

"Agent Morg, we want you to be at the top of your game."

"In that case, I'm afraid I'll be letting you down," Eytan retorted tersely.

"Even if you feel weakened by your recent injuries, we would never make the mistake of underestimating you. Before you ask the question, I can assure you that Mr. Karman is doing wonderfully and that I am seeing to it that he is treated with utmost respect."

"Don't expect me to thank you or even take your word for it," Eytan replied. He was getting angry and knew he had to watch what he said even more carefully.

"I'd never ask as much."

"How did you know about my injuries?"

"Ah, you must realize by now that our influence extends well beyond the simple realm of pharmaceuticals."

Eytan laughed. Of course. He had known all along. "So you're a member of the Consortium."

"We'll discuss this later. Tomorrow. Five thirty. Prague."

"Prague? I'm not going anywhere until I have proof that he's alive."

"Understood. I'll hand the phone over to Mr. Karman. He's sitting right next to me."

"Eli?"

"Yes, Eytan. Rest assured, I'm doing fine."

Eytan felt momentarily relieved at the sound of his friend's husky voice.

The phone exchanged hands again.

"There you go. You wanted proof. You have it. Ah, I almost forgot. Don't bother contacting Mossad or even informing them of the situation. If you do, the

48   David Khara

consequences will be dire," the man concluded before hanging up.

Eytan looked at the phone. In a few minutes, he would call Rose to tell her that he would bring her father back safe and sound, even if it meant setting the whole world ablaze. Then he'd call Captain O'Barr and ask for an emergency passage, which would cost him a pretty penny. That was the price of living as a recluse. But money meant nothing to Eytan, especially not today. Last, in order to obtain the necessary materials, he would have to activate his network on the continent, which he had built over the course of many missions.

Up to this point, the Kidon operative had led his missions the same way he had led the rest of his life. Alone. Relationships were luxuries with too high a price for someone whose existence was basically one long series of near-death experiences. Love was professional negligence. Yes, Eli was one of the few people— perhaps the only person—with whom he had deep and long-lasting bonds. And never before had he caused his friend's safety to be jeopardized.

Now Eytan clung to one reassuring thought. Sure, the Consortium was holding Eli hostage, but he also had a bargaining chip. Back at the BCI facility, Eytan had decided against killing off Elena. And at this moment, he was very pleased with himself for letting her live.

CHAPTER 8

MOSCOW, A FEW DAYS BEFORE THE INCIDENT IN PARDUBICE, EIGHT A.M.

The thick crowd slithered like a giant snake through the poorly lit tunnels, as if pulled by some gravitational force. Commuters lost their individual identities as soon as they entered the underground metro. They merged into one form, one faceless creature.

Oleg Kerzhakov observed this rush-hour performance at the Lubyanka station every day. It was hard to believe that not so long ago, more than three dozen people had lost their lives here in the 2010 Moscow Metro suicide bombing. How many of these expressionless commuters were masking gut-wrenching fear as they jammed themselves into the cars of the red line?

The member of Russia's intelligence agency, who was in his mid-thirties and had the buff physique of a boxer, had been among the first at the scene. He was a ten-year veteran of the service, and his experience with terrorist violence had protected him somewhat from the trauma caused by the horrific sight of shredded bodies and distraught survivors.

Every day that passes erases a bit more blood off the walls, he told himself as he made his way to his job with the FSB, the KGB's successor. After suffering a knee injury in a bad parachute landing, he had

50   David Khara

been disqualified from work in the field and was now overseeing security at the FSB headquarters near the station. It was a big change from his previous assignment, but at least he still got to carry a gun.

Oleg walked through the long subway tunnels, scanning each face and examining every movement made by the passersby. When he happened upon a pretty girl—and Moscow had plenty—he'd crack a flirty smile, and that usually did the trick. He had once been insecure about his nose, broken in more than one boxing match, but he quickly discovered that women in the capital found it fetching. His bad-boy image, accentuated by his unruly hair, definitely played in his favor.

Oleg was heading toward the metro exit with a little extra pep in his step, when a cute businesswoman, who appeared to be in her forties, caught his attention. Just as he was switching into seduction mode, he put on the brakes. A few steps away from the woman, two twentyish-looking men in hooded sweatshirts were walking briskly. Oleg froze in his tracks, causing those behind him to step on his heels. He crouched and pretended to tie his shoes. From this position, he spotted one guy's hand on the butt end of a gun sticking out of his pocket.

Before the pair could get lost in the crowd, he started shadowing them.

The police presence in the underground had been reinforced after the bombings of March 2010. Oleg thought it would be wise to hand the matter over to the first officer he could find. But why was it that there were never any cops around when they were needed? Oleg couldn't find even one. So he followed the two guys all the way to the platform and stationed himself behind them. The men were nervously rocking from one foot to the other like two junkies. A train pulled up, and as the hoard started piling into the cars, the two men shoved their way through, rudely elbowing the other commuters. An elderly man lost his balance, and if it weren't for Oleg, who just barely caught him by the raincoat, he would have fallen on his face.

Gramps leaned against him and struggled to stand up straight.

"Thank you, young man," he said, smoothing his coat and catching his breath.

"No problem," Oleg replied, anxious to catch up with the two thugs. Before he could move, the doors closed, and the train sped away.

"I'm so sorry. You've missed the train because of me."

"No worries," Oleg said. He had just spotted two police officers loafing on the other side of the platform. Their nonchalance bothered him only slightly more than the annoying old-timer.

"I'm going to leave you now. Will you be all right?"

"Yes, yes. Go on, my friend."

Oleg hurried toward the officers. When he reached them, he whipped out his badge and explained the situation. One of the men relayed the information via radio to a colleague in the next station. All around them, the commuters went about their business without paying any attention. A kid bumped into one of the officers and coughed.

"Cover your mouth when you cough," he reprimanded.

As the boy turned to the officer, Oleg took in his face. He was sickly pale. His eyes were red. He started coughing convulsively, and blood spurted out of his mouth. The boy tried to grab the police officer's sleeve before falling to the ground.

52   DAVID KHARA

Following protocol, Oleg stepped back and surveyed the platform. Everywhere he looked, people were throwing up, stumbling, and rubbing their eyes. Some were writhing on the ground, bathed in their own vomit. Blood was smeared across the walls and floor. Dozens of people, maybe a hundred, were dying before his eyes.

"Quick, tell them to shut down the metro!" he yelled at the two officers, who seemed to be too stunned to move. "And demand backup!" He didn't have to say it twice. The men shot off.

Oleg spotted the old guy in the raincoat. With his back turned to Oleg, the man was walking slowly toward the other end of the platform. Something wasn't right about him. Oleg could feel it in his gut.

"Sir!" he yelled. No response. He called again.

This time, the man stopped. He and Oleg were separated by about a hundred feet and a pile of bloody bodies. The sound of an arriving train thundered through the tunnel.

The old man turned to face Oleg, and he couldn't believe what he saw. The man was holding an ordinary-looking metal spray can and wearing a gas mask. The train slowed and stopped. The man raised his free hand and started waving good-bye to Oleg.

The agent opened his blazer and drew his weapon. He took aim as the doors were about to open and pulled the trigger. Three times. Three shots to the target. Straight to the chest. Gramps swung to the side before thudding to the ground. The train resumed its course without letting its passengers off, meaning the two officers had sounded the alert just in time.

Searching for survivors, Oleg moved from one body to the next. With one hand, he shielded his eyes from the glare of the overhead lights. His steps were becoming more labored. Just after his throat began to itch, an intense burning sensation ripped through his chest. Oleg propped himself against a pillar to catch his breath.

A coughing fit rose in his throat and shook his body with such force, he lost his balance and fell to the ground. The forensics team would determine the time of death: eight ten a.m.

CHAPTER 9

PRAGUE, THE DAY OF THE INCIDENT IN PARDUBICE

Eytan's afternoon flight from London landed at two forty-five on the dot. He was glad for that lucky break, at least. Mid-length flights were notorious for their delays. He knew the unfortunate passenger next to him was just as happy. The fiftyish-looking man in chinos and moccasins had been squashed against the window for the entire flight. Eytan's oversized frame was highly incompatible with the Embraer 170's narrow cabin. Any attempts the man made to negotiate a few extra inches of space were met with a scowl.

Once in the terminal, Eytan turned on his cell phone. No new messages or missed calls. No news was good news.

He plucked his army duffle off the baggage carousel, headed toward a newsstand, grabbed an English-language newspaper, and sat down in a bar bustling with arriving and departing travelers. He checked the time on his phone. It was three thirty. He had two hours to kill, and this was as good a way as any to pass the time.

Eytan spent the next one hundred and five minutes brushing up on the state of the world, first with an analysis of the financial crisis that had shaken Greece to its core and appeared likely to spread, followed by

THE SHIRO PROJECT   55

a superficial article on wildfires engulfing Moscow. That story was overshadowed by a Chechen militant attack on the country's parliament. He finished with a fairly complete assessment of the monsoon-sized floods that were hitting Pakistan. So basically, the Earth was spinning faster and faster and more and more out of control. Was the Consortium hiding behind any one of these catastrophes? That simple speculation got the wheels turning in his head.

At a quarter after five, he left his reading spot and made his way to the restroom. Dropping his duffle in front of one of the three sinks, he washed his hands and splashed his face with cold water. A thin man no older than twenty walked up to the sink next to him and did the same. He was wearing jeans, an I-heart-Prague T-shirt, and gold high-top sneakers, which made him look like any of the other youthful airport-trolling tourists. The two men didn't exchange a single glance. Eytan's sink partner picked up his duffle and left the restroom, followed a few seconds later by Eytan.

Outside the airport, a cool breeze was shooing away the day's warmth. It felt good. The Kidon operative sat down on a concrete bench, pulled out his phone, and made the requested call. Three rings, and he heard the same sugary-sweet voice from the day before.

"I appreciate your timeliness, Mr. Morg. May I assume that your current location is at the airport?"

"I wasn't going to swim here."

"That's unfortunate. The City of a Hundred Spires is quite breathtaking when viewed from the Vltava River."

"This may not be the best time to talk about tourist attractions."

"You're absolutely right, Mr. Morg. Maybe later. For the time being, I'd like you to go to the taxi stand

56 David Khara

across from Terminal 1. A driver is waiting for you there. He'll be holding a sign with your name on it. The man knows nothing, aside from the location where he's to take you. So there's no point in trying to push him for more information."

"So you think I'm that violent?"

"I've always believed that an ounce of prevention is worth a pound of cure." Eytan knew the man was trying to irritate him with his breezy cliché. "The ride won't take more than half an hour. Good-bye for now."

The conversation ended abruptly. But for Eytan, it had lasted long enough.

As the taxi bypassed the city, Eytan disregarded the view. Glancing over the driver's shoulder at the GPS, he had figured out that the address given by the mystery man was outside the metropolis. All he could focus on at this point was gearing up for the meeting, which meant arming up. He opened the bag he had switched with the I-heart-Prague boy and smiled at the sight of his requested arsenal. Eytan slipped a gun into his belt.

The Consortium wanted him in tiptop shape. He wouldn't disappoint.

After a quick thirty minutes, which included several traffic lulls that prompted the driver to go off on half-English, half-Czech cursing fits, the car arrived in an abandoned industrial park. In the middle of this weedy jungle stood two old buildings with shattered windows and caving roofs. Graffiti frescos in faded colors covered the walls. Perhaps it had been a playground for street artists before further deteriorating and acquiring its no-one-gets-out-of-here-alive vibe.

The taxi driver dropped Eytan off and drove away like a bat out of hell. The giant slung his bag over his shoulder and walked toward the middle of the industrial

THE SHIRO PROJECT   57

park, which he figured had gone out of business soon after the Communist Party closed up shop. At any other time, walking into a situation such as this would have been begging for a sniper's bullet. But Eytan wasn't worried about being taken out, at least not at this point. He was more curious than anything else.

Less than five minutes later, he arrived at a decrepit storage shack, where a black limousine was parked, looking laughably out of place in this abandoned lot. Reflexively, his eyes shot to the license plate. He memorized the numbers.

The shack's rusty metal door slid open. Two muscle men wearing gray suits and earpieces came out and motioned to Eytan. "He's inside," one of them said.

With his senses on high alert, Eytan walked toward the watchdogs. They stepped aside to let him pass.

"Would you like us to hold on to your bag?" the man asked.

"Thanks, I'll keep it with me," Eytan said.

"As you wish, sir," he replied. "We'll see you later."

The Mossad assassin entered the building. They were letting him keep his bag, and they weren't searching him. This was getting weirder by the second.

A stylish-looking man of medium height was standing about thirty feet away, next to a metal table. On it, a small laptop computer lay open.

"Come closer, Eytan. I won't bite," the man said. "Even unarmed, you have no reason to be scared of me. You can call me Jenkins."

Even unarmed? Eytan thought. What was going on?

He looked over this so-called Jenkins. He was wearing a short light-brown coat, Italian leather shoes with pointed toes, and a gray suit. His hair was swooped

58 DAVID KHARA

up and back. He looked like a model straight out of a menswear catalog. Eytan kept his appraisal to himself.

"Fine, stay there if you prefer," the man continued. "Since you're a bit late, I'll cut to the chase. If you want to see your pal Karman all in one piece, you'll have to do some work for us."

Eytan started to speak, but Jenkins waved him off. His hand was trembling, and Eytan noticed a facial tic. The metrosexual seemed to be overly excited.

"Before you object, I should tell you that you'd be helping a good cause, and I know you're a good Boy Scout. Oh, and by the way, it would be greatly appreciated if you'd release Elena."

This baby-faced amateur with the malevolent smile was speaking with such arrogance. He clearly knew nothing about the world.

"All right, Morgy. What do you say?"

Jenkins was trying to provoke him, but the man wasn't going to get the rise he wanted. "What do I say? Hmm, let me think a second," Eytan responded. "I'm a man of action, not an intellectual like you. I need some time to digest the ins and outs of the situation. You've captured Eli Karman in hopes of coercing me into working for an organization that's responsible for the death of millions of people, an organization that plans to kill even more people and, coincidentally, drastically changed the course of my own life. I would even venture to say stole my life. Does that sum it up?"

"Look," Jenkins said. "It's not like—"

"And you're asking me what I say about this?" Eytan pressed.

"Yes." The man wasn't smiling anymore. Eytan read a worried look in his eyes.

"Oh, I'm sorry. I'm being a little harsh, and I haven't answered your question. I say it'll be about a week in the hospital post-op and five or six months of physical therapy."

"What the hell are you blabbering about?" the man responded, clearly attempting to regain the upper hand. "I don't understand." His face was bright red, and beads of sweat were forming on his forehead.

"That's to be expected. I was being unreasonably vague," the Israeli agent continued. "Probably because of my disrupted upbringing. I was talking about knee-caps, busted ligaments, medical costs."

"Kneecaps? Ligaments? What knees?" The once confident voice was now embarrassingly squeaky.

"Yours," said Eytan.

He took out his gun, aimed at Jenkins's left leg, and pulled the trigger. Blood stained the man's pants as the bullet bit flesh. Jenkins fell backward, screaming.

Eytan made a pouty face, walked toward his wounded victim, and squatted next to him, gun in hand.

"Does it hurt, kid? It'll take some time to walk again. And as for jogging and playing squash, that all depends on how good your surgeon is and how much effort you put into therapy."

"What the hell did you do that for? Are you crazy? Your friend's going down. That's for sure!"

Eytan looked into the distance, as if the walls of the run-down building didn't exist.

"I doubt that. The problem with you and your huge head is that you make everything so complicated. Let me help you see things from my perspective. I hope you don't mind, but I'll be blunt, since we're friends now, and friends can be honest with each other. Your organization obviously needs me. Otherwise, you'd have shot me the second I walked into this shack. And if Eli dies, you can say good-bye to my cooperation. So

60   David Khara

basically, to speak your businessman language, you're negotiating blind. Normally, I'd suggest that you look around and savor a final opportunity to appreciate our beautiful world. Unfortunately, this disgusting joint doesn't allow for that. Plus, I'd like you to fully enjoy a long and painful recovery. So it's time to wrap this up, spare your life, and wait."

"Wait for what?" the man replied, gasping.

"Wait for your jackass of a boss to show up or call, depending on how he decides to make his entrance."

"But how…"

"Oh wow, you're not faking it. You really don't know anything. Here's a tip, you vain little power-hungry prick: to negotiate blind, a real pro sends a pawn. That's you, twerp. By the way, if I thought you were of any importance, I would've shot you between the eyes. Now I see why those men—the ones who supposedly had your back—let me keep my weapon. There you have it, little man. You were just played by a cast of honchos. I'd be surprised if they ever bring you back on board."

"Mr. Morg, thank you for your keen insight. You'd make a good human resources manager in my organization if you ever decide to leave Mossad."

The voice was coming from the small laptop on the table. Eytan recognized it immediately. The giant tucked his gun back under his belt. He leaned toward Jenkins and whispered in his ear. "I have to leave you. The adults need to discuss important business now. Remember: five or six months. Good luck."

He winked at Jenkins, whose mouth moved clumsily as he spit out a few venomous but restrained curses.

The disembodied voice spoke up again. "Would you be so kind as to pick up the computer, Mr. Morg? It's equipped with a camera. Please excuse my precautions, but I'd rather not be present during one of your angry mood swings."

"That's a wise move on your part. I'm a bit on edge at the moment," Eytan said as he lifted the laptop. It had two open windows. One displayed a close-up of the agent's face. The other showed the dark shape of a man. The light was conveniently positioned in a way that Eytan couldn't make out his features.

"I was wondering if you were going to kill him. Jenkins has a remarkable talent for annoying people, which amuses me. Well, that is until I no longer find his services useful. Don't worry. My men will take him to the hospital."

"Ah, so all this was just a way to get rid of a pesky employee?"

"That was, indeed, the plan."

"I'm not one to do things by the book, but wouldn't it have been easier to fire him the traditional way?"

"Of course, but that wouldn't have driven the message home. Jenkins has now learned that individuals are important to the organization, but they are never more important than the organization. While corporations last, employees are…"

"Expendable?"

"Exactly."

"They don't teach that in business school, do they?"

"You'd be surprised at how much business schools don't cover these days."

"And yet I've heard that tuition is through the roof."

"I don't mean to be rude, but we're not here to talk about the shortcomings of academia. We have more pressing matters to discuss."

"I agree."

"What do you know about the Consortium, Mr. Morg? Sorry, let me rephrase that: What do you think you know?"

"I know that your secret society supported Hitler's rise to power so that he'd create world chaos and, in the process, free scientific research of any ethical constraints. I also know that you used pharmaceutical companies to further a scheme to create a master race, but your plans hit a little snafu."

"Oh dear, your account appears quite sound, aside from a few details."

"That was the short version."

"Simplistic, to say the least."

"I'd love to know more, if only to glean some information that would help me set fire to your outfit, giving me the pleasure of watching it burn to the ground. But for starters, how about explaining what it is that you want from me."

"Well, to get straight to the point, what do you know about P4 laboratories?"

CHAPTER 10

With his bag over his shoulder and the computer in his right hand, Eytan left the storage building and took the cracked and weed-filled walkway around the building, as instructed by the man, who had identified himself as Cypher. The day had just a few hours of sunlight left, and the cool breeze rippled through the tall grass. The abandoned industrial park looked like a scene from an apocalypse movie. Rust was devouring the bleak structures. Inside the crumbling buildings, trees had taken root. Overgrowth covered what remained of the walls. Nature was gaining ground and would soon erase all trace of humanity from these parts.

Despite the circumstances, Eytan felt a unique poetry in the landscape. He wondered how he would paint it, and what he would name the rendering. But this was not the time to channel his inner impressionist.

He resumed his conversation.

"P4 laboratories adhere to extremely strict security standards and procedures, if memory serves me. They handle the most exotic and hazardous biological agents that cause infectious diseases. No vaccines have been developed for these potential plagues. Researchers are required to wear special suits with their own air supply. This kind of facility must have several showers, a UV-light room, a vacuum room, and airlock doors. The Centers for Disease Control and Prevention in Atlanta

64   DAVID KHARA

has a P4 lab. They're also called BSL4, or biosafety level 4 facilities."

"Commendable response," Cypher said. "Let me shed a bit more light on the issue. The extreme standards and procedures you outlined are necessitated by the kind of pathogens these facilities harbor. Just the mention of some of the viruses is enough to elicit widespread panic: Crimean-Congo, Marburg, Lassa, to name a few."

"Ebola—basically the worst viral scum out there."

"Exactly. Now for a little history lesson. In 1967, scientists at the Behringwerke laboratory in Marburg, Germany, were developing a measles vaccine. They were using kidney cells from imported Ugandan green monkeys. Sadly, the monkeys were carriers of a filovirus, which was unknown at the time. It was a strand of Ebola. Symptoms of the infection are terrifying: headaches, diarrhea, vomiting. Hemorrhaging kicks in after about a week, leading to death in most cases. I don't need to tell you that every researcher working with those cells at Behringwerke, plus two spouses, died within weeks. In all, thirty-one people were infected. No one knew the specific cause until much later."

Without missing a word of the explanation, Eytan had been trying to place Cypher's accent. Each sentence had brought him closer to figuring it out. He was now positive that the man was British. Cypher continued his story.

"The virus got its name from the location of the outbreak, the city of Marburg. There were also outbreaks in Frankfurt and Belgrade, Yugoslavia, that same year, but they were contained. They could have been much more serious. As a result, international authorities created the P4 accreditations and began enforcing the security measures."

The shadowy figure on the screen brought a hand to his mouth. Eytan heard the man inhale. A puff of vapor appeared, but there was no fiery glow. Cypher was smoking an electronic cigarette, and that was a prized piece of information.

"You see, Mr. Morg, I'm always amazed at the fuss people make over the dangers of nuclear power. Don't they know that scientists all over the world are working with microorganisms every day that have the potential to decimate the entire planet?"

"Images of Hiroshima and Nagasaki have left their mark."

"And most people don't give a deadly illness a second thought unless they have it, someone they know has it, or it's making headlines."

Eytan paused, rummaged through the pocket of his jacket, and pulled out a cigar.

"I agree," he sighed, lighting a match. "All right, this is all very interesting, but now I'd like to know what these labs have to do with me. I'm not usually an impatient man, but Eli Karman's kidnapping has given me the worst case of nerves. You know my reputation."

"Oh, Mr. Morg, kidnapping is such an ugly word. Let's just say your boss is our guest, nothing more. Once this situation is taken care of, he'll be back in the loving arms of his little family and his favorite agent."

"Your goon demanded Elena's release. Do you confirm this request?"

"Yes. We'll be trading Mr. Karman for my protégée. But before that, the both of you will be teaming up to take care of some business I have for you."

The thought of having anything to do with a fully conscious Elena repulsed Eytan. But he mulled it over for a few seconds and arrived at a simple conclusion: no one here had a choice. The two parties could leave

66   DAVID KHARA

as winners or losers, no guarantee on either side. For the moment, he'd have to grin and bear the man's terms. But the surprise end to this tale would be like Gunfight at the OK Corral, and that was fine by him.

"Okay. So give me the facts."

"We'll get there. For now, turn left, and then continue straight ahead."

The giant obeyed, and Cypher resumed. "Three months ago, a scientist working in one of our P4 labs disappeared, quite literally. This man came to work one morning, left that evening, and vanished without leaving a trace. His home was intact. His bank account had no suspicious activity before his disappearance, and it remained unused afterward. It's a complete mystery."

So these nutcases had their own P4 labs, and putting an end to the Bleiberg Project was really no serious setback for this new enemy. Now Eytan fully understood that their power to stir up trouble remained intact and even exceeded his wildest imagination.

"Tell me more about your Houdini," he said, concealing his anger.

"Given the sensitive nature of his work, this man was watched closely. We conducted a thorough background check before hiring him, and we didn't find a thing. He was a capable employee with no history."

"So now will you clue me in on the type of experiments this guy was conducting?"

"You're as sharp as a tack, Mr. Morg. I like that. This scientist was working on viral strains for military operations."

"Why am I not surprised," Eytan said with a sigh.

"Ah, but I'm not saying that he was developing bio-weapons. Just the opposite. He was researching ways to neutralize the stock amassed by the two blocs during the Cold War."

"Your magician ran off with the strains he was working on. He fled to a site with less surveillance than your intrusive research base. Is that it?"

"Just how do you do it, Mr. Morg?" Cypher said. Eytan could hear the derision in his tone.

"Simple. I always expect the worst. Chalk it up to experience. For fun, just tell me this: the Consortium is a big, powerful, and resourceful organization. Why me?"

"As the issue at hand is extremely sensitive, you can understand that we'd prefer to keep everything on the QT, at least for now. So why are we asking for your help? If you would allow me, I'd like to save my answer for a later time. You don't need to know my intentions in order to get the job done. All you need to know is that I have been thoroughly impressed by your talents. In some ways, I am greatly indebted to you, Mr. Morg. The dismantling of the Bleiberg Project, which I disapproved of, actually led to my own promotion. Now, as head of the executive committee, I've brought about a radical change in our approach. We're more, let's say, humanistic."

Eytan raised his cigar in the air. He was enticed by the opportunity to test this way-too-ass-kissing opponent.

"Hallelujah, boys and girls," Eytan shouted. "The hippies are making a comeback. If you really wanted to share a joint with me while singing Bob Dylan ditties around a campfire, kidnapping Eli Karman was a bit extreme, counterproductive even."

"Under other circumstances, I'd be entertained by your jokes, Mr. Morg," Cypher retorted.

Eytan could hear the man's smooth demeanor beginning to crack. He didn't like being on the receiving end of anyone's sarcasm. He was revealing his hidden and therefore dangerous temper, and Eytan was quick to take note. Later, it could be useful.

The shadow took a long drag of his electronic device and exhaled a large puff of smoke. The mystery man was clearly agitated. He paused, and a few seconds of silence followed. He's regrouping, Eytan thought.

"You're not taking my new strategy for the Consortium seriously," Cypher said in a cooler tone. "The supply of viral strains held by the two superpowers was an issue for our former leaders. But even though I'm not responsible for this incident, I won't leave it unresolved and allow the first terrorist who shows up to profit from it."

"Bingo, you've said the magic word! So I'm assuming the terrorist's motive hasn't fallen into your lap?"

"Let's be reasonable. People don't make a hobby of collecting viral strains. This kind of activity requires patience, a great deal of discipline, and a clear objective. Besides, the very nature of the stolen pathogens implies a desire to cause a large-scale bloodbath."

"But just for the sake of conversation, let's assume it's not a terrorist. Many governments might want to acquire this kind of bioweapon."

"Yes, Mr. Morg. Except that last week a warning letter reached officials in the Czech Republic. The creator—or creators—of said letter announced that a targeted biological attack would occur today somewhere within the nation's borders. That's as specific as they got."

"Did the letter indicate any demands?"

"No."

THE SHIRO PROJECT   69

"Is there reason to take the threat seriously?" Eytan asked.

"Yes."

"What is it?"

"The attack just occurred, Mr. Morg. It will no doubt have the same disastrous consequences as the recent strike in the Moscow metro."

Eytan remembered the newspaper story that he had read at the airport. "The one attributed to Chechen terrorists?" he asked.

"Yes, the Russian authorities blamed their favorite scapegoat to hide the truth. It was a bioweapon attack that was nothing close to the standard methods used by the Chechen militants. Ah, we've arrived! Look to your left."

Absorbed in finding clues in Cypher's speech, Eytan had forgotten his surroundings. He turned in the indicated direction and found a black Kawasaki ZZR 1400 and a yellow helmet.

"That's your ride. Your friend Karman told me that motorcycles are your preferred means of transportation. We got you the largest helmet available, which eliminated some of the more stylish options. I was also hoping to provide you with a leather jacket, but it appears that your lucky camo is all that you'll wear. I'm sure you're eager to discover the vehicle's surveillance capabilities and other technological features, so I'll let you know there's a GPS tracking device. Nothing else. But I assume you won't be taking my word for it."

"Nice work."

"The same equipment awaits Elena in the Hotel Imperial parking lot, which will serve as your home base. In the suite reserved under your name, there's a bag containing our friend's personal belongings, as

70   DAVID KHARA

well as two passports for her and a computer to help us stay in contact." Cypher paused. "Any questions?"

"None."

Cypher continued. "Go to the site of the incident, and scope out the scene. The coordinates were transferred to your navigation system. After your mission is completed, you'll release Elena. As for me, I'll be collecting as much data as possible to assist you. Use the provided phone number as soon as you uncover any important information. If you have any questions, feel free to call. We'll respond when possible. Good luck, Mr. Morg."

The call ended, leaving the Mossad agent feeling isolated and wary. Eytan was still trying to assimilate what he had just been told. He walked over to the motorcycle and examined it. The GPS was set for the Pardubice region in the eastern part of the Czech Republic.

The attack just occurred. The words ran through Eytan's mind. For well more than half a century, he had been fighting a brutal and merciless war in the shadows. His enemies had faces and bodies. All it took was a bullet or a punch. But biological weapons... How could he take on these invisible, intangible opponents?

Eytan turned around slowly, his hands inside the frayed pockets of his jacket. He no longer saw anything poetic in this wasteland. Man had long ago abandoned it to the forces of nature. Those forces had taken over, inch by inch. As far as Eytan was concerned, there was nothing of value to be found in this place.

The title of his imaginary painting was evident: "Prophecy."

CHAPTER 11

PRAGUE, THE NIGHT AFTER THE ATTACK IN PARDUBICE

Eytan didn't see the point in staying in the vicinity of the destroyed village. The disappearance of three special-forces commandos would draw even more attention to the area, and turning it into a battlefield would not help his cause. After disposing of the bodies, he retrieved his motorcycle and headed toward Prague.

It was now dusk, and his flight to Tel Aviv would be leaving moments before midnight. He'd have just enough time to stop at the hotel room, which Cypher had most likely reserved to keep an eye on him, take a shower, grab some grub, drop off his weapons, and leave to release Elena.

This last task made him sick to the stomach.

After all, this woman was responsible for killing the mother of Jeremy Corbin, the Wall Street trader who had helped him chase down Professor Bleiberg. She had also admitted killing Bernard Dean, the CIA agent who had watched over the young man for several years. She had even left her mark on Eytan in the form of a wound to his shoulder and another to his leg. Had Jeremy not saved him, his life would have ended altogether at the hands of this assassin.

Releasing Elena, rescuing Eli, and stopping a proven bioterrorist risk. Eytan's schedule for the week was

72   DAVID KHARA

filling up fast. The four-hour plane ride gave him time to harp on his unhappiness. On the plus side, the plane was practically empty at this late hour. So at least he didn't have to deal with a pesky seatmate.

Moments after the plane landed, Eytan was greeted in the terminal by three agents—two men and one woman—who drove him to Elena's place of detention. Eli had authorized her release without divulging any more information. On the way, the agents told Eytan about the prisoner's exploits.

Murphy's Law, the giant thought as he listened. He wondered if Jeremy had somehow passed all of his bad luck along to him.

Twenty minutes later, Eytan was greeting Dr. Lafner at the clinic entrance. The doctor looked bone-tired, but welcomed Eytan with open arms. From their initial introduction five years earlier, Eytan had liked the man. They shared an affinity for adventure. They both believed in bending the rules when necessary and had a certain disregard for authority. It wasn't lost on Eytan that the doctor never asked any prying questions about his unique genetic traits.

"Hey, Eytan! You have no idea how happy I am that you're here."

"Glad to see you too, Avi. But I'm afraid our reunion will be a short one."

"Not even enough time to grab a coffee? Our boss is going to get us a new machine, but in the meantime, I sneaked in this sweet espresso machine from home. Mum's the word. It's against the rules."

"Sorry, I can't, Avi. I've got a plane to catch."

They walked into the building. Eytan was relieved to know the doctor was alive, but he had no time to talk. Nothing could distract him from his objective. If he wanted to stop the downward spiral, he'd have to act fast.

"That's too bad," Avi said. "All right, I'll take you to her. I decided to keep the fireball locked up in a psychiatric cell until you got here. I put guards on her too, and with her being unconscious, I managed to perform a few exams."

"Oh, you know how I love a good experiment."

Avi held up a finger, wordlessly warning his friend that he was on the verge of going too far. "Watch it! You need to cut that act right now. I'm not conducting research on her. I'm checking her physical health. There's a difference. Would you like to meet the families of the soldiers she murdered? She didn't even try to hold them hostage. That madwoman killed them in cold blood. Had it not been for an enormous stroke of luck, I would have been dead too. I was scared shitless! So even though I enjoy a harmless prank or two, don't assume more than you should. Understand?"

"I might be going out on a limb here, but you seem a tad stressed."

"That's the understatement of the century."

Eytan placed his immense paw on the shoulder of this man, whom he considered his closest true friend at Mossad. "Look, I'm really sorry about the soldiers, but we were very clear about the level of harm that Elena was capable of committing. Obviously we didn't put enough men on her. How were you able to escape, anyway?"

"She was about to kill me, but she passed out before she could."

"And why did she faint? I mean, you're a charming guy and all, but this isn't the kind of gal who swoons so easily." Eytan gave the doctor a wink.

"Don't underestimate my powers of seduction, Eytan," the doctor countered. "I actually don't know why she passed out. I'm waiting to get the test results back. I'll give you an update as soon as I find out."

"Thanks, Avi."

"Yeah, well, anyway, I was glad to learn you'll be transferring her out of here."

Eytan rubbed his forehead. He was embarrassed to tell Avi his real reason for being there. "I'm here to free her, actually," he said.

"Excuse me?" Avi asked, confused.

"I didn't come here to transfer her, but to free her."

The doctor took a deep breath before throwing his arms in the air.

"This story's getting better and better! I love the intelligence service. If only you knew how its incomprehensible manipulations keep me going each and every day. Oh, and I guess there's no point in giving you any shit about your new cripple walk... I noticed your leg."

"You're such a pain." Eytan sneered.

"You know that's why you love me."

They arrived at a large door guarded by two heavily armed men. Avi stayed back.

"Alone," Eytan ordered the guards, who were about to follow him into the room.

The small space looked like a prison cell, with cement-block walls and a lone barred window. Elena, wearing blue pajamas, was seated in a chair at a small rectangular table. She was handcuffed.

"Hello, Elena."

"Morg, if you've come here for information, spare yourself the effort. I'll die before I say anything." Giving him a hateful look, she brought her hands to her mouth and fingered her injured lip. "Enjoy your little victory parade while it lasts."

"Do you rehearse these quips in front of a mirror at night, or does this crap come naturally?"

She scowled, and Eytan knew he had struck a chord. He sat down in front of her. "Why did you have to torture those four men before killing them?"

"We were just play fighting. Then the security guard came at me with his gun. It wasn't difficult to get his weapon. I thought I'd add to the fun by shooting out the lights. Long story short, I lost the gun, but not before he lost the use of a leg. In the end, they all lost their lives. All's fair in love and war. Isn't that what they say?"

"Wow, and I thought I was a hard-ass."

"You would have done the same."

"I don't kill in cold blood."

"Such compassion."

"Or fair play. It depends on your point of view."

"Did you come here to teach me semantics or give me a lesson on morality? In either case, you're wasting your breath. You won. I didn't. Nothing else matters. So get on with it if you—"

Eytan interrupted the would-be long-winded speech. "I have good news and bad news. For me, it's all bad news. That alone should make you happy."

"Make me happy? We'll see about that. But I'm curious to know where this is going."

"The good news: I'm freeing you. The bad: it's so we can work together."

"I don't understand."

"I'll leave the explanation to one of your pals," Eytan said as he pulled out his cell phone. He punched the speaker option and placed it on the table. It rang a few times before a voice responded.

"Mr. Morg, what news do you have for me?"

"I'm with Elena. She can hear you."

"Hello, my dear. How are you doing?"

Elena sat up straight in her chair.

"Cypher?"

"I understand your surprise, dear, but there's no time for gushing. You'll have to settle for listening to and following my instructions."

"Yes, sir."

She leaned forward, her cuffed hands stretched out on the table. Eytan was soaking up her body language. She was a star student glued to her favorite teacher's every word. So this woman, who was harder than stone, was actually capable of acting obediently. How intriguing.

"We're dealing with an emergency. I've called on Mr. Morg for help, and you're to work together. He'll explain the rest."

"All right," Elena said. Eytan could see the confusion on her face.

"Now this applies to both of you: set aside your differences for the time being. Mr. Morg is aware of the consequences, but Elena, I'm expecting an equal amount of cooperation from you."

"You can depend on me, sir," she said.

"I would expect nothing less. Good luck to both of you."

Eytan ended the call and twirled the phone in his fingers before putting it back in his pocket. A long silence set in. He fixed his sharp gaze on Elena's dark eyes.

"Well, there you have it," he said. "As you can see, we're both screwed."

"Agreed."

"Your clothes are in the next room. Our plane to Prague leaves in an hour. I'll fill you in on the details during the flight."

"Why are you following Cypher's orders?" the woman asked.

"I could ask you the same question."

She slid her palms over the table.

"I see. Neither one of us is going to cave."

"Nope. This is shitty for the both of us, but we have to deal with it. Just to get things straight, I'm your superior in this operation. You do as I say and when I say. As for your equipment, I'll give it to you once we've arrived. You'll have no weapons or means of communication unless I decide otherwise. If you'd still like to eliminate me, you'll have the pleasure of trying to do so once we've completed this mission."

"Sounds good to me. I don't have to kill you today. Tomorrow will work just as well."

"Great," he said.

He motioned to Elena to hold up her shackled wrists, and he unlocked the handcuffs with the key Avi had given him. But just as the cuffs were springing apart, Elena stood and knocked Eytan against the wall. With her right forearm, she pinned his neck against the cement blocks. She used her left hand to dig into his wounded thigh. For the second time, Eytan felt the killer's breath against his face. The first time was during their encounter at the BCI facility. Only now, Jeremy wasn't there to save him.

Her jaw tight, she upped the pressure on his neck. "I'm very tempted..."

She released him.

"But I'm a good girl. If Cypher wants us to work together, so be it."

Eytan wouldn't be caught like that again. Through the whole confrontation, his look had remained impassive. He knew his refusal to react had disappointed her. He walked to the other side of the cell and opened the door as if nothing had happened.

She passed by him, and they headed toward the next room.

"You're welcome to take a shower if you want. We're leaving in fifteen minutes. Be on time."

The woman went into the room where her clothes awaited her. Eytan checked his watch. The prospect of having to fly yet again was ticking him off.

He spotted Avi Lafner coming down the hallway.

"Ready for your flight?" the doctor asked.

Eytan gave him a frustrated look.

"You don't look too excited about going back to Prague," his friend said.

"It's been a tough week."

CHAPTER 12

PRAGUE, THAT SAME NIGHT

Branislav was hyped. Holding a cup of scalding tea, he paced the living room of the apartment outside the capital that he shared with his wife, Lucie. Shaken by the day's events, he knew falling asleep would be impossible. Never in a million years could he have imagined himself at the wrong end of military machine guns (or on the right side, for that matter). Nor could he wrap his head around all those bodies or the mysterious knight in shining armor. Nope, there's no way I'll be finding my Zen tonight, Branislav thought. Worse yet, he still hadn't talked with his parents. He tried calling them one more time but once again got the automated message. "Your call cannot be completed yada yada."

He threw the phone on the couch before collapsing into it himself. Even though things had been chilly between Lucie and him, and he had been sleeping on the futon in the spare room, he liked having her around. Now, however, he was glad she was working on location for two days, on a made-for-television movie. "At least she won't be involved in this god-awful mess," he said and sighed.

Branislav placed his cup on the coffee table and rubbed his skull. In the past, he had been irritated

80   DAVID KHARA

by all the time she spent on film sets, but everything was different now. If she'd give him the chance and if there was even the smallest glimmer of hope for their marriage, he'd stop wasting energy on inconsequential things. It's the fool's curse, he thought bitterly. Why is it that you can't appreciate what you have until everything goes to hell?

Two in the morning. Another pot of tea. He decided to put his faith in chamomile. He needed to calm down and think. Maybe with a cup or two, he could even get some sleep.

He had become completely paranoid on his drive back to Prague. He could hardly take his eyes off the rearview mirror. Were people pursuing him? He even considered hiding out in a hotel room for a few days before returning to his apartment. But who would be trying to find him? Three guys had seen his name and address, but they weren't a problem now. Only God and that strange bald motorcyclist knew where their bodies were stashed. As for the police blocking the road, he hadn't given them any reason to take down his license-plate number. After reviewing everything, he decided to dismiss his concerns.

It's good to be careful, but let's not go overboard, he told himself. He'd give it until the morning—just to make sure he was safe—then hit the newsroom with this.

Shadows animated by the headlights of passing cars danced on the living room walls. Branislav lit a cigarette and went into the spare room. At this hour, even the floral-patterned futon looked inviting. He lay down and fell under the trance of his smoke rings as they pirouetted in the air and vanished before reaching the ceiling. After a few more puffs he crushed his cigarette butt in the ashtray. And as his questions grew

THE SHIRO PROJECT   81

murkier, his ideas less precise, and the room less present, Branislav drifted into a heavy sleep.

A shrill buzz pierced his dream. "I just got to sleep," he muttered as he opened an eye. But it wasn't dark anymore. The light coming from the windows felt blinding. It was too soon for that much sun. Now the noise of the cell phone next to him was hurting his ears. He answered the call just before it went to voice mail.

"Bran? Are you all right?"

"Mom?"

"Where are you, dear? Your father and I have been worried sick."

He stood up with a great deal of effort. The wheels were back in motion. He headed toward the kitchen to wet his dry throat with some much-needed coffee.

"I'm at the apartment. I tried calling yesterday, but—"

"You weren't caught in the wildfire?" his mother asked.

"Wildfire?" He had to be half-asleep still. What wildfire?

"You didn't hear?"

"Um, no. What are you talking about?"

"A huge forest fire broke out late yesterday afternoon. The roads were closed, and the telephone lines were down until this morning. We were so scared that you—"

"No, Mom, I'm fine. The police officers made me turn around, and I couldn't get hold of you. So what happened? Did you have to evacuate?"

"No, the firefighters got it under control. Two of them came by earlier to tell us we have nothing to worry about. But on TV, they're saying the neighboring village was completely wiped out. Can you believe it?"

82   DAVID KHARA

"Mom, I have to run to the office. I'll call you back when I have more information. Worst-case scenario, take Dad's boat and go to the other side of the lake if the flames are close. Okay?"

"You know your father. He's already taken care of everything if we have to leave."

"Give him a hug for me. I'll talk to you later, Mom."

"Talk later, dear. And give Lucie my love."

Branislav ended the call and went into the living room to turn on the TV. He clicked the remote to the news channel where he had gotten his start as a journalist. Horrific images came up. Planes were flying above the forest he had known so well. They were showering monstrous flames with tons of fire retardant. An impressive number of firefighters had spent the entire night battling the blaze, according to the reporter.

A scroll bar at the bottom of the screen relayed news of the fiery destruction of the small village. All the residents had lost their lives.

Branislav couldn't believe his eyes—or his ears. His reporter's instincts egged him on. The fire was a cover-up for what he had witnessed the day before. They were using the scorched-earth strategy.

Half an hour later, after a hot shower, Branislav was feeling reinvigorated. He rushed to his car and headed to the paper. A story like this could catapult him out of the professional rut he was in. He was tired of covering the same old sporting events. This could be his big break. But he needed more information. He had to put the pieces together. He knew what had happened to him, and he had seen the village himself. But what had caused this bizarre event? He had to keep his wits. Only yesterday, he had been staring death in the face. What personal perils would he be risking by taking on

THE SHIRO PROJECT   83

this story? That giant, Eytan, had warned him not to say a word about it, but now that it was on the news, it must be okay.

Playful heckling greeted him in the newsroom. He had made up an excuse for cutting his vacation short: an unfinished story about an obscure soccer club had been nagging at him, and he couldn't enjoy his time off until it was done. The reporters covering the Pardubice fire were paying no attention. The fire would be filling many pages of the next day's paper, and there was much news to gather. Three veterans were heading up the team. They were shooting off one phone call after another in search of the facts. A reporter and a photographer had been dispatched to the scene to conduct interviews with firefighters and eyewitnesses. The palpable tension in the newsroom discouraged Branislav from asking questions.

He sat down at his desk, took out the sandwich that would serve as his lunch, and logged onto his computer. He read the wire stories and those filed by his paper's reporters. They all contained intriguing information. Or intriguing misinformation. He would have to do his own research. A wizard behind the curtain—perhaps more than one wizard—was doing his best to make people believe something that wasn't real. And Branislav knew exactly where to start.

At about three in the afternoon, the news channel sent out a report announcing the firefighters' victory over the disaster. The area where the fire originated would continue to be closed off. The cause of the blaze still hadn't been determined, although there was speculation that it was fireworks-related. The exact number of fatalities still wasn't known.

Branislav's curiosity and determination were in high gear. Answers to initial queries e-mailed to the

84   DAVID KHARA

paper's regular informants started flooding in. The reporter had been careful not to reveal the reason for his questions. After the previous day's death scare, he was in no rush to draw unwanted attention. The smallest misstep could alert the government, the military, or other secretive authorities. Certain habits tied to the Czech Republic's complicated past were still very much alive. If any doubt remained about that, this somber affair was clear proof.

Branislav was focusing on voter records for the village where the massacre had taken place. Most of the people on the list were retirees, but one puzzling name stood out. When the phone rang, he didn't bother to take his eyes off the document to pick up the receiver.

The melodious voice of Svetlana, the receptionist, flowed through the line. "Bran, there's a package for you at the front desk."

"What is it?" Branislav asked, uneasy.

"It's a camera with an envelope. Are you coming down, or should I bring them up to you?"

The journalist was silent.

"Bran, are you there?"

"Yeah, yeah. Who dropped them off?"

"A big guy with waxed eyebrows. Kind of stocky but not bad looking. If he's a friend of yours, feel free to slip him my number."

"I'll think about it. That would be great if you could bring them up to me. I'm swamped right now."

"Okay."

In his excitement to solve the mystery, Branislav had almost forgotten about his camera. Actually, he had half hoped that his rescuer would forget about it. Seeing how easily and brutally the man had eliminated those three commandos was disturbing, to say the least. Clearly, it was best to stay on this guy's good side.

Svetlana showed up moments later, drawing the usual lustful looks. As she handed Branislav the camera and accompanying letter, she gave him a flirtatious smile. The receptionist's visits to the newsroom had the ability to cheer up the male reporters on even their worst days.

Branislav plugged his digital camera into his computer. He was both surprised and relieved to see that it worked smoothly. Even more shocking, all his pictures were still there. Taking a closer look, he saw an additional folder in the list of thumbnails. A double-click later, and the image of a bistro appeared on the screen. And this wasn't just any bistro. It was the small joint across the street from the newspaper. The time at which the picture was taken revealed the photographer's intentions: five minutes before Svetlana's call.

The envelope contained a short note with an obscure message: "Print photo DSC_00081. Large format." He transferred the indicated image onto a thumb drive and made the requested print.

Branislav collected all the papers scattered across his desk and put them in a plastic folder. He disconnected the camera, threw on his jacket, and jetted out of the office. Against all logic, he was going to RSVP this rather unusual invitation. He just didn't know if he was confusing wishful thinking with a death wish.

CHAPTER 13

The newspaper offices were in a part of town devoid of tourists, and the street was virtually deserted this afternoon. Branislav scoped out the scene in search of a stakeout car or any suspicious-looking characters. He saw no one but a woman leaning against a bus-stop sign. Even if she had been in a crowd, she would have caught his attention. This woman was eye candy. Black pants and a tapered leather jacket accentuated her thin—but not scrawny—figure. Her body language, however, was enough to put off all but the most daring flirt. Her arms were folded across her chest, and her expression was nothing short of prickly.

Seeing no immediate danger, he crossed the street.

Branislav took a deep breath before entering the bistro. Colleagues would pick up their morning coffee here before heading to the office. They would stop in for lunch and meet after work for drinks. In the middle of the morning or afternoon, one could usually find a reporter conducting an interview or using his laptop at one of the tables. If the paper ever relocated, bistro owner Venceslas would certainly lose the bulk of his business and be forced to close.

Venceslas was in his fifties and welcomed all patrons, regulars or not, with infectious enthusiasm. No matter the season, the former rock guitarist could always be seen sporting a short-sleeved polo, which allowed him to show off his tattoo sleeves and rippling muscles.

Photos of Venceslas's idol, Henry Rollins, adorned the walls, alongside posters from the music legend's LPs. This thematic décor choice was a startling contrast to the classically styled furniture: booth seats upholstered in sumptuous purple velvet and marble-topped tables with cast-iron legs.

"Hey there, champ," Venceslas shouted as he filled a half-pint of brown ale to the brim.

Branislav responded with less energy than usual.

"Your date is waiting for you in the back. Go have a seat. I'll bring you some liquid fuel in a couple of minutes. Hey, what sport does this guy play? Those guns on him are hard-core!"

Branislav replied with a raised eyebrow and crossed the main room, acknowledging various colleagues with a simple nod. With each step, his heart pounded a little harder. He passed the small bar leading to the backroom and located the man whose face was etched in his mind.

The tank truck was sitting coolly, his arms stretched along the top of the backrest in a booth on the far wall. His nonchalance only reinforced Branislav's anxiety. He could feel the knot in his throat getting bigger.

With a wave and a huge smile, the giant invited Branislav to join him.

Don't let him see your fear, Branislav was thinking as he approached the man who had saved his life twenty-four hours earlier.

"I took the liberty of ordering your favorite drink. Venceslas is also bringing us a plate of Prague ham. I figured I'd take advantage of my forced vacation to taste the local cuisine. And, uh, chill out, would you? You look pathetic."

Branislav glanced at the mirror next to the bathroom door. Staring back was a gaunt face. Under his eyes were dark circles and bulging veins. He was a walking poster child for clinical insomnia, thanks to a cocktail of stress, adrenaline, and nights spent on the futon.

The young man removed his raincoat and folded it over the back of his chair. He sat down, placing his camera and plastic folder on the table, just as Venceslas showed up, tray in hand. Once the order was served, and the two men had the room to themselves again, Eytan pushed the plate of smoked ham in Branislav's direction, never taking his eyes off his guest.

Branislav was starving, and he figured it wasn't a good idea to get on the guy's bad side by refusing to eat what he had ordered. So he picked up a slice of ham with his fork and put it on his plate, as Eytan, an amused look on his face, looked on.

"How..." he stammered. "How did you find me?"

"Your wallet."

"Why did you contact me?"

"You know very well why." He nodded at the folder.

"How did you know I'd be doing my own investigation?"

"You're a reporter. Need I say more?"

Branislav laughed and adjusted himself in his chair. The guy was terse, but he was on point.

"You got that right, but—"

"Yes?"

"I have more questions to ask before..."

"No time now. Later, we'll see."

"I guess I don't have a choice?"

"I had a similar conversation in a slightly tenser setting a couple of days ago," the giant said. "We always have a choice. We just have to accept the consequences."

Having seen this man dispatch the three guys from special forces, Branislav understood the truth of his statement. If the man had wanted to take his life, he

THE SHIRO PROJECT   89

would have done it already. Branislav knew this. But he still wanted some assurance, even if it meant getting no more than a hypothetical response.

"Just tell me what role you play in this story and if I have reason to be afraid of you."

"I'm here to figure out what happened and to prevent those responsible from doing any more harm. As for your second question, well, I love watching my future victims devour a plate of meat. It's so thrilling."

Branislav practically choked on his ham. But when he looked up, he saw the playful smirk on the giant's face and relaxed a bit. He managed to swallow the food lodged in his throat and spoke up again.

"I see. All right, I'm warning you, though. I'm working more on speculation than foolproof facts."

"All investigations start out that way. Let's hear it."

"Okay. What did we see yesterday? Dead people and guys in protective suits—that implies a nuclear, biological, or chemical problem."

"We can forget nuclear. That doesn't match with the deaths or the state of the village."

"I agree. What else do we have? Excessive military measures and commandos prepared to take out witnesses, which proves that the problem is supersensitive."

"They're saying it's a fire," Eytan said. "They're hiding the real incident from the public and the media. Do you think it might have been a botched military operation?"

"That's possible, but I doubt it."

"Why?

"What I saw yesterday looked more like a response to an emergency situation."

"I agree."

"Based on this information, I followed your advice to lie low," Branislav said. "Instead of probing army,

90   DAVID KHARA

police, or government officials, I focused on the village. I thought I might find a motive there."

"Not bad."

"Thanks. First, I got hold of a list of registered voters. Then I got my hands on some tax information to find out more about the villagers."

"Sneaky," Eytan said.

Branislav was flattered. He took out the records and pushed them across the table.

"Check them out. Just about all of the residents were retired. The odd thing is that I couldn't trace work histories for most of them. In fact, that was true for everyone over sixty-five."

"Go on."

"These people worked and paid taxes—some of them paid huge amounts. But it's impossible to determine what they did for a living. I have no idea what this means, but it's troubling. And I found something else. A former colleague and friend of my father's lived in that village. I called him Uncle Ivan when I was a kid. I didn't know he lived so close to my parents. I hope he wasn't one of the victims. Actually, I haven't seen him since my father left Paramo. I can't believe it's been that long."

"Your father worked at Paramo?"

"Um, yeah. Why?"

Eytan sat up and grabbed his overstuffed army bag. "Get your things. We'll take care of the photo I asked you to print later. Is your car nearby?"

"Yeah, but—

"I have a sudden urge to meet your folks. Let's go. Chop-chop!"

And just like that, before even realizing it, Branislav was on Eytan's heels. Once outside, he pointed out his Skoda.

THE SHIRO PROJECT   91

"Do you think my parents are in danger?" he asked on the way to the car.

"That's exactly what I want to prevent. But you should still call. It'll make you feel better. Don't mention my name. Their phones might've been tapped. Okay?"

"Got it."

The call was quick and the conversation casual enough not to raise his parents' suspicions. Branislav was relieved to know that his mother and father were all right. He cheerfully told Eytan that the firefighters had returned to his parents' home earlier in the afternoon to tell them that they were safe.

Seeing Eytan's grave reaction, Branislav became alarmed.

They got to the car without exchanging a word. Branislav slid behind the wheel. Eytan got in and adjusted his seat all the way back to keep his knees clear of the glove compartment. As he was struggling to find a semi-comfortable position, the back door opened. Branislav jumped in his seat and let out a high-pitched yelp. In his rearview mirror, he saw the stunning woman who had been loitering at the bus stop half an hour earlier.

"Don't freak out. She's with me," Eytan muttered as he fought with the seatbelt.

"Elena," she said.

"Branislav," the reporter responded, trying to sound suave.

She gave him a smile. Branislav could tell the facial gesture was painfully difficult for the woman. With the completion of the smiling exercise, she seemed to lose interest in any small courtesies. "Can you tell me why I'm stuck in the backseat?" she asked.

92   David Khara

Eytan's response made it clear that these two weren't exactly amiable travel buddies. "Because I'm bigger. That's why! Damn, you're getting on my nerves."

Branislav decided to stay out of the way. Without delaying any longer, he turned on the ignition. This was going to be a fun ride.

CHAPTER 14

Less than half a mile into the trip to Pardubice, Eytan asked Branislav to stop the car.

"All right, I won't subject you or me to this any longer. I'm getting out of your clown car made for dwarves and away from Ms. Elena's crosshairs. Our motorcycles are parked across the street. We'll follow you the rest of the way."

Branislav thought he saw the woman crack a smile at the giant's frustration. He wished he owned a bigger, more comfortable car. But then again, he didn't usually serve as taxi driver for grumpy goliaths.

With his passengers gone, Branislav turned on the radio. He wouldn't have dared to listen to KC and the Sunshine Band's "Shake Your Booty" with those two strangers in the car. He turned up the volume all the way. One disco hit after another filled the Skoda. The music temporarily washed away his anxiety. He allowed himself to daydream. He was doing his own investigative piece, and if he played his cards right, he'd soon be working elbow-to-elbow with the paper's news reporters.

Every so often he checked for the two bikers in his rearview mirror. He wasn't sure why, but he was actually proud to be accompanying them. Admittedly, Eytan inspired more confidence than cold-eyed Elena, who looked as though she would cut him at any moment.

94   DAVID KHARA

Following Eytan's suggestion—really, his demand—Branislav took the southern route to his parents' home. Eytan thought the main road would still be blocked, and discretion was key.

The strange procession got off the highway. They took secondary arteries and then poorly paved roads that were more difficult to navigate. Two hours after leaving Prague, the trio arrived in a parking area next to an artificial beach on the edge of a lake. Branislav parked his car. Eytan pulled his motorcycle up to Branislav's right, and Elena stopped hers to his left. They all kept their headlights on to illuminate the small sandy stretch of land. Lead-colored rain clouds filled the sky, but they could make out a large wooden hut and two pontoons, which confirmed that this was a small water sports club.

Despite himself, Branislav ogled Elena as she removed her helmet. Eytan opened the trunk and took out his bag without saying a word.

"You're sure your dad's coming to get us?" the giant asked as he looked around.

"Yep, he's already answered the text I just sent. He's on his way. It's crazy. Everything's so quiet here. It seems like the past two days were just a bad dream."

"Your cushy little life is collapsing, my dear. And unfortunately, you are in a bad dream. It's one you may never wake up from." Elena spoke without even glancing in his direction. Her raspy voice and the eerie phrasing gave Branislav the unnerving feeling that he had just heard a prophecy. The woman headed toward the beach and scanned the lake.

Branislav shuddered and walked over to Eytan, who was shaking his head.

"Jesus, that colleague of yours is a delight."

Eytan gave him a look. There wasn't much he could do about Elena's attitude.

"You know, this is where I covered my very first story."

"Oh yeah?" Eytan said, sounding more polite than interested. He rummaged through his bag.

"Yeah, I was doing a portrait on a rowing champ who trained here. I don't remember his name. The headline was 'Song of the Paddle.'"

"Rowers use oars, not paddles." Elena corrected him without taking her eyes off the water.

Branislav muttered under his breath and kicked the sand. "The copy desk didn't think 'Song of the Oar' had the same kind of poetry."

In the distance, the three of them heard an engine. A small boat maneuvered by an enormous figure appeared about a nautical mile from the bank. The skiff drew alongside the pontoon. Eytan flicked off the headlights and joined Elena and Branislav, who were already climbing aboard. Branislav exchanged a few words with his father and then sat down with his travel companions. No one made a peep during the ten-minute journey across the lake.

As they approached the shore, a large house loomed on the horizon. It was impressive enough that the young Czech's father owned a boat, Eytan thought as he stared at the villa. But the boat was a dinky inflatable pool toy compared with this imposing structure. Built on a hill, the two-story house with white stucco walls and red roof clearly offered a stunning view of the magnificent landscape. Its many balconies were covered with pots of geraniums. Eytan had the fleeting feeling that he was in Bavaria.

96   DAVID KHARA

The agent was already familiar with Bohemia. Reinhard Heydrich, one of Heinrich Himmler's henchmen, had cracked down so hard on the territory, he had been called the Butcher of Prague. But this lake showed Eytan all the beauty that the region had to offer. Nature had the ability to purge the planet of humanity's vilest sins and served as a reminder that mortals were transient, alive one day and dead the next. These mountainous landscapes would survive much longer than the human race.

Branislav's father got out of the boat first and tied it up. The man had a round face, bald head, and big nose. His solid build was accentuated by a barrel chest that made him look strong rather than overweight. His chinos and shawl-collar cardigan over a classic polo gave him the look of a country gentleman, despite his muscular stature. He wasn't a talkative fellow, and he had remained loyal to his reserved nature by revealing no sign of surprise at seeing his son with two perfect strangers, both of them a good foot taller than he was. Having reached his home turf, he abandoned his reticence and offered Elena a hand as she started to climb out of the pontoon.

True to form, she coldly declined the offer and jumped out herself, causing the boat to rock. Branislav was nearly swept overboard, but Eytan caught the hood of his raincoat just in time.

All of them were standing on the front porch two minutes later. Through the elegant glass entry doors, they could make out a lavishly decorated living room. And before Branislav's father could even take the doorknob, a stylish woman with a full head of white hair came rushing toward them. She opened the door and, ignoring the others, rushed up to Branislav. She took her son in her arms and looked at him with a face full of love. They chatted softly.

"Mom," Branislav said, taking his mother's hand and turning to his companions. "I would like you to meet Eytan and Elena."

The two guests nodded. Eytan smiled as he did this. Elena didn't bother.

"Nice to meet you. I'm Branislav's mom," she babbled, still clinging to her son.

His father introduced himself next.

"Vladek Poborsky. Come in. Let me fix you drinks, and we can talk. That is, unless anyone's hungry?" His English was impeccable.

"I'm fine with just a drink," Eytan replied, heading into the living room.

Everyone else followed suit. They sat down, and Branislav's father poured each of them a glass of chilled herbal liqueur. His mother brought in dishes filled with small appetizers. Eytan was tempted to slump into the couch, but he was afraid that getting too comfortable would upset his formal hosts. Elena, sitting with one foot over the thigh of her other leg, let out a big yawn.

Eytan was grateful. At least she wasn't thinking about killing him at the moment.

Stuck between his mother and father, Branislav didn't look like a worldly reporter. He looked like a child.

As Eytan stared at Branislav and his sixtyish father, he tried to find the hereditary connection between them. It was impossible. The two didn't seem to share a single trait, either in appearance or in behavior. Branislav seemed like a nice guy—the quiet, intelligent type who preferred to do his own thing without offending anyone. He also seemed to take a lot of pride in his profession. Vladek on the other hand, personified the kind of overbearing father who left an indelible imprint. Eytan surmised that any act of resistance was quickly quashed. Vladek did have inquisitive blue eyes that gave him a bit of approachability, but Branislav bore a closer resemblance to his more genteel and affable mother.

When the questions died down, Eytan decided it was an opportune time to cut to the chase.

"Thank you for your hospitality, Mr. and Mrs. Poborsky. Unfortunately, we're not here for a friendly visit."

The father leaned back in his chair and folded his hands over his chest. He looked the two strangers in the eye and made it a point to stare at the bag for a few seconds. He leaned over to his wife, and whispered something in her ear. Smiling, she got up and left the room.

"Who are the two of you?" he asked Eytan.

"Let's just say, we're allies. The less you know, the better we'll all be."

"Sir, I've spent over half my life in a country under communist rule, and I've put up with all the inconveniences that that implies. It takes more than fake firefighters and two secret agents on a mission to intimidate me."

The rebuke seemed to snap Elena out of her drowsy thoughts. She showed fresh interest in the conversation.

To Eytan's surprise, Vladek motioned at the duffle.

"An expert eye quickly detects the shape of gun barrels in a bag."

"Fake firefighters?" Eytan said, smiling. That was all he intended to respond to.

"I've been following the news on TV since this morning. I would have been completely suckered by the whole fire story if those men hadn't paid us a visit last night and again this afternoon. For over ten years, I was production director at a company that stocked highly flammable and explosive products. So believe me, I can recognize a firefighter when I see one. And anyway, their questions weren't directly related to the fire."

"What exactly did they want to know?" asked Eytan."

"If we visited the village frequently, if we were there the day before, if we noticed anything different. They gave the appearance of taking no more than a casual interest in our answers, but they might as well have been wearing secret-police badges."

Eytan saw the man in a new light. The former Eastern Bloc countries were chock-full of these rogue characters—masters in the art of dodging roadblocks and quick to catch any booby traps. Vladek definitely belonged to this group of gritty individuals.

"Did they question you about your time at Paramo?" Eytan asked point blank.

Branislav's father was caught off guard. But he didn't flinch from the question.

"They did not. I see where you're going. No need to beat around the bush."

Eytan seized the opportunity.

"Mr. Poborsky, did you ever work on Semtex?"

"Semtex? What's that?" Branislav asked, sitting up in his chair.

That was Elena's cue to show her host that her vocabulary consisted of more than a few monosyllabic words. Plus, she didn't see any threat in the Poborsky household—mother, senior, or junior.

"Semtex is one of the most powerful explosives ever created. It was invented by a Czech man named Stanislav Brebera. This explosive gets its name from

Semtin, the city where it was created. If I'm not mistaken, that's just a few miles from Pardubice. And here's a juicy tidbit: Semtex was once the preferred plaything for many terrorists."

"Dad, is that true?"

Vladek shrugged.

"You would know if you had been more interested in my line of work and less obsessed with soccer. Obviously, we produced it, but for industrial purposes, mostly for demolition companies. We also manufactured it for military use, but I didn't work on that until the very end of my career. We had absolutely no intention of letting it get into the hands of terrorists."

"What exactly did your work consist of?" asked Eytan.

"I was responsible for the addition of a chemical tagging agent. In its raw form, Semtex is basically undetectable. After the product was used in terrorist attacks, we were pressured by the international community to add certain substances that would make the explosive detectable. The substances we added produced a signature vapor emission."

"And according to Branislav, one of your former colleagues, Ivan, lived close by. He might have been one of the victims. Could you tell us what his contributions were?"

Vladek was silent for a few moments.

"Ivan was part of my team. That's all. Can you tell me why you're asking these questions? What really happened in that village yesterday?"

Eytan turned to Branislav and gave him a nod.

"Dad, on my way here, I saw something that they're not talking about in the news."

THE SHIRO PROJECT 101

Branislav started telling his story, and despite his father's rapid-fire interruptions, objections, and questions, he made it to the end of his account.

"We're hoping your connection with Paramo will give us a lead," Elena intervened before Eytan had the chance to open his mouth. He didn't protest. In fact, he was rather pleased to see her participate.

"What agency do you work for?"

"For the moment, all you need to know is that we're trying to stop any more disasters from happening," Eytan replied, beating Elena to the punch.

"Dad, he saved my life. I think you can trust him."

"Let me be the judge of that. Answer the question."

"We work for an antiterrorist branch of Mossad. We have good reason to believe that what happened yesterday is just the opening act for a whole wave of bigger and deadlier attacks. Vladek, any information could be vital."

"Branislav?"

"Yes?"

"Go see your mother."

"What? But—"

"Just do what I said!"

Branislav glared at his father, but did as he was told.

"Promise me my wife and son have nothing to be scared of."

"As we don't know anything further at the moment, I can't promise that," Eytan said. "But they have no reason to be frightened of us. We'll do everything to ensure your safety."

"You're barking up the wrong tree by going after Semtex," Vladek muttered as he rubbed his chin.

"What do—" Eytan didn't have the chance to finish his question.

"But Branislav was definitely on the right track by scanning through the list of village residents."

Elena spoke up. "Be more precise."

Vladek rose from his armchair and walked over to a desk. He opened a drawer and started rummaging anxiously. Eytan slid a discreet hand toward the weapon hidden in his jacket. After several seconds, a visibly relieved Vladek extracted his hand and waved a chocolate bar in the air.

"My wife is going to yell at me. She gets all hysterical whenever my cholesterol rises."

He ripped open the wrapper, broke off a hunk of the chocolate, and offered it to Elena. She declined, but Eytan couldn't resist.

"Bad memories die hard," Vladek continued as he sat down again. "And the Czechs trained their fair share of demons. From 1950 to 1990, our country played a crucial role in developing psychoactive substances for the Soviet Union. Our chemists were considered the best in the Eastern Bloc. And as it turns out, a lot of people who worked in those labs were residents of that village. I can't tell you what their specific fields of expertise were. I gleaned this information from casual conversations. It's highly likely that the village had fewer innocent victims than we've been led to believe."

"It didn't look like a planned military operation but, instead, an emergency response," Eytan interjected. "The fire and the media coverage attest to that. The government authorities have two objectives: first, to steer attention away from the real problem, and second, to understand and fix said problem. In that regard, things appear to be taken care of."

"A backfire is a highly effective way to control a wildfire," Elena said, a contemptuous smile on her face.

"It's the oldest trick in the book," Vladek said. "I'm sorry I can't offer you more information. You know as much as I do now."

Eytan leaned over his bag and took out the folder with Branislav's papers. He pulled out the enlarged photograph, stood up, and handed it to Vladek. Then he sat down next to him. With catlike stealth, Elena glided over to join them.

"Examine this image carefully. Do you notice anything?"

Vladek absorbed the blow. The sidewalks were littered with bodies. These were people he had known for years. He had enjoyed fishing trips with some of them. Feeling the weight of the agents' eyes, he collected himself and examined the photo in detail.

Eytan pointed to a spot in the picture. "There, on the wall, behind the man in the protective suit."

"It looks like a series of drawings or maybe some uppercase letters. That's strange."

"Have you ever seen this inscription?"

"No. Never," Vladek said, sure of himself.

"Given the profile of these residents, I wouldn't have pegged them for graffiti artists. Now, in that corner, what do you see?"

"Another guy in a white suit, but it looks like he's photographing the wall."

Eytan took the picture out of Vladek's hands.

"We have a couple of leads, at least," Elena said. "They're not the ones we were expecting, but either way, this is helpful."

"There's only one way to know for sure," Eytan said.

"By capturing one of these military men who were at the scene," Elena chimed in. "And making him talk."

104 David Khara

Eytan couldn't miss the change in the woman. Just a few minutes earlier, she had been ready to nod off. Now she was fully invested in the case.

"You won't have to go far," Vladek said as he got up. "Headquarters are only a mile northeast of here. And since I suspect the firefighters are part of the army's special forces, you should be able to find what you're looking for. You can walk to the camp by cutting through the forest."

After logging thousands of miles on land and in the air, Eytan was looking forward to seeing a little action.

Elena's face looked positively gleeful. She rubbed her hands together in excitement. Yes, Eytan thought, they were both up for a little action.

CHAPTER 15

The room was as silent as a grave. Eytan stared at a Flemish-inspired painting, one of four in the same style hanging in the living area. This canvas depicted a blithe group of bourgeois men gathered around a farm table that was filled with baskets of fruit and glasses of wine.

How depressing. You'd have to put a gun to my head to make me have these in my home, he thought. He preferred Claude Monet.

He wanted to scratch the work just to see if a more valuable painting lay underneath this rendering. It was highly improbable, but taking just a bit of the paint off was still tempting.

"Are you interested in art?" Vladek asked.

"No," Eytan lied to avoid a long and pointless conversation. "I was just wondering if—"

"What?" Elena and Vladek asked in unison.

"Czechoslovakia played a very specific role as an Eastern Bloc country, and, uh, I'm not sure of the exact connection yet, but—"

"But what?" Elena pressed. The woman simply had no patience.

"Forget it. I was thinking out loud. We should get a move on. But Vladek, I need to ask your son to join us."

"Excuse me?"

"We don't have a choice," Elena intervened. "If we discover something important while we're scoping out the camp, we'll need to act quickly. I don't speak Czech, and I'm assuming the same goes for my partner."

Eytan nodded as confirmation.

"How do you expect us to get any facts if we don't understand the language?" she said.

Elena's insistence elicited the expected response.

"Absolutely not," Vladek barked.

While he had appeared calm and poised up to this point, the man was now red in the face. Eytan could tell he had raised a lot of hell in the factory.

"Without an interpreter, we're stuck," Elena said and sighed.

"Take me. I speak Czech." Vladek had a defiant look on his face and his fists on his hips. Eytan felt Elena looking at him. He would have to settle this.

"Mr. Poborsky, that's not a good idea," Eytan said. "Going with any civilian will slow us down. But we don't have a ton of options. We need someone who knows the area and can move quickly if something goes wrong. If we have to get out of there, Branislav will move faster than you. Besides, he has already put a considerable amount of work into this, and I'm sure he would object to being left behind."

"There's still plenty of gas in the tank at my age," Vladek protested.

"I believe you. But this isn't a pissing contest. It's going to be a dangerous mission with many variables."

"How can I trust that you can achieve your goal and protect my son?"

Eytan remained silent for a moment and then locked his blue eyes with Vladek's. Eytan could almost feel the shiver shooting up the man's spine at the sight of his cold determination. If Vladek hadn't understood before, he did now. Above all else, Eytan was a soldier.

THE SHIRO PROJECT 107

"Mr. Poborsky, there's no one more prepared to protect your son or better suited to lead this kind of operation," Elena said with a soft voice.

This woman never failed to surprise Eytan, who hadn't thought she was capable of coming off as kind or understanding. Her tactful intervention managed to appease Vladek.

"All right," he said. "He's a big boy. If he wants to go with you, I won't keep him. My wife is going to kill me." He gave the two agents an anxious look and left the room to get his son.

Eytan leaned toward Elena. "What's your game?" he asked in a hushed voice.

She squirmed in her chair and tapped the armrest with her long, thin fingers.

"Did you want to spend all day arguing with gramps? I said what he wanted to hear. That's all. I'm just as anxious to be done with this as you are, 302. I plan on doing everything it takes, as surprising as that may seem. Plus, what I told him wasn't all lies."

She shot him a smile that he couldn't quite decipher.

"Meaning?"

"No one can compete with us."

"That's true, I suppose," Eytan said as he sank back into the sofa. Her sense of superiority annoyed him. For years, he had prepared his missions without relying on his superhuman strengths, but instead on rigorous practice, focus, and determination. Elena figured she intrinsically had the upper hand, end of story. And while he welcomed this flawed attitude in his enemies, he did not tolerate it in his partners—as rare as they might be.

Vladek returned with Branislav, who agreed to accompany them without further discussion.

Eytan and Elena exchanged a look and rose in unison from their seats.

"If all goes well, we'll be back here in about two hours. Until then, don't leave your house," the Kidon operative ordered Vladek. He turned to Branislav. "Keep your cell phone and documents here. Oh, one more request."

Two minutes later, the crew was regrouped on the terrace. A strong breeze was rippling the lake and making the treetops sway. Vladek mapped out the lay of the land for Eytan. His arms at his sides, Branislav stared at Elena like a puppy dog.

"I look like an idiot," he grumbled. "Plus, this dumb thing itches!"

"No, it's fine. Seriously, you look way better in this getup," Elena teased.

"I doubt it," he muttered.

She pulled down the midnight-blue ski mask that Eytan was making their impromptu translator wear.

"There, that's better. Now we can see only your eyes. If you have to look like a bozo, better to wear the thing properly."

"So I really do look like an idiot."

"Branislav," she said and sighed as she put her hands on the reporter's shoulders, "how could you not?"

She left him with his wounded vanity and, with a light step from this little ribbing session, rejoined Eytan and Vladek. Branislav followed.

With his bulky military bag on his shoulder, Eytan signaled that it was time to go.

They disappeared into the woods.

As Vladek watched them leave, he reassessed the evening's revelations—those made by Eytan and his son, as well as his own.

He went back into the living room, where his wife was waiting, and silently sat down on the couch.

"They're going to bring him back safe and sound."

She shot him a look. "How do you know that for sure?'

"Intuition," he muttered.

He grabbed the remote and flipped to the news channel, which continued to display the firefighting planes circling the forest. The same shot had been playing on a loop for hours, even though the water bombers had returned to their base ages ago. Again and again, the news anchor praised the teamwork of the firefighters and the army. They had contained the catastrophe.

Nothing but fabrications, he thought as the national motto ran through his head. Pravda zvítězí: truth prevails.

CHAPTER 16

The moon rose in the Bohemian sky, casting a hazy glow on the forest. Usually nighttime travelers welcomed such illumination, but for a stealth mission, it was clearly less favorable. For the last twenty minutes, the team had been trekking in contemplative silence. The undergrowth and damp soil muffled the sound of their footsteps. Bringing Branislav had proved to be a smart decision. In fact, the reporter had become pack leader and was shepherding his friends at a decent pace up the steep footpaths.

As the caboose, Eytan watched the young man forge ahead with his little flashlight. Both agents had objected to his using it. They wanted to remain as discreet as possible. But he had insisted. "I already look like an ass in this mask. I'm not going to sprain an ankle for your amusement too."

It was a convincing argument, considering the terrain. They even let him ditch the balaclava—temporarily.

The Kidon was keeping an eye on Elena. Her behavior was erratic, mysterious, and unpredictable. At times she was withdrawn, and at other times she was fully engaged. She was impatient and downright dangerous. He hadn't forgotten her promise to take him out once their mission was over. She was also capable of deluding people into thinking she had compassion. Eytan was annoyed to see Branislav gallantly holding aside the shrub and tree branches for her. Then she

THE SHIRO PROJECT 111

would sadistically let them snap back and hit him in the face.

Half an hour after the start of their hike, they were out of the forest and had reached the summit of a green hill. The location offered a sweeping view of the valley, which was intersected by a small stream.

Eytan stopped and carefully placed his bag at his feet. He unzipped it and took out a gun.

"I'm going to scout the area. Wait here," he ordered, handing the pistol to Elena.

"Do you trust me, 302?" she asked, sliding her hand over the weapon.

"I'm not going to waste my energy babysitting you. Either kill me, or do what I say."

And with that, he hiked off.

Elena took out the magazine and checked the contents. Satisfied, she reassembled the weapon and slipped the pistol into her belt.

"So that's how secret agents joke around?" Branislav asked hesitantly.

"What?"

The woman didn't seem to understand the question.

"You call him by a number, not his name. He says he doesn't have time to babysit you, and he invites you to kill him. Looks to me like you guys have that Odd Couple routine down pat."

Elena smiled. Just because she was forced to collaborate with the Israeli agent, she didn't have to make his life easy.

"Eytan is not my partner. He's my guard. We're not colleagues. We're enemies. I've been assigned to kill him. The number is not any type of ID. It's his guinea pig number. So that should clear up your little misunderstanding over what we are to each other."

112 David Khara

"Are you making fun of me?"

"Does it look like I am?"

"I can't tell. By your face, I'd say no, not really, but…"

Elena was growing tired of the conversation. She turned away from Branislav. "Sit down and shut up before I'm tempted to show you what secret agents really laugh about."

Branislav obeyed without objection.

Some three hundred feet away, Eytan was stretched out on the ground at the edge of the woods and using his binoculars to scope out his objective. The camp appeared to be roughly the size of a soccer field, maybe one hundred and twenty yards long and eighty yards wide. It was surrounded by fire trucks and light tanks and illuminated by a dozen floodlights. An octagonal camouflage tent and three satellite dishes on tripods were in the middle of the field. Cables at the back of the tent were connected to an enormous gray generator on the bed of a white tractor-trailer. Eytan was familiar with this kind of generator. It was designed for specific military purposes. Between the satellite communications system and the energy supply, it was obvious that this big top was serving as the operation's headquarters. Two military men with machine guns were standing guard.

Another heavy vehicle was parked about a hundred feet to the right of the camp. It was of no particular interest, but what it was towing attracted the agent's attention. It looked like a mobile home with four ventilation stacks on the roof. A black door with a translucent window was at the back of the unit. A ramp extended from the door to the ground.

Just as Eytan was taking a closer look, a thick cloud of vapor rose from the ventilation chambers. Moments later, the door opened, and a woman with curly brown hair emerged. The woman, who was wearing black pants and a white coat, descended the ramp and approached one of the camp guards. He saluted her, and they talked for a couple of minutes. The guard handed her a pack of cigarettes and a lighter. She nodded and walked over to a nearby fire truck. Leaning against it, she lit a cigarette.

Operation headquarters and a mobile quarantine unit. Bingo! Eytan made a mental note. He left his observation point to return to Elena and Branislav. He found them sitting more than fifty feet apart, looking like well-behaved angels. Almost too well-behaved.

"Everything all right?"

"Not a worry in the world," responded Elena. "Right, Branny?"

"Yep, just peachy," the Czech said with a nervous smile.

"Great. Elena, we're going to take action. There are about thirty of them, forty at most. And since I didn't spot any sleeping quarters, it probably won't be long before our little party clears out."

Eytan unzipped the bag to reveal an impressive arsenal: two M14 assault rifles, several Heckler & Koch MP5 submachine guns, two metal cans, and a bunch of magazines.

"Not very Mossad but still a nice stash," Elena said.

"I could have brought an Uzi, a few Desert Eagles, and a Lonely Planet guide to Tel Aviv. Oh, I don't have any more masks, but I could give you my yarmulke to wear if you'd like."

"That's enough," she said. He had hit a nerve.

114 David Khara

Meanwhile, Branislav could not take his eyes off the frightening smorgasbord of weaponry spread out before him.

"Do you always travel with these?" he stammered.

"Nyet. But because I didn't know what I'd be up against, I decided to go big or go home. It so happens that I believe I made the right decision."

Eytan pulled a small black case out of the bag, opened it, and took out three tiny earpieces. He inserted one in his right ear and held the other two out to Elena and Branislav.

"They're already set to a secure frequency."

The Czech journalist examined what felt almost weightless and appeared to be a simple earplug. "There's no microphone," he said, surprised.

"No need. It picks up sounds. Its only flaw is a short battery life."

"Impressive," Branislav said.

"The guys in R&D should be locked up in a loony bin, but I have to admit, they do pretty good work."

Eytan turned toward the young man.

"Branislav, no matter what you hear, stay put, and don't move a muscle until we return. But if your earbud goes silent, run into the woods and back to your parents' house as fast as you can."

"All right, but do you really think that just the two of you can take on a group of thirty-some military guys?"

"Yes," Eytan responded as he slipped the magazines into his jacket pockets. "It's never the army with the most soldiers that wins, but the side that can outsmart the opponent. I'm sure they've jacked up their security in response to the disappearance of those three men who were after you. But believe me, there's no way they're anticipating an attack. And besides, even the

THE SHIRO PROJECT 115

best-trained soldiers are never fully prepared for the unexpected."

"But still, you're not planning to kill all those men, are you?"

"After regaling us with your misadventures from yesterday, I'm surprised by your reluctance," Elena said while attaching an MP5 holster to her thigh. "Did you object when Eytan eliminated those three dudes who were prepared to destroy you?"

"No, obviously, but that situation was more like legitimate defense," he said.

"I see. Mr. Noble has a highly flexible moral code, depending on his self-interest from one moment by the next."

Her sarcasm infuriated Branislav. "What the hell is your problem, anyway?"

Elena started walking in his direction. She looked ready to rip him apart. Eytan abandoned his preparations to address the acrimonious pair.

"Cut the crap," he ordered. "Elena, get your equipment. We're leaving. Now!" He turned to Branislav. "As for you, I thought you had a little maturity. I thought you were better than this."

Looking like two scolded children, they both obeyed and silently stepped away from each other. Elena shot Branislav a wicked smile and finished arming up.

Branislav grabbed Eytan by the sleeve before the giant could join her. "Don't kill those people," he said.

The Kidon agent leaned in, took out his earpiece, and shushed the journalist. "I think you're a nice guy, but you're really starting to piss me off. From now until we get back, I want radio silence, unless something happens." He pulled down Branislav's mask.

116 David Khara

Branislav held back, sheepish and unsure how he felt about the imminent massacre. He watched as Eytan and Elena headed off to their combat positions.

When the two of them got to their perch above the camp, they stretched out side by side. The giant handed his binoculars to his fellow assassin.

"The command tent is our primary target. I'd like to hear your plan."

"You're asking for my input?" Elena replied, clearly surprised.

"So it would seem."

She observed the location's layout for a good minute.

"The area is too exposed for a discreet approach. I recommend a frontal attack with heavy weapons, capitalizing on our high position. You enter on the north side so they're forced to take cover and turn their backs on me. Then I open a second front here, from the south. I shoot at the entrance to the tent to keep them from escaping while you cut the power supply and communications systems. Once the threat is lowered or under control, we enter. How does that sound?"

"You've got it all covered."

"What do you plan on doing with that truck on the right? It's a mobile quarantine unit, meaning it's heavily reinforced."

"That's not our main objective. I'm not worried about its fortification. I'm more concerned about what's inside."

"Yeah, you're afraid it's full of contagious corpses, right?"

"The ones that are left, yes. I spotted tire tracks that match the tires on the unit here. That means they've already loaded some of the bodies and taken them out. There's no point in taking the risk of going into that quarantine unit. We should be fine with just capturing a doctor or someone in charge of the operation. Open fire on my signal."

They looked at each other in agreement. All animosity and mistrust vanished in this acknowledgment of their mutual goal.

Eytan ran to his combat post a few hundred feet to the north. After placing a metal can and three magazines at his feet, he shouldered his assault rifle, adjusted his advanced combat optical gun sight, and took aim at the satellite dishes next to the command tent.

"It's showtime."

CHAPTER 17

Special-forces members Karel and Jan were patrolling the camp with extra caution. After the attack on the village and the disappearance of their three army brothers, extreme vigilance was in order.

The Czech government was deploying massive measures to cope with the most extreme terrorist threat that the nation had yet encountered. At least all those years of intensive daily training would be put to good use. Up till now, the special forces hadn't seen much action.

In the command tent, the tight-lipped higher-ups and military researchers had been assessing the situation and were now getting ready to dismantle the camp. For hours, the two men had been prepared to take on any enemy, but no opponents had presented themselves. They were tired. To keep alert and beat the boredom, Karel, a precision-firing specialist, was enlightening close-combat expert Jan on the many benefits of yoga, particularly its ability to help the practitioner hone his breathing—an essential skill for a sniper.

A metal clink caught their attention. It was followed by a dozen more. The noise was coming from the satellite dishes. They rushed over to see what was going on. Karel examined one of the dishes. There were impact marks, and the wires leading out from it were letting off sparks. But before he had time to get up and report his findings to Jan, a lieutenant emerged from the tent. He was shouting something about interrupted communications. As the lieutenant approached the two soldiers, the floodlights started shutting off one by one to the sound of shattered glass. They were all out in mere seconds. The men didn't have time to respond. An enormous explosion came next. It blew a fire truck off the ground in a whirl of apocalyptic flames.

Karel felt his heart racing and pearls of sweat dripping from his temples. He gripped his gun and tried to channel the breathing exercises taught by his yoga master. As he did this, another fiery explosion ripped through the camp, and he saw a fellow soldier go flying in the air. All around, he heard panicked shouting. Officers were emerging from the tent, only to be hit by bullets. They took several rounds each, and looking like contortionists, they spun in circles before falling to the ground. The invisible assailants were aiming with diabolic precision. The bodies were piling up. Karel and Jan heard frenzied orders, as well as cries for help. Ducking for cover between the generator and the tent, they didn't know exactly how to respond. Where were the assailants?

When he heard two more explosions over his shoulder, Karel realized they were being attacked from behind.

On the hill overlooking the camp, Branislav was appalled and powerless. Tears streamed down his face. Through his earpiece he could hear Eytan's directions. He was telling Elena where to shoot or toss a grenade and letting her know when he would lob the next explosive. The giant had mercilessly slain the three commandos who had threatened his life the previous day. Branislav had no reason to believe the killer would soften up overnight. But this massacre was too much to take. And there was nothing he could do to stop it.

Eytan took aim at the satellite dishes, which were defenseless against his precise eye. He pulled out his empty magazine, replaced it on the spot, and focused on the lights to his left. Just before pulling the trigger, he shouted, "She's all yours, Elena."

Elena had been waiting patiently for Eytan's orders to open fire, and as soon as she was given the go-ahead, she eagerly blasted each and every light.

"Okay," Eytan said. "Let's keep up the pace. Take care of the generator. Then blow up the trucks. I'll deal with my zone, and afterward, we'll blast this place to smithereens. Go!"

A slit in the tent opened, and an officer appeared. Before the entry flap closed again, Eytan spotted the brown-haired woman who had been smoking a cigarette a few minutes earlier. She was now hunched over a laptop.

At that moment, the electricity went off, thanks to Elena's aim.

"Revised plan: blow up the quarantine truck to create a diversion."

"There's no risk?"

"It's armored. Aim for the tractor. That'll do. Now."

No sooner had the words come out of his mouth than the deed was done.

The cab of the truck rose into the air, as if propelled by an invisible force. Seconds later it crashed to the ground, landing on its side with a thunderous boom. The trailer, which the cab had dragged into the air with the force of the explosion, broke free of its hitch and landed nearby.

THE SHIRO PROJECT 121

Eytan surveyed the back door for a few moments, but no one came out. He continued.

Karel was watching his world collapse before his eyes. An unstoppable tidal wave of chaos was sweeping through the camp. He tried to calm himself so that he could do something—anything—but it was impossible. Between the endless rounds of gunshots, the wailing victims, and the explosions punctuating the nightmarish darkness, he couldn't even think. He knew that Jan wasn't doing any better. His breathing was noisy, and his eyes were filled with terror.

And yet Jan managed to dart off—so quickly, Karel couldn't stop him. He was seeking a better refuge, Karel was sure. Another blast went off. Karel covered his head. He was okay. The tent, on the other hand, wasn't as lucky. It was now full of holes. He would have said it looked like a hunk of Swiss cheese, but that would have been putting the whole grisly scene in a bizarre context.

Silence. Karel risked assessing the situation. In only a minute—two at the most—his peaceful post had turned into an Armageddon. What was next?

"What an asshole!" Elena spat as she spotted a runaway and squashed his escape with a bullet to the shoulder.

"What's going on?" Branislav asked frantically.

"You, shut up!" Elena responded.

"Stop, both of you. Elena, keep your foul mood to yourself. Branislav, stay quiet, and let us do our job. Elena?"

No response.

"Elena!" Eytan pressed.

"I'm here!"

"We're going in. We'll meet at the command post."

She strapped her M16 over her shoulder, drew her MP5, and descended to the camp to finish off the scraps, which were a bit too spoiled for her liking.

Fifteen feet from each other, the two men were exchanging conflicting signals. They were arguing over how to proceed. Karel wanted to lie low until they had a better idea of what was going on. Jan thought it was best to take shelter in one of the trucks that hadn't been blown up.

Karel saw a shadow in the distance—the offensive was entering a new phase. He scanned the scene in search of other assailants, but aside from the massive silhouette that appeared to be making huge strides in their direction, he saw no one on the horizon. As the oppressive shape walked by a wounded victim struggling to get up, he stopped and delivered a bullet to his throat.

Karel hunkered down a few more inches in hopes of remaining unseen. The shadowy figure's cold and murderous determination enraged the guard. "Shit, if this guy wants a war, he's got one!" he fumed.

Now was the time to show off his sniper skills. He craned his neck and spotted the man as he continued to eliminate the wounded, one by one. Karel took a deep breath and adjusted his aim. That bastard was as good as dead.

"You have no idea how much I'd like to see you do that!"

He jumped at the sound of the voice coming from behind him. A woman's voice? Karel's basic English was limited to simple commands, so he couldn't grasp the exact meaning of the sentence. He thought it wise to drop his weapon and put his hands in the air. It was a universal symbol.

THE SHIRO PROJECT 123

"Lie down!" barked the stranger.

That he understood, and without attempting any heroism, he obeyed before losing consciousness.

Assuming any movement would lead to his demise, Jan remained motionless on the ground, playing dead. The dampness of the earth penetrated his uniform and chilled his flesh. He caught a glimpse of Karel just as the butt end of a rifle knocked him out cold. Considering the graveyard all around him, it could have been a lot worse.

Elena and Eytan met in front of the command post, having systematically neutralized the remaining occupants of the now-devastated camp.

"Cover your eyes!" the Kidon operative ordered.

Elena obeyed without hesitation. Eytan threw a can, which he had been saving since the start of the operation, into the tent. He turned around and covered his own eyes. There was a flash of blinding light inside the tent.

"Would it have killed you to let me know that we'd be shooting rubber bullets?" she screamed when she opened her eyes.

Several hundred feet away, Branislav was leaning against a tree trunk. He slid all the way to the ground.

"Rubber bullets," he said and sighed as he held his head with both hands.

Ignoring the woman's accusations, Eytan opened a slit in what remained of the command post and peered inside.

"I don't see how that would've changed anything," he responded distractedly, noting with satisfaction that all three occupants—two men in uniform and the woman wearing the white coat—were unconscious.

He was about to enter when Elena crept up behind him with her arm cocked. Eytan turned around at lightning speed and diverted the attack with his palm. Before she could react, he grabbed her by the neck. Her jaw dropped in awe of his grip. He leaned in close and locked his cold blue eyes with hers. It wouldn't take much for him to crush her windpipe.

"Did you really think we were going to kill all these people? You've been a huge help so far. Don't ruin it," he said with disarming calmness.

He released his grip and stepped back. Elena was tempted to launch a full-on attack that would settle things once and for all. But she was still shaking and decided to opt for a stalemate.

"You should have warned me. That's all," she muttered, rubbing her throat.

"Sure, but I didn't. No deaths, but plenty of injuries. You'll have to wait to get your dose of blood. End of discussion."

"Could you at least explain why you brought these weapons?"

"I came to Prague hoping to beat up your little buddies from the Consortium. And I was planning to take prisoners. So I armed up. Is that explanation good enough for you?"

"No."

"Whatever. I'll get over it. Czechy?"

"Uh, is that my new nickname?" asked Branislav, surprised to be addressed at all.

"Yes, I'm not going to say your name out loud while we're here," Eytan responded.

"Ah, all right."

"I'm bringing you the person we'll be questioning. So pull your mask down. Elena, take the laptop and the files next to it. Over and out."

THE SHIRO PROJECT 125

Elena was still frustrated. But she did as she was told. She quickly unplugged the PC cables and grabbed the computer. Eytan lifted the woman's eyelids to make sure she wasn't faking her unconscious state and picked her up.

Crouched under a truck, a stunned Jan watched them leave the camp. Without any means of communication or backup, he knew this was no time to take action. Following them was the smarter move.

Reaching the top of the hill, Eytan had barely lowered his prisoner to the ground, when Branislav rushed to meet him. He shook his hand vigorously.

"Thank you, thank you, thank you," he said. "I honestly believed you were going crazy."

"That's not how his holiness operates," Elena said as she walked up to the two men.

She squatted beside the brunette and tied her wrists together with the nylon rope from her partner's bag. Then she ripped off a strip of the woman's coat and used it to blindfold her.

"I'm not some naïve goody-two-shoes. If I had considered these people real enemies, not a single one of them would have gotten out alive," Eytan responded. "In this case, killing them would have accomplished nothing for our mission."

Branislav didn't know if the statement merited any praise, but it would do.

Elena guarded the unconscious brunette while Branislav scanned the disk files with the Kidon agent at his side. Most of the documents were obscure medical reports riddled with terms that were impossible to comprehend. Branislav expressed his frustration in a string of swear words and grunts.

Eytan gave up and walked over to his bag. He picked up the pile of documents and was flipping through them when he found something that put him in a good mood. It was a series of enlarged photographs. He flashed a predatory smile.

It was time to question the prisoner and move out as quickly as possible.

"See if you can wake her up," Eytan ordered Elena.

For once, his command was met with enthusiasm. A series of slaps to the face ensued. The scientist strained to lift her head after several attempts. Branislav approached Eytan and whispered in his ear.

"Why am I wearing this mask if she can't see anything?"

"Safety first."

Elena unceremoniously pulled the woman into a sitting position.

The interrogation proceeded with surprising simplicity. Eytan asked the questions. Branislav translated them as well as he could, and the terrified prisoner replied compliantly. Five minutes later, it was all finished. Eytan, however, was unsatisfied with the sparse information they had been able to glean.

"Tell her not to worry," Eytan said. "She has nothing to be afraid of. I'm going to drop her off at the camp. Pack everything up. I'll be quick." The woman yelped as Eytan threw her over his shoulder like an old rug and disappeared into the forest.

From his hiding spot behind a bush, Jan didn't have a good visual of the inquisitors, but he had heard everything. He had learned, to his astonishment, that the region had been subjected to a viral attack.

He knew he had to capture one of these people. But he didn't want to act recklessly, and he had only his handgun. His rifle had been lost in the chaos. "Damn, I wish Karel were here," he said and sighed. "He would have known what to do." Jan still failed to grasp how two people could have led such a violent frontal so effectively. Fortunately, the giant had cleared out. The masked man appeared to be unarmed. So the woman with the red hair appeared to be the only serious challenge.

With Eytan and the prisoner gone, Branislav could finally remove his mask. He soothed his itchy face and swore that he'd throw the knit concealment into his parents' fireplace the next chance he got.

"Who told you to take that off?"

As per usual, Branislav couldn't tell if Elena was serious or pulling his leg.

"Uh, what's the big deal? We're finished here, right? I don't see why I need to keep it on."

Branislav stopped and raised his hands in the air.

"You don't have to be a drama queen about it. I was joking," Elena replied.

With a subtle move of his chin, Branislav instructed Elena to look over her shoulder. She obliged.

Behind her, a man with a gun was moving toward the two of them. He signaled her to raise her hands. She complied.

"On the ground, both of you," the soldier ordered in patchy English.

Elena did as she was told. But Branislav stalled. He was hoping to spot Eytan coming back from his drop-off. Nervous, vexed, and impatient, the soldier leaped at Branislav and hit him in the face with the butt of his gun. Branislav fell flat on his ass. He held his injured and bloody nose with both hands.

Like a world-class gymnast, Elena pushed down on the ground with all her strength, jumped to her feet, and swung her legs at the man's chest. He dropped his weapon and tumbled backward but regrouped by rolling into a perfect summersault. Stabilized once again, he adopted a Wing Chun stance—hands open in front of his torso—and advanced toward the woman.

Elena froze as straight as an arrow, arms by her side. With a quick chest rotation, she dodged the first impulsive jab and countered with a low kick to the man's shin.

"I have a feeling that you and I are going to hit it off," he said with a sinister smile.

Elena found the first few moves entertaining. She was waiting patiently for the perfect moment to finish the poor guy off. Bring it on, she thought silently.

But this man knew what he was doing. As she registered her opponent's prowess, Elena's arrogance vanished and was replaced with serious concentration. His masterful hand-to-hand combat skills forced her to rely on a full range of blocks and sways. She wasn't gaining an inch of ground. And she was beginning to pant.

A slight duck by her opponent gave Elena the opportunity she needed to take the advantage and bring the battle to a close. She seized it. She faked a right hook, forcing the man to block an absent attack. It was time to seal the deal. She circled in on him and wiped him out with a punch to the face. Before he had time to respond, she struck his forearm from below with her right hand and completed a reverse maneuver with the left hand. At the unmistakable sound of fractured bones, she knew she had successfully landed her move.

THE SHIRO PROJECT 129

She heard a howl of pain followed by a loud thud as his body hit the ground. But as she stood over her victim, Elena wasn't feeling victorious. She couldn't understand why, but she couldn't see him. In fact, she couldn't see anything.

Eytan placed his gift at what was left of the camp. In a few moments, the soldiers would be pulling themselves together, and despite the inevitable broken bones from the nonlethal bullets, they'd be quick to sound the alarm. The authorities would surely be baffled by the use of rubber ammunition; this confusion would slow down their decision making and muddle their judgment. He would have preferred using other measures, but only a quick, violent, and deliberately exaggerated act could be effective in such an emergency. He was prepared to do anything to get Eli back. But had he crossed a line? He hated to admit it, but Cypher and he had a common goal. They both wanted to eliminate this threat, which was becoming more serious by the second. It was a sad truth: as much as government leaders went on and on about the quest for peace, the research into chemical, biological, and nuclear weaponry seemed to be gaining momentum. Death was already an inescapable truth. Did the world's power brokers have to work so hard to hurry it along? And how many more innocent people would pay the price for their megalomania?

A wave of heat snapped Eytan out of his thoughts. Rivers of sweat were pouring down his smooth-shaven skull. His veins were throbbing. He lowered himself to the ground and rested his back against a tree. He pulled out a small case that looked like it held cigars. Inside was a syringe filled with greenish liquid. His heart was beating at a dangerously fast clip. Trembling, he planted the needle in his right forearm and injected himself. The serum, which he always had with him, had been the source of his survival for decades. His heart slowed, and at the same moment, the world around him froze.

CHAPTER 18

RESEARCH CENTER UNIT 731, HARBIN, MANCHURIA, 1943

He had been told the trip would be rough, and so far it was delivering on that promise. The young man felt homesick, but he hid it from his colleagues. Compassion was not a virtue valued by the Imperial Army, even in its medical unit. In fact, it wasn't considered a prerogative at all. Loyalty and devotion were all that mattered to the emperor of Japan.

Hirokazu Shinje considered himself a highly capable professional. It was an opinion that had been bolstered by his rigorous medical studies at Tokyo Imperial University. But since arriving on the continent, his confidence had been shaken by the center's strict disciplinary practices.

He was extremely proud to have been awarded this assignment in Manchuria, a region that had been occupied by Japan since the early nineteen thirties. Shrouded in secrecy, the research center near the city of Harbin focused on issues of water purification and the prevention of contagious diseases. Unit 731 dealt with vital questions concerning the protection of the Empire of the Rising Sun, and being invited there was quite an honor.

In reality, however, living conditions and the nature of the work were far from satisfying. Researchers

132 David Khara

had to show absolute obedience or risk being hazed, a common practice in the army. And while the staff had access to recreational facilities, it was easy to feel trapped by the fifteen-foot-high fences and the watchtowers that bordered the grounds.

Ruling this impressive kingdom was Lieutenant General Shiro Ishii. One hundred and fifty buildings on grounds that covered three and a half square miles were under his command. The man was charismatic, but he was also given to indulgences that shocked those inside and outside the military. He liked his booze and women and wasn't inclined to show the least bit of restraint. Some people attributed his behavior to psychological problems. Hirokazu didn't care about the cause or causes. He just thought the man was bat-shit nuts.

Fortunately, they rarely crossed paths. This wasn't surprising, considering the number of people working at the massive research center. In addition to the thousands of Japanese employees, there were Chinese and other Asian prisoners, as well as some Caucasian internees. Every day, the occupying government's swift and radical justice system imprisoned another batch of criminals.

Hirokazu had no problems with this. As far as he was concerned, criminals, especially Chinese criminals, were an unworthy, insignificant subspecies. And even though society had no use for them, they were quite helpful in his line of work: vaccine research. His sector relied heavily on a steady flow of human guinea pigs. The research they permitted him to do was much more reliable than animal testing.

Three months into his assignment at the research facility, Hirokazu had established a predictable routine. After a light morning workout, he would survey the infected test subjects and monitor the progression of their ailments. Then came the inoculation phase, in which he would administer vaccines and new pathogenic strains. In the afternoon, he would attend a lecture given by an expert in a field such as biochemistry, hematology, virology, or surgery. Every once in a while he would go to the lab to hone his dissection skills.

He followed this routine seven days a week. But he never complained. And neither did any of his colleagues, whose professional lives were almost identical to his. After all, Japan had taken on the Americans in the Pacific. The Japanese soldiers were willing to sacrifice their lives for the cause, but researchers like Hirokazu were making a significant contribution, as well.

Hirokazu fought the monotony of the job by measuring his progress in the understanding and mastery of infectious agents. This knowledge would be helpful not only in the war effort, but also in his career.

At the moment, he was impatiently waiting for his snooze-fest anatomy seminar to end. The ten other students in the lecture hall appeared to be just as bored as he was. But they were all jolted awake when a gray-haired man in a uniform with legal department insignia barged into the auditorium. He whispered a few words in the professor's ear and addressed the small crowd.

"We're going to conclude our class with a new exercise. Leave your things here and follow me."

Hirokazu and the others complied. With their instructor leading the pack, the group left the room and then the building. Together, they walked to the closest prison and down to the locker room in the basement.

134 DAVID KHARA

Once there, they were told to change into protective clothing and leather aprons.

They were led down a long corridor to a door guarded by two men. One of the guards opened the door and ushered them into a large area resembling a crude operating room. It contained only wooden tables and wheeled carts holding various surgical instruments. Hirokazu had to blink several times to adjust his eyes to the blindingly bright ceiling lights.

Without having to be told, the students formed a semicircle in front of their professor. The man in uniform entered behind them.

"Today, you're going to practice surgery under simulated battlefield conditions. I'm expecting your very best work, as the fate of our soldiers depends on it."

He then gave an order to the guards, who brought in two Chinese men in chains. The first was approaching fifty, while the second looked like he was in his early twenties. The two men resembled each other, and Hirokazu thought they were father and son. They had identical birthmarks in the corners of their mouths.

The prisoners appeared to be disoriented and terrified—less by the soldiers who handled them roughly than by the scholarly assembly of men in white shirts. Unlike the human guinea pigs used for viral tests, these men didn't look malnourished. The students were told that the men hadn't come from the prison, but from a nearby village. Hirokazu reflected on this and what it could mean. His questions were quickly answered.

The man in uniform took out his handgun—a Type 14 Nambu pistol—and shot two bullets into the stomachs of the Chinese men. At the sound of the gunfire, Hirokazu's heart stopped for what felt like many seconds. Terrified, he looked at the two injured

THE SHIRO PROJECT 135

victims curled up on the ground and squirming like earthworms.

"The first group's task will be to extract the bullets from the younger subject. Act as if he's one of our own soldiers. The second team will amputate the four limbs of the older subject and then examine the viscera. The materials you will need are at your disposal, but no anesthesia. You'll be judged on the survival rates of your subjects. Get to work!"

The excitement in the room felt almost electric. Many of the students were jazzed by the unique nature of the experiment. The opportunity to operate on live subjects was extraordinary.

Hirokazu elbowed his way to the table that had been tasked with bullet extraction. The young man was screaming in agony while the students strapped him to the wooden table with his arms crossed. A gag was placed over his mouth to muffle his shrieks. The students at the other table gave the father the same treatment. His agonized screams were even louder. Four students, two for each specimen, examined the men for breathing, cardiac rhythm, and the other vital signs.

Behind a large glass window, Shiro Ishii, surrounded by a throng of military men, doctors, and researchers, some of whom were taking notes, was observing the surgeries. Hirokazu saw they were all fully engaged in the procedures.

Hirokazu glanced at the other table, where one of the doctors was using a saw to slice into the older man's right leg. He could feel his lunch coming up with the sounds that followed—breaking bones and smothered shrieks. Throwing up in front of the officials and his colleagues would mean the end of his career, so he used every bit of his discipline to quell the churning in his gut. His own operating table bore a closer resemblance to his idea of surgery as an art. The precision and thoroughness of his work calmed him down.

After an hour, the judge announced the father's death. The old man had survived the amputation of his right leg and an arm, but his heart had given out with the first cuts on the remaining leg. A heated discussion broke out between the medical team and the officials. Hirokazu caught a few snippets as he handed his surgical instruments off to an impatient colleague.

The observers considered the survival time remarkable, but they were highly critical of the quality of the amputations. The students started to argue with the observers, but their professor quickly cut them off. He scolded them and then improvised a full-length lecture around the cadaver.

At the other workstation, the operation on the still-living patient continued. Hirokazu just wanted it to end. He was exhausted. The longed-for release came an hour later, when the man died. The students feared they would be dressed down like the first team, but they were simply told to proceed with the dissection.

Hirokazu Shinje felt battered as he mustered up the will to dissect the body. He knew this day would leave deep scars.

But he had no idea just how much those two Chinese men would haunt every night of his existence.

CHAPTER 19

NEAR THE CZECH ARMY CAMP, 2010

A thick veil of clouds covering the night sky seemed to accentuate the ghostlike shapes of the trees. Elena rubbed her eyes and looked at the softly glowing moon. Little by little, she was regaining her sight, shedding the uncomfortable feeling of perceiving the world through a filtered lens. Relieved, she stroked the coarse, damp bark of the oak tree that she was leaning against. Then she closed her eyes again and took a deep breath. The mossy aroma rising from the earth comforted her.

"Are you hurt?"

Elena felt Eytan's warm hand on her arm. Her partner was back. She chided herself for being so self-absorbed she hadn't heard him arrive.

"What do you care?" she replied, angrily jerking her arm away.

She opened her eyes. Silhouettes, colors, and details had all come into focus. At last. Nearby, Branislav was attempting to pull himself together. He gently touched the bump on his nose. Eytan saw the beginnings of two black eyes, sure signs of a broken nose. A few feet away, a stranger with bound hands and feet was sitting on the ground. He was breathing heavily.

Eytan glared at Elena. "What happened here?"

138 DAVID KHARA

She pointed her chin at the man on the ground. "That jackass jumped us out of nowhere. Don't worry about your buddy. He just got a little bump on the nose. The other guy looks like he has a broken arm."

"He saw Branislav's face without the mask?"

"What do you think?" Elena said.

Eytan squatted beside her. "You and Branislav need to scram," he said in a low voice. "I'll take care of the guard and then meet up with you."

"I'll deal with him. I'm the one who—"

"No," Eytan interrupted. He pulled out his gun. "This needs to be handled by someone who doesn't take pleasure in it."

No blow could match the violence of the Kidon agent's words. For a long time, Elena had considered killing one of her job rewards. But her position had other important responsibilities, as well. Eytan had just reduced her to little more than a psychopath. That was harsh. After all, what was the difference between the two of them? How was he in a position to judge her? What gave him the right to think of himself as her moral and emotional superior?

In the end, she was angry with herself. She had failed to carry out the mission that had been assigned to her. This was unbearable. She hid her discomfort and walked over to a dazed and confused Branislav. Together, they headed into the woods.

A few minutes later, Eytan caught up with them.

The trek back to the family abode was awkward. Elena didn't say a word. Eytan fretted over Branislav's swollen nose. It was getting bigger by the minute. "I'm habink sub trouble breathink, but it's find," Branislav said when Eytan asked him how he was doing. Eytan had no trouble understanding.

Vladek paced in his living room. For two hours, he had been subjected to bitter rants and fits of weeping. That's how things always played out between him and his wife whenever they got into a Branislav-related disagreement. His good sense told him that he should never have entrusted his son to the strange and obviously dangerous duo. But this was a situation that required a bold solution. He had always been a man of action, and he should have been the one to go in. His son wasn't cut from the same cloth. Should he have let Branislav stare danger in the face just because he himself had never flinched?

As the two parents faced off for yet another confrontation, the terrace door opened. Branislav came in with Eytan and Elena.

"Oh sweetie, you're hurt!" his mother cried.

She leaped to her feet and rushed to her son, once again snubbing the other two. "Let me take care of you." She acknowledged Eytan with a harsh glare. "Congratulations! You've returned my son with a broken nose. God knows what else could have happened to him."

Vladek was relieved. A broken nose was nothing. His own had been broken more than once. With his son home, and his marital spat on hold, he greeted the two agents with a solid handshake.

"Thank you for keeping your word."

The giant forced a smile.

"You didn't find what you were looking for?"

"No, we did."

"How much damage done?"

Eytan's stony expression said all that was necessary.

"I see," Vladek muttered as he lowered his eyes. So, what's your exit strategy?"

140 David Khara

"We got what we wanted and even a bit more. The less you know from here on out, the better it'll be for you and your family. Now if you could, please take us back to the other side of the lake. We have to be on our way."

"Hold on," Vladek responded. "Do you really intend to keep me in the dark?"

"That's how it needs to be, Vladek, and you know it. Follow my advice. Don't try to find out anything more. And tell Branislav to stay here. People will probably show up with questions in the next few days. What will you tell them?"

"Oh, don't worry about that," Vladek said. "Lying to the authorities is a national pastime. I saw nothing. I heard nothing. I know nothing."

"Perfect. Let's go."

Vladek grabbed his heavy jacket and accompanied Eytan and Elena to the pontoon. As he prepared to embark, Branislav came rushing out of the house, cotton stuffed in his nose.

"Are you leavink?" he asked.

"We have to," Eytan replied tersely.

"I was hopink..."

"To get on with your life? Well, no problem there. Your wish is granted," Eytan said. He gave the journalist a wink. "Besides, a doctor needs to take a look at that nose."

"Will we see each oder again?"

"Not likely. As you may have noticed, bumping into me is usually a sign of trouble."

"Yeah, well, you know, if you eber neeb anythink..."

"Happy trails, Branislav!"

Eytan settled into the boat.

THE SHIRO PROJECT 141

Branislav smiled and felt his nose again. Then he turned to Elena, who was about to board the boat. She looked worse than ever—pale and grim, like an angel of death. He offered her his hand. She didn't take it.

"Thanks."

She stared down at him and looked like she might smack him.

"Why are you thanking me? I failed," she said. There was bitterness in her voice.

This was an entirely new facet of Elena's personality. The whole time Branislav had known her, she'd behaved like an emotionless machine designed to get the job done. Unlike Eytan, she lacked empathy. But now she seemed disheartened. A feeling like this had to be something new and strange for her.

"You were supposed to protect be, and I'm still alibe. I don't call that failink," he said as he stealthily took her hand.

His persistence seemed to throw Elena off even more than she already was. She glanced at Eytan. Branislav wondered if she was worried that he'd think less of her if he saw any chink in her armor. But he was watching stoically. She pried her hand away and joined the men in the boat.

Branislav sat down at the water's edge and watched the boat get smaller as it made its way to the other side of the lake. Oddly, the pair had grown on him. Of course, their feats during the raid on the camp were beyond his comprehension. Their road trip was far from the vacation he had envisioned, and watching them leave was surely a relief for his mother and father. Nonetheless, he knew that no matter what the future had in store for him, he'd never forget Eytan and Elena.

They'd be continuing their mission elsewhere, as Branislav tackled his new three-part task: comfort his overprotective mother on the verge of a nervous breakdown, cheer up his depressed father as he confronted the reality of old age, and fix his derailed marriage.

Branislav thought about Eytan's last piece of advice. Maybe that was the takeaway from all of this: it was time to get on with his life.

CHAPTER 20

PRAGUE, ELEVEN-THIRTY P.M.

Eytan and Elena checked into their hotel, motorcycle helmets in hand. The receptionist, a short, plump young man, left his desk in the office behind the counter, where he had been watching a TV show on his laptop, to accommodate them. Seconds after he placed their suite's magnetic key card on the counter, Elena snatched it up and darted toward the elevators. Like a shadow, Eytan followed close behind. She fidgeted as she waited for the doors to close and then compulsively pushed the button to their floor several times. She was more tightly wound than a Jack-in-the-box. Eytan thought it best to keep his mouth shut.

She rushed into their suite, threw her jacket on the floor, and spouted icily, "I'm taking a shower." She disappeared into the bathroom, slamming the door behind her.

Eytan dropped his bag with a heavy, tired sigh. He was no stranger to the fatigue that accompanied his work or the stamina and exceptional skills that it required. But he hadn't been prepared for a fellow assassin's mood swings and what appeared to be hurt feelings. At least he'd have the next few moments all to himself. He took off his jacket and hung it meticulously on the back of a chair. He picked up Elena's carelessly strewn article of clothing, folded it, and placed it neatly on the couch.

He rummaged through the minibar and found a sugary soda, then sat down in an armchair and stretched out his legs. It was a rare moment of peace and quiet. He could now assess the situation What he had learned during their nighttime adventure hardly inspired optimism. If anything, it had reinforced his opinion that the days to come would be full of harsh realities. He hadn't quite figured out why Cypher had enlisted his help and forced him into this partnership with Elena. Several theories were starting to percolate. Still, it was too soon to know for sure.

Eytan had to admit that the Amazon was a worthy ally and an impressive enemy. During their time together, he had gotten a better grasp of her personality. She was antagonistic and conniving, yes, but she was certainly more complicated than that. If she learned to manage her anger and acquired some humility, she could probably surpass him. Yet he doubted there was hope for this woman. Their collaboration would certainly meet a brutal end.

Elena appeared in the doorway. She was wearing a white cotton bathrobe, and her hair was wrapped in a blue towel. As he looked her up and down, he acknowledged a new and puzzling piece of information. He had been so consumed with the mission, he hadn't assimilated the fact that she was a knockout.

"Feeling better?" he asked.

"What's it to you?" she snapped.

No charm. No surprise there. He stood up and eyed her scornfully.

"Let's call Cypher. I'm beyond excited for this to be over."

"Same," she muttered, drying her hair with the towel.

THE SHIRO PROJECT 145

Eytan sat down at the table, punched the number provided by the Consortium, and put the cell phone on speaker. Three rings later, he heard Cypher's nauseatingly sweet voice.

"Hello, Mr. Morg. What's the latest from Prague?"

"I want to hear Eli."

After a few moments, his friend's lively voice confirmed that he was okay. "I'm fine, Eytan. Don't worry."

Cypher returned. "Good, now that we've taken care of the formalities, shall we get back to business?"

"We know the nature of the attack but not how it was carried out," Eytan began. "Autopsies were still underway when we intervened, but the ones that had already been completed indicated that the victims' airways were practically liquefied. And the blood vessels in their eyes had burst."

"Were there blisters or burn marks on the skin?"

"No. I also thought it could be mustard gas, but that doesn't fit. According to my source, the weapon was not chemical, but viral. However, the type of virus was still undetermined. Does this imply a link to the research conducted in your lab, Cypher?" It was more of an accusation than a question.

"I'm afraid so."

"Why am I not surprised?"

"I had no reason to divulge the nature of the stolen strains without knowing for sure that they were involved in the Czech and Russian attacks."

"Now you know, so I suggest that you spill everything."

"First, you need to understand that these operations were organized by the former leadership and that I do not approve of them."

146 DAVID KHARA

"I don't give a shit about your guilt trip. I want reliable information!"

Eytan was yelling, and now even Elena looked startled. She had never seen him lose control.

"The lab was working on an improved version of the Crimean-Congo virus."

"Improved? How so?"

"Ten times more aggressive, a new method of diffusion via aerosol cans, a limited lifespan to prevent epidemics, and several other enhancements. I'll skip the details for the sake of brevity. The goal was to create a viral weapon that could be carried in a container."

"You're a bunch of madmen! You make me sick."

"That's one of the symptoms."

Eytan swiveled his chair to face Elena.

"Wow, the man's got a sense of humor too!"

She shook her head. He threw up his hands and turned back to the phone.

"Developing this kind of weaponry using the stolen strains would require various resources: appropriate facilities, specific materials, a high level of expertise, and thus considerable funds. This gives us lots of new leads to work with. We'll use your ties to the pharmaceutical industry to dig deeper."

"I'll take care of that, if 302 allows it," Elena jumped in, as she leaned over the phone next to Eytan.

She questioned him with her eyes. He couldn't help noticing an intoxicating fragrance was radiating from her skin. He caught himself inhaling. Was he crazy? Eytan collected himself and pulled away. He silently approved Elena's proposition.

"I'm delighted to see the two of you collaborating so effectively."

"There's more," Eytan responded. "We made another discovery at the scene. There was a strange motif in one of the photos. From far away, it looked like graffiti. But actually, it's a series of ideograms, or characters. I'll send you the photos."

"Hmm, characters. That's surprising, indeed. And intriguing."

"It is, as is the rest of this story. Translate the characters as fast as possible. I'm anxious to learn what they mean. And here's another crucial tidbit: we have every reason to believe that the Pardubice victims were not chosen by accident. I'm not a hundred percent sure, but there could be a connection between them and the studies led by the Czech laboratories. I've acquired a list. If you could take a look—"

"Send me the names. I'll check. Is that all?"

"For now, yes."

"You've both done great work, but we still have a lot on our plate. Get some rest. I'll contact you as soon as I have more information."

Cypher ended the call.

Elena went back into the bathroom.

Eytan proceeded to send the files, as he had promised. The task took a good fifteen minutes, much to his annoyance. Most things technological gave him a massive headache, and this computer was no exception. Silver lining: he wouldn't be spending yet another night on a plane.

Elena opened the bedroom door. Eytan looked up instinctively. She had slipped out of her robe and into a white T-shirt and jeans.

"Hey, 302, how about we get a bite to eat?"

Eytan looked at her for a moment. What the hell? His whole routine—getting missions from Eli, carrying them out, and starting over again—had been shot to hell in a handbasket over the past couple of days. Eli had been kidnapped, and to save him, he had to work

148 David Khara

with this trigger-happy dragon lady. A cold beer and some sustenance, even with a woman out to kill him, was just what he needed.

"Sure, I'd like that," he said, stretching his arms and legs.

"What do you want, 302?" she asked, scanning the room service menu.

He closed the laptop and got up from the chair.

"Call me Eytan or any other damn name that pops into your head. Just quit it with the 302."

"Is Superman losing his legendary cool?" Elena asked, still examining the hotel's dinner selection.

He grabbed his jacket, threw it on, and started walking toward the door. "First, to hell with my cool. And second, Superman is too hungry to fight you right now. Come on, let go for once. I'm taking you out to a real restaurant. I could use some fresh air."

Elena let out what sounded like a sincere, delightful little laugh. Eytan was surprised at how captivating it sounded. Then she smiled. There was no trace of scorn or sarcasm. It looked genuine. Elena took a deep breath and exhaled, as though she were finally releasing all her pent-up stress and anger.

"I'm in!" she declared.

The knockout had just blown Eytan away.

CHAPTER 21

Eytan was asking the guy at the front desk about good restaurants that weren't tourist traps and still open at this late hour. Elena was seeing a totally different Eytan—one who could be affable and even charming.

Eytan regaled the man at the reception desk with a couple of jokes, which Elena didn't find particularly amusing. Then the man picked up the phone and made a reservation at a well-known brasserie. Who is this person I've been spending all this time with? Elena asked herself.

As they walked away, she heard Eytan say, "Thanks, Thomas."

"No problem, Eytan," the other replied.

A few minutes of conversation, and they were old pals. It irked every fiber of her being.

Following directions provided by Eytan's new friend, they meandered the narrow cobblestone streets of Prague. Eytan took in the sights, admiring the city's storied architecture, and especially the many towers and church spires that seemed to float above the red rooftops. The seemingly illogical mix of building styles—Gothic here, Baroque there, and functionally communist just around the corner—intrigued Elena. They gave the old city an almost Kafkaesque feel.

When they reached their destination, a waiter led them from one room to another through a maze of narrow hallways. They arrived in a small intimate space that was nothing like the noisy and busy setup at the front of the restaurant. He showed them to the only open table.

A hot spot for night owls, the restaurant provided a multilingual menu. While the main course options were limited, there were at least a dozen types of beer. Eytan decided on a caramel-flavored brew, which paired well with the daily special: honey-glazed roasted pork and vegetable soup in a bread bowl. Uninspired by the meat selections, all of which seemed to have some kind of sauce or glaze, she went for a plate of bramborák, potato pancakes flavored with oregano. They were a Prague specialty.

"Now you can enjoy the local delicacies and also add some meat to those bones," he said.

"I'm not worried about my figure," she retorted. "I was just suggesting that we get something to eat, not go off on some culinary romp in the city."

Despite the waiter's suggestions, she stuck with plain water. Eytan gave the waiter the menus, and the man walked away, leaving the two superagents alone.

"So you're one of those weird people who eats only because it's necessary for survival."

"Do you have a problem with that?"

"Does the concept of pleasure mean anything to you?"

Deeply offended by the comment, Elena looked around to make sure no one could hear before leaning toward her partner.

"Do you expect me to believe it has any more meaning in your life?" she taunted. "By the way, you eat pork?"

Seeing the waiter coming back, she stopped short. He was skillfully carrying a tray loaded with five beers and one glass of water. He served up Eytan's brew and

THE SHIRO PROJECT 151

Elena's water, then sauntered off to deliver the rest of the drinks to the other tables.

"I thought you knew everything about me," Eytan replied.

"Just the important stuff."

"In that case, you probably know that I've lived through hard times—deprivation, starvation, and worse. As a child in the Warsaw ghetto, I swore that I would never turn down any sort of food that was offered to me. Being held in Stutthof only reinforced that decision. Since then, I've allowed myself to indulge in life's delights from time to time. And in response to the subtext of your question, I have a very personal relationship with God, but I eat whatever looks good to me." He took a swig of his beer.

"That makes sense."

Eytan took another swig and held out his glass to Elena. "It's tasty. You should try it."

"I'll pass."

"Your loss."

A welcome silence fell as their dishes arrived.

Eytan dug into his meal, but Elena merely pushed the food from one spot on her plate to another. She was too distracted by her thoughts to enjoy the meal.

"It's not true, what you said back in the forest," she blurted out. She looked at Eytan with her dark eyes. "What's our profession again? Oh yeah, we execute orders, and ipso facto, we execute people. Despite your insinuations, I don't get off on killing. I take pleasure in doing it the right way and for the right reasons. I like leading successful missions. That's my job, and I'm committed to it. So in that respect, I see no difference between the two of us."

152 David Khara

Eytan put down his fork, pushed aside his plate, and tried to read the fierce face in front of him. He couldn't. Was this the hateful Elena whom he knew all too well, or were there other emotions that she had never dared to show? What had pushed this rigid character into defending herself so vehemently?

"We're not the same, and here's why," he responded. "I take out the guilty, those who threaten the innocent. But you and your friends live by some philosophy that continues to elude me—you are the threat."

He stopped himself. He didn't want those at the surrounding tables to overhear. "Similar means, different ends," he muttered, thinking back to their first encounter in the Sonian Forest.

"If I'm such a menace, why did you ask for my advice before the raid?" Elena pressed.

"Because I wanted your take on the situation. We're a team at the moment. We may not like it, but that's no reason to botch the mission. It makes more sense to rely on both of our skill sets."

"I failed."

It was hard to miss the dejection in her voice. At least his theory back at the hotel was right. She was in a bad mood because she couldn't handle failure, especially her own.

"Only those who never try never fail. Our mistakes have dramatic consequences. It's inherent in our line of work."

"But you never mess up."

Her naïve comment amused Eytan. He leaned back in his chair and crossed his legs. "Don't be so sure about that. I've made lots of mistakes, and I'll make plenty more. You're traumatized by failure. But for me, it's like rocket fuel. It pushes me to be even better at my job."

"Okay, I admit, I can be a little impatient at times," Elena confessed.

Eytan joined his hands together like the Shaolin master in the nineteen seventies TV show Kung Fu, which he had watched on occasion. "Knowledge is only acquired with age, young grasshopper."

Elena didn't know what he was talking about, because she never watched television, but she relaxed a bit.

"I haven't figured you out yet, but I am taking your promise on face value," he began again. "The one you made to Cypher. I don't know what you two are to each other, and to tell you the truth, I don't care. But I believe you will keep your word."

"Don't waste your time trying to get to know me," she responded coolly. "We're working together today. Don't get your hopes up, though. The time will come—"

"Since you insist so much on that, I'd like to make one request."

"Shoot."

"Wait until we've finished our mission."

"Seems like a fair request. But you'll always wonder if I play fair, won't you?"

"What's the point in seeing a movie when you already know the ending?"

Elena let out a genuine laugh, which Eytan had been hoping for since their arrival at the restaurant. The shadow of melancholy on her face disappeared, and her catlike eyes sparkled mischievously. Eytan appreciated her natural beauty, untouched by makeup. Under other circumstances...

"Does the world have to go mad for us to have a peaceful conversation?" she asked.

"You took the words right out of my mouth. But wouldn't we be out of place in a sane world?"

"Touché! Anyway, you mentioned my relationship with Cypher. But what about you? How is it that the mythical Eytan Morg, a former master in the art of solo combat, would agree to work for an organization that he should be fighting with all his might? What made you sell your soul?"

Eytan brushed some stray crumbs from the bread bowl off the table. He looked at his hand as he answered. "You'll probably find this hard to believe, but your boss kidnapped one of my closest friends to force me to collaborate with you. Anyone who has ever been important to me is already dead. Many of them died before my eyes, and some of those deaths were my fault. Eli is the only person left."

"What exactly does this man mean to you? Sounds as if you love him like a father."

"You have no idea."

CHAPTER 22

Somewhere in the middle of the Mediterranean Sea, November 1953

The ocean liner broke through wave after wave. As buckets of blue-green water crashed on the deck, a dozen children giddily challenged each watery crest. Glued to the railing, they would wait for the next swell. Seconds before it arrived, they would run away in a flurry of screams and laughter. They never moved fast enough or far enough—or maybe that was the point. The children met each drenching peak with glee. The oldest, who looked about eleven or twelve, was leading the game with all the bravery of a war hero. Like a Royal Air Force fighter, he was wearing a blue polka dot scarf around his neck and a leather jacket with extra-long sleeves that covered his fingers.

Eytan watched from a distance. The children's playful shenanigans entertained him. But he was even more amused by the boisterous parade of parents who appeared one after another to retrieve their offspring and take them inside to warm up. The brisk late-November weather seemed to indicate that a harsh winter would sweep through Europe. But in a few days, the passengers on this ship would be enjoying the milder climate in Israel.

156 DAVID KHARA

After losing some of his steam, the little RAF cadet left his battleground and sheepishly followed his furious father. This bold and energetic kid would soon epitomize the new Jewish man. In no time, his strong jaw and muscular arms would trump the anti-Semitic stereotypes that portrayed Jews as stooped and frail people with big noses.

Ten years earlier, Jews all over Europe had been teetering on extinction. Yes, millions had been lost in the extermination chambers. But now another era— one that Eytan couldn't have envisioned in his darkest days—was beginning. And the survivors were sending down roots in a new land.

Eytan returned to his drawing. The soft squeaking of his charcoal against the sketchpad lulled him into a daydream, temporarily displacing any nostalgia for London. Based in England since the end of the war, he had never fantasized about going to Israel. But the bigwigs at MI6 and Mossad were sending him there, so that's where he would go.

Equipped with the means to execute his missions, along with the serum he needed to stay alive, Eytan was now attached to the Israeli services. He would have the British military at his disposal on an as-required basis. He alone would decide on his targets and the appropriate time to take action. He would never have to answer to anyone. All issues concerning his missions were under his complete control. With his extraordinary strengths, incredible past, and almost unbelievable success rate, anyone betting on someone other than Agent Morg would have been crazy. And British Prime Minister Winston Churchill was far from crazy.

After the war, Churchill, had suggested just executing the Nazi leaders instead of going through the motions of the Nuremberg trials. A clean and simple solution for those who had schemed to bring about the Final Solution. Franklin Roosevelt and Joseph Stalin had dissuaded Churchill, but Eytan admired this pragmatic and witty British prime minister. In fact, the bulldog and the giant had become good friends over the years. Thanks to Churchill, Eytan had developed a fondness for cigars. Eytan would miss his British comrade in his new yet ancient home.

"Hey, mista!"

A shadow was hovering over the sketchpad. Eytan looked up. The boy in the leather jacket and RAF scarf had broken away from his father and had returned to the deck. He was planted in front of Eytan with a confidence that most adults couldn't pull off.

"I heard the grown-ups talking about you. They say you're a Nazi hunter. They say you made Wilhelm Stuckart's car crash, the guy who wrote those anti-Jewish Nuremberg Laws. Is it true?"

For a second, it looked like the kid was about to throw down the gauntlet.

"Ah, to be young and uninhibited," Eytan said under his breath as he rose to his feet. The boy's eyes grew wide as he took in the man's size.

"So, is it true, mista?"

"What do you think?"

"Come on, be a pal!"

Eytan laughed at the boy's insistence. He leaned over to pick up his coffee thermos and poured himself a cup.

"Can I have some?"

"You're too young. Is there no one else around here for you to bug?"

"I want to be a fighter pilot or a Nazi killer when I grow up."

"It's good to have goals," Eytan replied, securing the lid on his thermos. He sat down again and picked up his charcoal and sketchpad, hoping the little squirt would get the hint.

"How did you get to be so big?"

The kid had tenacity. Eytan didn't look up. Making eye contact would only encourage the pesky pipsqueak.

"I ate all my carrots. Now leave me alone!"

"And how come you got no hair? You're not old."

Was this how the whole voyage was going to go?

"So? How come you got no hair?"

"Scram, or I'll drag you back to your dad."

"He's not my dad," the boy said, wiping his nose with the back of his hand. "My name's Frank."

"Good for you. Now go someplace else."

"My parents died in a camp. I was little when the Germans took them away. I don't remember them. I try to, but I can't. A new mom and dad are waiting for me in Israel."

Eytan put down his sketchbook. The kid didn't look sad.

"My parents were taken too. I'm big so that I can scare people who want to send us back to the camps. As for Wilhelm Stuckart, I just think he was a bad driver." Eytan winked at the boy.

The boy grinned. "It's true then! You kill Nazis!"

"You've got a one-track mind, champ, I'll give you that. Let's just say I make sure the bad guys who got away aren't able to hide under their rocks for very long. But it's a secret, okay?"

The kid put down his index finger over his mouth, indicating that he would, indeed, stay quiet, and held out his other hand to shake on it. The hand disappeared in Eytan's gigantic mitt.

An adult passenger loomed up from behind and grabbed Frank by the collar. "This child is out of control! Go back with the others," the man ordered.

The man was bald, wore glasses, and looked like he was in his fifties. He easily could have been mistaken for a strict German headmaster who had time traveled from the eighteen hundreds.

"I hope he wasn't bothering you too much, sir. He's a mischief-maker."

"You should be proud of his liveliness. It's a rare quality. And no, he wasn't a problem at all. Frank and I are pals."

Eytan's response seemed to ease the man's mind. Before being shepherded back to his cabin, Frank glanced over his shoulder and waved to Eytan, who raised his hand in return.

Eytan couldn't help but wonder: How many orphans like Frank were on this ship? Five? Fifty? And how many more of them were scattered around the globe? Fifty million deaths. It was nearly impossible to comprehend all the parents, wives, husbands, and children who had been forced to live without their loved ones because of World War II. Always on the move, he had never dwelled on the statistics until this moment. Now they were almost too much to think about.

Unlike Frank, Eytan remembered his parents. Just as clearly as he remembered the face of the soldier who killed his little brother. He put that face on every enemy he tracked down. The memory of it fueled his relentless drive. But he drew his strength not so much from hatred for his torturers but from compassion for the victims. As long as he maintained this balance, and the scales didn't tip, he would be all right.

Eytan spent the rest of the day sketching passengers who braved the wind and the cold to get a breath of fresh air on deck. At nightfall, he returned to his cabin. It was so cramped, he could barely move. But for someone who had experienced the cages of Stutthof, the cabin was as good as the presidential suite in a five-star hotel.

After dropping off his things, he went to the common room, where all the travelers took their meals. He sat down at a table with a dozen other people and ate his dinner while eavesdropping on small talk. His tablemates were chatting about their respective careers, family members who had already relocated in Israel, and what they planned to do when they got there. Their words were loaded with life and hope.

Eytan stayed true to his daily routine by waving a polite good night and heading in the direction of the deck to savor an evening cigar.

After that, he usually went back to his cabin. He would try to make it as late as possible, because his bed was too small to allow for much sleep. He sometimes spent most of night reading. It was a way to make up for an education that had been cut short thirteen years earlier. And he didn't need much sleep anyway, no more than four or five hours. This evening, he would be reading Stefan Zweig's wonderful novel The Royal Game.

Eytan was still savoring his after-dinner Cuban cigar, when he heard a woman calling him. He turned, irritated at the interruption, and saw the ship's nurse in white uniform running in his direction. She had curly brown hair and appeared to be about his age. She was cute, too.

"I'm sorry to bother you, sir, but we need your help in the infirmary."

"The infirmary? What—"

The nurse stopped him before he could finish his sentence.

"No time to explain. Follow me."

Cute, but firm. He had no choice but to comply. He was hoping to deal with the matter as quickly as possible, because he was eager to get back to his book.

Three hallways and two staircases later, he entered the infirmary behind her.

Eytan was expecting a small room, like a sick bay with a single bed and a medicine cabinet. What he saw shocked him. Some thirty beds were packed into the space. A child lay in each one. There were kids of all ages. This wasn't an infirmary. It was an orphanage. The room was warm and surprisingly calm.

The nurse approached one of her colleagues. Eytan could see only her massive back as the woman leaned over a table covered with a white sheet. The two women spoke a few words, which he couldn't hear, and then turned around and started walking toward him.

Eytan could tell that the older—and larger—woman was a Mrs. Bossypants. She looked determined—probably a necessity given that she looked after nearly three dozen children with no parents. In fact, she had one of them in her arms.

She gave him a head-to-toe look-over before saying hello. It was a bit intimidating, even for a man like Eytan.

"I've been told you work for the government?"

"Actually, to be honest…"

"Yes or no?" she pressed.

"Well, yes, in a way. But who told you that?"

"The young man behind you."

Eytan turned around and saw Frank's adorably guilty face. It was bright enough to melt the ice caps. The giant didn't have time to scold the boy before the

162 DAVID KHARA

matronly nurse started talking again, drawing Eytan's attention to the young child she was holding in her arms.

"We've asked everyone on board, and nobody will take him," she said.

"That's unfortunate, but…"

"Frank told us you were traveling alone. You must have a lot of free time. Could you at least watch this little tyke for the rest of the trip? You'd be doing us a huge favor. We already have so much to do," she said, nodding in direction of the beds. "And after we dock in Haifa, perhaps you could find trustworthy people to take him in. It's hard to find homes for boys so young. With your government connections, it would be a cinch."

Her last sentence felt like the slam of a judge's gavel.

"No, no, no, wait a minute. I'm the last person you'd want for something like this," Eytan said, pointing at the younger boy in the nurse's arms. "I can't take care of him."

He turned to Frank, who was standing next to him, proud as a peacock. The kid had cojones. "What crazy lies have you been spewing?"

"Um, I didn't…" the boy sputtered.

The nurse had been shifting her weight from one foot to the other. The child she was holding, as frail as he looked, was getting heavy. She put him down on a nearby table and began telling off poor Frank, whose bedtime was long overdue.

As he watched the scene, Eytan felt a small, soft hand grab his index finger. The younger child could barely wrap the hand around his finger, but he held on. Eytan looked down at the boy and tuned out the nurse's reprimands.

"What's his name?" the giant asked, interrupting the nurse.

"Eli, sir. Eli Karman. His mother died of tuberculosis, and his cowardly father ran off long before the boy was born."

There was a pause, as Eytan observed Eli, who was still gripping his finger. The boys eyes were filled with joy, curiosity, and a certain twinkle. Eytan looked up to the nurse.

"Listen, I won't be able to take care of him full time, but I can make sure he gets everything he needs, including a good education."

The faces of the two women lit up. Frank was thrilled too. "Really?" he exclaimed.

With his right hand still held for ransom, Eytan kneeled down and spoke to the child in a soft voice.

"So, Eli, how about we go for a quiet stroll, just the two of us?"

The offer was greeted with a pure and earnest smile. The deal was sealed.

So off they went on their walk together.

One that would last a lifetime.

CHAPTER 23

PRAGUE

Elena and Eytan walked through Prague's streets back to their hotel. A light rain was falling, and the pavement was wet. A group of teenagers emerged from beneath a canopy where they had taken shelter and dashed toward the two agents like a herd of wild colts. One of the boys bumped into Eytan. The giant didn't budge, but the kid fell flat on his butt. Eytan cracked a smile and leaned down to give the young man a hand. Obviously perplexed by this odd bald man in a military getup, the teen hesitated before accepting the help. His friends, who had frozen and gone silent, eased up and started laughing again. The boy gave Eytan a thumbs up and joined the group, which stampeded off saying good night in German-laced English.

The whole incident baffled Elena. If the same thing had happened to her, she wouldn't have helped the kid. And she certainly wouldn't have given him a friendly smile. She wasn't mean or hateful. It just wouldn't have occurred to her. She didn't waste time socializing with others. Playfulness and creativity had been trained out of her. She had given up her past, her parents (her father, in particular), and even her blond locks, which, as a child, she had spent hours brushing in her Brussels bedroom.

Over the years, she had carried the weight of the Consortium's security operations on her shoulders. This job meant everything to her. It was her reason for living, a way to give back part of what had been given to her. And she was frightfully good at it.

Then one day, she heard a name, a name that spread throughout the secret organization like a mystical incantation, a name that became legendary: Eytan Morgenstern, Patient 302, the first subject to live through Professor Bleiberg's genetic manipulations, a survivor who tracked fugitive Nazis around the globe.

From that point on, all the Consortium higher-ups became obsessed with recruiting 302 away from Mossad. If that were not possible, they'd do away with him. The idée fixe consumed even Bleiberg. Elena rarely got face time with the brilliant geneticist, but when she did, he would constantly talk about his guinea pig's exploits. In the end, he—and therefore the others—began treating her like any other subordinate.

Patient 302 stripped her of her uniqueness and hijacked all the attention she had been getting from her new family—her real family. Elena channeled everything into reclaiming her position and status. But nothing worked. And without realizing it, she sank to the same cruel level as everyone else in the organization. Then one day she saw the solution. It was so clear, so pure, so simple.

She had to kill a legend to become one.

The opportunity presented itself at the BCI facility. Patient 302 had stood right in front of her, disarmed and more vulnerable than ever. All she had to do was pull the trigger, and the mythical monster would be fairy dust. She had wounded him twice—once in the shoulder and then in the thigh. But some unknown force had stopped her from firing a bullet into his head

166 David Khara

or heart. She had to summon up all her hatred toward this man, whom she didn't even know, to fuel her discipline and finish him off once and for all. But she had missed her chance.

Tonight, she was walking alongside him in Prague. The more she watched him, the more she admired him, and the more her hatred grew. Eytan Morg represented the perfect nemesis. He was comfortable interacting with others, always effortlessly attentive, super professional. He reminded her of the famous poem by Rudyard Kipling, which she had read years ago:

> If you can keep your head when all about you
> Are losing theirs and blaming it on you,
> If you can trust yourself when all men doubt you,
> But make allowance for their doubting too;
> If you can wait and not be tired by waiting,
>
> Or being lied about, don't deal in lies,
> Or being hated, don't give way to hating,
> And yet don't look too good, nor talk too wise...
>
> You'll be a Man, my son!

Elena, locked inside her fortress of solitude and anger, had to admit the unbearable fact that under other circumstances, in another lifetime, the two of them...

A dull buzz interrupted her thoughts.

"Cell phone," Eytan said. He pulled the phone out of his pocket and put it to his ear.

"We'll call you from the hotel," he told the caller.

"No more dawdling. Cypher has new information."

And with that, their peaceful stroll came to an abrupt end. The two walked briskly the rest of the way.

Barely settled in their suite, Eytan once again pulled out his cell phone.

"Are you in your room?" Cypher asked, answering the call.

"Yes, but before we begin… You know the drill."

"Of course, here's your friend."

Eli reassured Eytan that he was okay, and Eytan agreed to proceed.

"As a preface, getting information from former Soviet Bloc countries is complicated."

Goes with the territory, Eytan thought. Some habits die hard.

"Still, you're a powerful man with influence," he said.

"You get the idea," Cypher said. "Your source on the victims of the village guessed right. Most of the residents worked in secret labs in the Pardubice region during the Cold War. As a reward for their service and to keep them from talking, the government provided them with homes and comfortable pensions."

"What fields did these people work in?"

"Bacteriology, psychoactive substances, poisons, all Czech specialties."

"Was their profile in any way similar to that of the Moscow metro subjects?" Elena asked.

"No. I'm afraid those were merely civilians without any obvious ties to the village residents. Their only connection appears to be the way they died."

"It's hard to find a motive that would give us any kind of lead," Eytan said.

"Yes, the motive. Speaking of which, I have good news and bad news, Mr. Morg. Which one would you like to hear first?"

"I'm not a fan of these little games, but give me the good news first, for a change."

"We've translated the characters."

"And the bad news?
"We've translated the characters."

CHAPTER 24

"The characters are Japanese, and they mean 'the children of Shiro.' Add that information to the biological attacks, and I'm sure you grasp the magnitude of our problem."

Eytan took a moment to digest the news. He ran his hand over his head and looked at the ceiling.

"Hell... Shiro Ishii."

"Yes," Cypher said.

"Do you mind filling me in?" Elena asked, taking a bottle of water out of the minibar. She held out another bottle to Eytan, but he declined.

"Mr. Morg will explain everything, my dear. As for me, I must be off. Call me back as soon as you have anything on the lab materials."

Cypher ended the call without any formalities. Eytan made his way to the window overlooking the Vltava River. Elena followed, leaned her shoulder against the wall, and waited for his explanation.

"There was this one German concentration camp doctor I arrested," Eytan said in a monotone. "I offered him a quick bullet to the brain, but he chose to go to trial. During his interrogation, he pretty much shrugged off the horrors he and his buddies committed. His words stuck in my head. 'Compared to the Japanese, we were choirboys.'"

"I don't know very much about the Pacific War," Elena said.

Eytan sighed.

"From 1931 until the Soviet invasion of Manchuria in 1945, the Japanese had research centers in the occupied Chinese region. The most horrific and well known of them was Unit 731. Its official name was the Epidemic Prevention and Water Purification Department. A nice little euphemism to cover up the facility's true purpose. Under the command of Lieutenant General Shiro Ishii, Unit 731 developed an advanced biological and chemical warfare program that included experimentation on human subjects. The Kempeitai, the Imperial Army's military police, a sort of Gestapo, provided some six hundred human guinea pigs every year the unit was in existence. Many more human subjects came from other experimentation sites. Nearly three-quarters of them were Chinese. But the rest were Russians, Pacific islanders, and Southeast Asians. It's believed there were even some Allied prisoners of war. Once medical ethics were thrown out the window, it was anything goes. You needed a heart of steel to hear the horrors committed: vivisections, amputations, the infliction of all possible and imaginable diseases on women and children."

"That's insane," Elena replied, genuinely disgusted.

"They were also frozen, gassed, and hanged upside down to see how long it would take to choke to death. Even if a subject survived an experiment, he was immediately forced to endure another one. And it went on and on until he was eventually killed. Victims were jokingly referred to as 'logs,' meaning lumber, and the center was called the 'sawmill.' Basically, all you have to do is imagine the worst abominations in the world under the most nightmarish circumstances, and you should get the picture."

THE SHIRO PROJECT 171

Eytan stopped. He listened to the muffled street noise below and the gentle tapping of rain against the window.

"That's awful," Elena said after a few minutes of silence. She took a sip of her water. "But what's the connection between the horrors committed in the Pacific during World War II and the attacks in Czechoslovakia and Moscow?"

"I'll get there. Let me finish first. After studying medicine, Ishii served in the army as a high-ranking surgeon. During a two-year trip through Europe, he researched chemical weapons used during World War I. This was a huge eye-opener for him. He came to the conclusion that victory over the USSR and the United States could be achieved through chemical and bacteriological warfare."

"There were no such attacks during World War II, to my knowledge."

"That's partially true. At one point, the Japanese did launch thousands of incendiary balloons over the Pacific. Only a few managed to land on the West Coast. Six people died, but those balloons could have done much more harm if the plan had succeeded. The Japanese then loaded a submarine with biological weapons, but it sank before the weapons could be used. Undaunted, they devised Operation Cherry Blossom, which would have involved filling planes with fleas infected with the plague. Kamikazes were supposed to crash their planes near San Diego. That plan was thwarted when a message was sent by the US government to Japan. I'm paraphrasing, but basically it said, 'We know where the emperor is hiding. Send your bombs, and we'll turn him into birdfeed.'"

"They were telling the Japanese government that they'd drop an atom bomb on the emperor?"

172 DAVID KHARA

"Yep, the Americans originally planned to hit Berlin, but the Third Reich collapsed before the bomb was ready. Unfortunately, the people of Hiroshima and Nagasaki weren't as lucky."

Eytan turned his back to the window.

"Anyway, between the Japanese writing on the wall and the nature of the attacks here and in Russia, I'm worried there's a Unit 731 copycat."

"Do you think the two events are connected?"

"Your boss, Cypher, seems to think so. Two attacks in the same week. That can't be a coincidence. The real problem will be identifying our terrorists and understanding their motives so we can keep them from striking again. I'm anxious to receive more information from your network."

"That shouldn't take long. Do you have any theories?"

"Too many. It's hard to isolate the most credible one."

"So what happened to Ishii at the end of the war?"

"Nothing."

"You're shitting me, right?" exclaimed Elena.

"I wish. The man gave up all the details of his operation in exchange for immunity. He died of lung cancer in 1959, a free man. He was sixty-seven. Quite a lifespan when you consider that some of his victims didn't make it to their first birthday."

"I'd like to know how the guy managed an exchange like that. Why didn't you target him? I bet you would have loved that."

"I was focused on the part of history that affected me personally. And that kept me busy enough," Eytan said. "And besides, if I had decided to seek justice for what Ishii and his cohorts did, I would have faced a major obstacle."

"It must have been a big one."

"The Americans protected Ishii and his team so they could get hold of his work. His experiments were a gold mine for the United States. The wholesale disregard for ethics made it possible for Unit 731 to make major discoveries. For example, they sent naked subjects outside in below-freezing temperatures. It would sicken most people to know that those studies yielded critical advancements in the treatment of frostbite, treatments that are considered standard procedure today. So there was no way the United States was going to put Ishii on trial. And going after him myself and getting on Uncle Sam's bad side in the process wouldn't have been an especially smart move right in the middle of the Cold War."

"And even after all that, you still consider the Consortium your enemy?" Elena asked. "We're angels in comparison."

"I've already heard that line of reasoning. The people who finance evil are as guilty as those who implement it. As far as I'm concerned, there's no difference between Ishii and your Bleiberg. Both were obsessed with inflicting their repugnant visions on the rest of us. And the Consortium is continuing Bleiberg's quest."

"There's no point in arguing. Neither of us is going to budge," Elena said. "So let's get back to business. There's someone out there who is aligned with Shiro Ishii—perhaps ideologically. They've stolen biological material from a Consortium lab, and they've been having a grand old time testing it out in Moscow and the Czech Republic. Does that pretty much sum it up?"

"So it seems."

She reflected for a few moments.

"But what exactly is this person or organization's goal in creating weapons? Why Moscow? Was it because Unit 731 had been developing weapons to attack the Soviet Union? If so, why would the terrorists go after the Czech Republic?"

"The country did play an important role in similar research for the Eastern Bloc. But like you, I'm having a hard time finding a direct connection."

Elena and Eytan heard a ding. Elena had just received an e-mail on her laptop. "Maybe that's the information we need," she said.

Five long minutes filled with the sound of Elena typing on her keyboard followed. Then came a brief silence.

"Morg, I think we've got our lead."

"Let's hear it," he said.

"I'll need a moment to explain. Do you have your doctored passport?"

"Of course. Where are we going?"

"Tokyo."

CHAPTER 25

Tokyo, autumn 1947

The hotel's banquet room looked like the command center of a hectic military base. Men in US and British dress uniforms filled the room. Peter Aikman had to bite his lip to keep from laughing. He already stood out in his civilian clothes, so even the slightest guffaw would certainly bring all eyes on him, which was the last thing he wanted.

At least for now he was flying safely under the radar.

Peter scanned the sea of officers. Grouped in threes and fours, they were all conversing and sipping their drinks. Peter stood on his toes to get a better view of the room. Finding a man who wasn't even five feet tall in the midst of all these decorated lumberjacks was going to be a challenge.

If only these assholes weren't so big and cozy with each other, he thought as he elbowed his way to the bar. The room was hot, and the bodies exuded pungent smells of BO, cheap cigarettes, and spicy aftershave.

He noted with a smirk that the generals had taken the best spots beneath giant fans whose blades were spinning at full speed. The privileges of rank.

Life had to be good at the top.

Peter finally arrived at a circular bar carved from exotic wood. Behind it were three Marine Corps

176 David Khara

bartenders hustling to fill the drink orders. Members of the Japanese serving staff were waiting in line to pick up the drinks and deliver them to the foreign military officers. Their hotel, just like their country, had been invaded. Peter wondered what feelings these men held behind their impassive faces. Did they hate the officers? Or were they relieved that they could get on with their lives? He brushed off any urge to find answers to those questions. What was the point? The Pentagon agent had seen some grotesque images since the end of the war, including the emaciated survivors of Poland's concentration camps. In his opinion, the invading Allies were far more humane than the enemies they had vanquished. Still, he had developed an uncharacteristic bit of compassion for the ordinary civilians who had nothing to do with the atrocities committed by their governments. Maybe he was developing a conscience? Maybe a grain of morality was sprouting inside his cold and calculating mind?

"Peter! I almost thought you wouldn't find me!"

The treble voice came out of nowhere, and its unique nature left no doubt as to its owner. A small man with a limp popped up between two captains and pushed his way through. He was wearing a broad smile. No matter the occasion, that wide smile was always evident on Elliot Garnikel's plump face.

"Sorry, excuse me, thanks," he repeated as he shoved aside the obstacles in his path with his cane, which was as much a part of him as his portly build and bald head. And the bastard knew how to use his handicaps to his advantage. He had a ravishing beauty on each arm.

"You've really got to tell me how you do it," Peter joked. He checked out his friend's female companions as they took their leave.

Elliot let out a laugh—a sort of restrained chirping that morphed into a wheeze.

"Women don't care as much about a man's looks as his ability to meet their needs, my friend. And in that respect, I am the uncontested champion. Don't let it get to you, pretty boy," he said with a wink.

Peter smiled but was quickly irritated. The noisy fans and the loud conversations were drowning out "In the Mood," one of his Glenn Miller favorites. He changed the subject. "The conquered territories have become one big board game for high-ranking military officers, secret agents, and tipsy scoundrels. And yesterday's enemies, now tamed, have become meek business associates. Makes you wonder the point of the whole war."

"What do you expect?" Elliot replied. "The world has gone mad. You know, Japan has always had a strange relationship with war. They call it bushido— the way of the samurai. It's an entire philosophy based on the concepts of frugality, honor, mastery of the martial arts, and loyalty to the master. These warrior values are stripped of all emotion. And sacrificing your life in the name of the emperor is considered the highest form of valor. Honestly, I don't get it. What I do know is that many poor souls have died because of the absurd notion. But anyhow, now's the time to make up and play nice, which means there's money to be made."

"You're nothing but a crook," Peter said as he took out a pack of cigarettes from his jacket.

"What can I say? I've got beginner's luck," Elliot said. "Follow me. They're probably waiting for you."

The unlikely duo made their way through the crowd toward the hotel's main staircase.

"What about MacArthur?" Peter asked.

178   David Khara

"Oh, he's doing his job well and is a master in the art of seduction. The Japanese are very grateful for his help in protecting Hirohito. I must admit, he did well there. Getting the major war criminals to keep the emperor blameless—that took real skill. By preserving the historical symbol of their independence and identity, he's been able to strip the Japanese of their power quite easily."

"Surprising. I always took him for a dangerous and out-of-control lunatic," Peter said, going up the stairs with his friend. Because of Elliot's disability, the slow climb felt laborious, and Peter was anxious to get to his meeting.

"Out of control? It's possible," Elliot said. "As for your other postulations, he may be dangerous, but he's definitely not crazy. Look around. We're at peace with Japan. Ten years from now, they'll be drinking our Cokes and eating Oscar Mayer hotdogs, even though we gut-punched them with two atomic bombs. Pulling off that kind of accomplishment takes qualities that men like you could never understand, my friend."

"You're right. I care only about the results, not the methods for achieving them. I just hope that MacNutcase's envoy stays the course, because we're dealing with an important matter today."

"I don't know the specifics of this meeting. No offense, but I'm still surprised that you were chosen for this mission. You're not exactly famous for your negotiating skills."

"I'm not here to negotiate but to make sure the terms of the contract are respected," Peter responded as he wiped his forehead with the back of his sleeve.

The small man stopped in front of a door and knocked three times with his cane. A Japanese man who looked as stiff as a board answered. He was

THE SHIRO PROJECT 179

wearing a stylish broad-shoulder jacket with wide lapels. He was also sporting a pair of Ray-Ban aviator sunglasses.

What a ridiculous getup, Peter thought.

"Hello, I'm the colonel's translator. Please come in," the Japanese man said, removing his sunglasses. He bowed, and the two visitors did the same.

"Thanks, but I won't be joining you," Elliot said as he turned to leave the room. "I'm only an intermediary here, and my job is done. Peter, I'll be waiting for you at the bar."

"I didn't have time to inform Mr. Garnikel of his greatly desired presence," Peter said.

He nudged his friend. Elliot grumbled, but nothing intelligible came out of his mouth. The Japanese man started leading them to another doorway. Peter smiled and pushed his fussing pal forward. His limp seemed more dramatic than usual.

Peter stooped and whispered in Elliot's ear. "You have to be here for this meeting. I need an objective witness. Don't worry. A nice fat envelope awaits you."

"Please warn me next time. You know how much I hate getting mixed up in your affairs."

Peter swiped his finger in front of his mouth. It was time he zip his lip. The message was loud and clear.

The three men entered a mostly unfurnished room filled with smoke. The walls hadn't been painted, and old newspapers covered the floor. High class all the way, Peter thought. The hotel had been built six months earlier and wasn't supposed to open to the public until the spring of 1948. In the meantime, the army had commandeered the ground floor for soirées and the unfinished rooms upstairs for meetings.

A beat-up circular table with five chairs was conveniently positioned under a ceiling fan.

180 David Khara

Two cigarette-smoking men were standing in the room. Peter recognized both of them. While preparing the contract, he had met the first one, Simon Dickel, a member of MacArthur's staff. Tall and broad shouldered, Dickel was dressed in an impeccable uniform. His brown hair was cut short, according to military protocol. The arrogant prick was as cold and calculating as they came.

Peter had never met the other man but was certain of his identity, nonetheless. Colonel Nagoshi was both revered and reviled. Some considered him a reasonable person open to negotiation and focused on rebuilding his country. Others called him a bloodthirsty devil who had no respect for human life—one of the worst war criminals the world had ever known.

Some chips and playing cards, and this could have been a back-alley gambling room, Peter thought. But a more thorough observation of the poker faces dispelled any temptation to challenge them to a game.

The translator placed himself beside Nagoshi, and a new round of bows marked the start of the meeting. Dickel asked everyone to take a seat and initiated the discussion.

"Mr. Aikman, you may begin, since it's your responsibility to lead this meeting."

Peter ignored the tinge of jealousy in his voice. Clearly, the American military man was used to being the one in charge. Peter placed his briefcase on the table. He inserted a small key in a lock on each side of the handle. With the press of his thumbs, he opened the briefcase and wordlessly took out two folders. He placed one in front of MacArthur's man and the other before the icy colonel.

"Gentlemen, following our specialists' examination of your credentials, I am pleased to confirm the terms of our collaboration. This contract will finalize our agreement. You have two copies, one in English and the other in Japanese. As your translator can verify, the two versions spell out the same conditions, point by point. As this meeting will be our last, I invite you to read over the memorandum of understanding carefully, and if there are any terms that need to be clarified, now is the time to do so."

Colonel Nagoshi leaned over to his translator. They spoke for a few minutes in Japanese and then proceeded to read the contract. After a good fifteen minutes, they exchanged folders.

"The requests made by Lieutenant General Ishii have, indeed, been honored, and we are thankful for that," the translator said.

Another bowing session ensued. These men could use the most overly polite formalities to mask their savage behavior, Peter thought. Despite his distrust, the Pentagon agent bowed in return.

"A quarter million in cash and a top-secret classification for all activities carried out by the lieutenant general in exchange for the entirety of his research. Your boss has been granted immunity from prosecution, and Uncle Sam has been quite generous. However, if our little soviet comrades should come into possession of your discoveries, the contract will become null and void, and you can imagine the consequences if that were to happen."

"Your warnings are unnecessary. The lieutenant general does not hold the Soviet Union in high regard. He would take his own life before collaborating with Stalin."

"The lieutenant general is a man of honor," Peter said. No one could miss the mocking tone in his voice.

182 DAVID KHARA

"Okay," Dickel interrupted. "The funds will be delivered to Mr. Ishii's residence within three days. Your communication with Proconsul MacArthur's services will end once the exchange is executed. At that point, the lieutenant general will work directly with our intelligence service. Is that correct, Aikman?"

"Absolutely," Peter responded. "And I'll be serving as your liaison officer until further notice. By the way, our specialists appreciate the value of your unit's scientific research. If they wish to meet the lieutenant general and his team, would you see any harm in that?"

"Provided that there is additional compensation, your request would be welcomed," the translator announced after consulting with Colonel Nagoshi.

The five men remained still and observed each other for several long seconds.

"Perfect, I believe we are finished here, gentlemen," Dickel said.

He rose from his seat and headed toward the door.

The colonel followed, as did his translator and Peter. A round of military handshakes and Japanese-style bows finalized the meeting. The two Japanese men and Dickel left. Elliot, however, was still glued to his chair. No one had bothered to say good-bye to him.

"You really screwed me over," Elliot seethed as he rose from his chair.

"I don't get what you're insinuating," Peter responded casually. He leaned against a wall and lit a cigarette.

Elliot swung at the briefcase, and it went flying across the room. The agent could hardly believe the little guy had it in him.

"Do you know what these madmen have done in Manchuria?"

"I have a vague idea, but until further notice, that's not my responsibility," Peter said and sighed.

"You can't get off that easily, not after what you told me about the camps in Europe. These guys committed worse crimes than the Nazis. And shit, people like me were at the top of the Germans' kill list!"

Peter stared into space. "Jewish and handicapped—you're right. You would have been a prime candidate for Hitler's killing machine. But with your trafficking activities and notorious scheming, you're in no position to give me any lessons on morality."

"I do business, Peter, but not at any price. This... This is another beast altogether. What Shiro Ishii has gotten here is blood money, paid for with thousands of lives. The stories circulating around Shiro Ishii go far beyond what I've heard about the Nazi death camps. And to think he has immunity now." He was shaking.

"You should settle down, Elliot. What just happened here is bigger than the both of us. It's politics."

"No! It's exploitation of human suffering, all for military gain," Elliot shouted as he pounded the floor with his cane.

"Do you honestly think we have seen the end of warfare?" Peter asked. "The defeat of Germany and Japan does not mean peace. Our former ally, Stalin, has become our enemy. We supported him so that he could control the Eastern Front against Hitler, and we knew him well enough to understand that nothing would stop him from turning on us when the time was right. So we're acting accordingly, even if it means wiping the slate clean on the experiments conducted by Ishii and his men. This kind of compromise is for the good of our nation's security."

"Compromise? To me, it sounds more like you're rushing blindly into the arms of war criminals!"

"You shouldn't react this way. Need I remind you of the integral role you played in this transaction?

Without your contacts we wouldn't have been able to meet with these men. You're just as involved in this as I am."

"If I had known... For God's sake, Peter. What did you do?"

"I'll tell you what I've done, Elliot." Peter walked over to the door and locked it. Turning around and walking back, he slipped a hand inside his jacket and pulled out a gun. He pointed it at the small man and pulled the trigger. The swooshing fan blades drowned out the sound of the gunshot.

Elliot Garnikel remained speechless for several seconds. He dropped his cane and brought both hands to his stomach. It didn't take long for pain to replace the confusion.

Peter put his weapon back in its holster and approached the wounded man. How could such an apparently weak man continue to stand his ground with a bullet in his belly? He bent down to look his dying friend in the eye.

"I'm sorry, Elliot. But if it's any consolation, all the other participants in this transaction will drop off, as well. A little plane crash awaits that moronic Dickel. Honestly, I would have preferred avoiding this, but your reaction proved just how important it is to uphold the secrecy of the agreement."

Elliot keeled over, seized by convulsions, his bulging eyes never leaving Peter Aikman's impassive face. The latter placed two fingers on his victim's neck. After confirming that there was no pulse, the man from the Pentagon got back up and headed toward the door. He turned the handle, then peered back.

"You know what we did in this room, Elliot? We made a good deal."

CHAPTER 26

PRAGUE, 2010

He slid the razor over his skull with military precision. Each stroke reinforced his resolve to keep hold of his true self, or at least stray from it as little as possible. This daily routine, seemingly insignificant, was symbolic of his resistance. Naturally brown-haired, Eytan could never accept the blond hair Professor Bleiberg's experiments had given him. And so he observed the same ritual every day. An act initiated out of anger and defiance had become a few meditative moments of introspection. As he caught a glimpse of the faint orange sun rising above the rooftops of Prague, he obsessed over his execution of the unfortunate Czech soldier. He felt dishonorable. He had lived by a strict code of conduct, and with this murder, his code was wobbling on a thin edge—razor thin.

It was the only way to protect Branislav and his family. Killing war criminals was one thing, but here, the victim was only doing his job. Damn Elena, arrogant and negligent once again, and that kid, who showed his face too soon. Mistakes that forced him to break his code, changing him from an assassin into a cold-blooded murderer.

And who were these children of Shiro? They were spreading chaos and costing blameless people their

186 David Khara

lives. That was the very definition of terrorism. He'd have to stop them, whatever the cost. If only to relieve the weight of shame pressing on his conscience.

Elena was still asleep in the next room. With their flight to Tokyo scheduled to leave late in the morning, they had agreed to treat themselves to a little extra rest. He had let Elena have the bed and had settled for the fold-out couch in the common room. It didn't quite accommodate his size.

He leaned over the sink and splashed water on his face.

Through the slightly ajar door, Elena watched her "genetic brother," which was what she called him in private. As a kid, she had mastered the art of faking sleep, and when the giant crossed the bedroom as quietly as a mouse, she tried not to spoil his valiant attempt to respect her slumber. She couldn't tear her eyes away from the titan's back. His many scars impressed her far more than his muscles. His body was a virtual altar to pain and suffering.

A few minutes later she jumped out of bed and went to the common room, where a breakfast ordered by the Kidon agent awaited her. She sat down at the table and poured herself a cup of tea to go with the decadent Viennese pastries. Eytan arrived just in time to grab a slice of toast and a croissant before everything was gone.

"Sleep well?" he asked, unwrapping a pat of butter and slathering it over his toast.

"Like a baby. And yourself?"

He nodded affirmatively as he grabbed a porcelain cup, which looked tiny in his hand. A killer who played tea party! Elena giggled at the absurdity of the scene.

"That was a good call with Japan," he said, spreading the jam on his toast.

"I don't deserve that much credit. There aren't many manufacturers who make materials for P3 and P4 labs. According to my contacts' cross-references, the Shinje Corp., also known as the S. Corp., has acquired materials from various companies that are essential for this kind of setup: a bunch of Class II biosafety cabinets, positive-pressure protective suits, fluorescence microscopes, nitrogen tanks, that kind of thing. The list goes on. The orders were spaced out over a long period, most likely to avoid unwanted attention. The company works in the medical sector. However, it doesn't claim to have any P4 labs."

"How suspicious."

"Yes, especially since the Shinje Corp. doesn't make vaccines or medications. It makes prosthetic limbs. In fact, they're at the forefront of traumatology and bionic technology. I did a little Internet search while you were in the shower. And the results are quite interesting."

She stood up, picked up a hotel note pad from the table, and sat back down.

"Check it out. Shinje Corp., created in 1949. Like several other Japanese companies, it was a major player in the nation's postwar economic miracle, the boom that catapulted Japan onto the world's financial stage. Seeing what was left of the nation at the end of World War II, the term 'miracle' is no exaggeration." Elena stopped to pour herself another cup of tea. "I was more interested in the company's founder, Hirokazu Shinje. Fascinating character. This man was one of the first people to talk openly about Unit 731's crimes and acknowledge his own involvement. The media wasn't terribly interested in his revelations. That disgusted him so much, he decided to live as a recluse."

"Doesn't sound like your typical terrorist," Eytan said. "Are you sure about all this?"

"That's what I read online. There are a lot of sites that talk about him, and they all say more or less the same thing. Are you ready for the cherry on top? In the nineteen sixties, Shinje created a charitable foundation."

"I don't get it," Eytan said.

"You don't? It's so simple. Maybe the guy isn't as apologetic as he wants to look. He could be using his good deeds to cover up what he's really doing: continuing the work of his mentor, Ishii. He might be following the model of the Aum Shinrikyo cult, which was responsible for the sarin gas attack in the Tokyo subway, and have his own group of zealots."

"Do you really think that at the age of ninety, maybe even older, Shinje would have the energy and drive to undertake such an endeavor?"

"I wouldn't waste my time trying to understand the deranged thoughts of a crazy old man. All I care about is ending this as soon as possible. Now that we know where the materials were delivered, we're back in business."

"But why attack the Russians and the Czechs?"

Elena put down her notes.

"That's the last piece of the puzzle."

They both continued their breakfast in silence. According to Elena's theory, the missing piece of the puzzle could be in Japan. Still, there was something about Shinje that wasn't adding up. And there was another matter, which had nothing to do with the Japanese entrepreneur or any biological weapons that he might or might not be working on. Eytan was in a good mood, and Elena looked, well, relaxed. This was as good a time as any to test his luck.

"Elena, I've got a personal question for you. It's been on my mind for a while now."

"Shoot," she replied as she folded her napkin and put it on the table.

"Why—"

He hesitated.

"Why what?" she asked.

"Why did you accept Bleiberg's treatments? What exactly were you expecting?"

The woman's face tensed.

"That's none of your business," she said, getting up from the table.

"I don't want to upset you, I just want to understand. The survival rate was only thirty percent with Bleiberg's genetic modifications. Why take such a risk?"

Elena headed toward the bedroom. She stopped at the doorway and looked over her shoulder. "Because thirty percent is always better than zero."

CHAPTER 27

BRUSSELS, 1955

An endless parade of adults in white coats filed through the hospital hallway. A little girl, no stranger to the scene, was waiting patiently on a long red bench outside the doctor's office. Despite the pain, she swung her legs to the beat of a nursery rhyme that her mother had taught her the night before.

A nurse approached, her hands clasped behind her back. The girl had always admired her red hair, cut in a boyish style.

"Right or left?" she asked with a heavy Dutch accent.

The child got a kick out of this ritual. She had cracked the code a long time ago, and even though there was no longer any element of surprise, winning a mint lollipop was an exciting prospect.

"Right," the girl said softly, pretending to guess.

The nurse made a pouty face that quickly became a huge smile. She brandished the candy in her right fist.

"Thanks, Hanne," the child exclaimed, hamming it up as she took the lollipop.

The woman gently stroked the little girl's cheek. "Your daddy should be here soon," she said.

The little girl didn't reply. She was focused on unwrapping her treat. The nurse and the child sat quietly, oblivious to the pediatric ward and the rest of

THE SHIRO PROJECT 191

the world around them. Time stood still, giving them this singular moment of peace.

A squeaky hospital bed pushed by an orderly jolted them from their trance. Duty called. The nurse stood up, smoothed her white coat, and directed the new arrival to his room.

A short time later, a stylish man appeared. In the eyes of the little girl, he was the tallest and most handsome person in the world. The black patch over his left eye, along with the Russian accent, commanded respect and added to his seemingly serious demeanor. But the little girl knew that a kindhearted soul was behind that formidable façade.

Waving his black hat, he held out his arms.

"Come, my sweet pea. The doctor wants to see you."

The little girl got down from the bench and walked stiffly toward her father. When she finally reached him, she tackled him with a bear hug. He tried to hide the tears welling in his eyes, but she knew they were there.

Only her father was present for these consultations. Her mother could no longer cope with her daughter's worsening condition and the painful exams she was subjected to.

Andreï Kourilyenko would never forget the moment the doctor revealed the diagnosis. "Your daughter has amyotrophic lateral sclerosis. ALS for short. It's a degenerative autoimmune disease, and it's very rare in children. I'm sorry."

He didn't need to hear the prognosis from the doctor to know there was no hope for his daughter. His days during the war as a political commissar in charge of scientific research had given him a solid enough medical background to understand. On a diplomatic assignment in the West, he had joined the secret society

Consortium. Andreï had traded a life full of fear and distrust for a comfortable existence with his wife and daughter. The Russian, hardened by years of Stalinism, could have lived in total bliss. But any prospects for that bliss were swept away by his little girl's illness, followed by his wife's depression. The fatal diagnosis destroyed everything. Not even Andreï himself knew how he had mustered the strength to bear the unbearable reality.

"How much time?" he had asked.

The doctor removed his glasses and rubbed his face, as if to avoid eye contact.

"Your daughter's life expectancy is a matter of months, two years at the most."

Andreï felt his throat tense up.

"Is she going to suffer?"

"This form of sclerosis causes numerous muscular and respiratory complications. But I cannot predict exactly how it will manifest for your daughter."

"You didn't answer the question," Andreï insisted.

"It doesn't look good."

Six months had passed since the doctor's devastating news. Denial hadn't changed a thing. The unstoppable illness continued to advance. First came constipation, followed by excruciating joint pain, which led to weakened motor function. And yet she never complained. She made every effort to stay cheerful and downplay her symptoms. It broke Andreï's heart. There was no reward for her bravery. Signs of muscular atrophy were intensifying, mostly in her lower body. She could still walk, but for how much longer? Soon she wouldn't even be able to breathe.

The exam dragged on, as usual. While the doctor jotted his findings on his clipboard, Andreï stroked the little girl's hair and whispered words of encouragement. Lies.

"Don't worry, Elena, everything will be all right."

Another six months, and now Elena was bedridden. Her lungs were failing. She was pretending to sleep, because her father didn't cry as much when he thought she was resting peacefully. But she opened her eyes a bit when she heard someone talking to him.

He was wearing a beige raincoat buttoned all the way to the neck. A wide-brimmed gray hat hid his features. His voice, however, sounded stern. Her father, who always enjoyed talking with people, was strangely quiet. He even seemed to be afraid of the stranger.

"How have you been holding up since our last encounter?" Despite the seemingly sympathetic words, the man sounded indifferent.

"Why are you asking, Bleiberg?" her father said. "Isn't it obvious?"

"I was just being polite. There's no need to take offense."

He walked around the room, examining the furniture, as if he were conducting an inspection. He stopped at the foot of the bed, put on a pair of glasses, and picked up her chart. He scanned it.

"Stop wasting time with this charade. You never do anything without a reason. What do you want?"

"Oh, me? Nothing. Wouldn't you expect a courtesy visit in a dire situation such as this, especially since I have the resources to cure your daughter?"

Elena almost cried out. She wanted so badly to be healed, to say good riddance to her aching body and the aloof doctors with cold hands who treated her like she was a thing, not a person. She still hoped for some life-saving treatment. And here it was, in the unexpected form of a strange visitor saddled with an ugly German accent.

"How?" stammered her father.

"Oh, come on! You know very well," said this man named Bleiberg. "A simple injection, and the big bad illness will be nothing more than a memory."

The man made a fist and blew into it. Then he revealed his empty palm, as if he had performed a magic feat.

"So, there it is," her father replied, shaking his head. "You've accomplished miracles, but at what price? Your secret experiments for the SS send shivers up my spine. Assuming I do accept your offer, what would you expect in return? You're not the kind to hand out gifts."

"You've kept your keen soviet insight," Bleiberg said. "I'm not asking for much, compared with what I'm offering. Of course, I can't guarantee success for the treatment. But a thirty percent chance is better than zero, right?"

The two men stared at each other. The stranger's calm demeanor was a stark contrast to her father's anxiety. Bleiberg pointed at her.

"If she survives my treatment, I want her," he announced.

Elena watched her father put his hands over his face. "Never! I can't let you take my daughter and turn her into a guinea pig."

"Surprising. You're prepared to watch your only child suffer an agonizing death out of respect for what moral code? One only you understand?"

"Real doctors are taking care of her here. Nobody is pretending to be God."

"And what good is that doing her? What results are these real doctors achieving? Pity, compassion, and even this illusion that you call love won't save your daughter. Take time to think over my offer. Weigh the good against the bad. I'll come back tomorrow for your final decision. Have a good night, Commissar."

Bleiberg adjusted his hat and held out a hand to Andreï. He didn't take it.

How could her father so quickly refuse an offer she had been praying for? How could he deny her this chance to live? The realization kindled a feeling deep inside her. A feeling that would never leave her. It was hatred.

Elena opened her eyes wide. The man glanced at her while her father wasn't looking. Elena gave him an almost imperceptible nod. He smiled and left the room like a puff of air.

Andreï remained silent for several minutes. He looked at his daughter, who had closed her eyes again. Just thinking about her in this man's clutches revolted him.

The next day, Professor Viktor Bleiberg showed up bright and early.

Elena survived the injection and soon enjoyed a full recovery.

She saw her father only one more time.

The day she killed him.

CHAPTER 28

PRAGUE, 2010

Just before leaving the hotel, Eytan made a quick call to the Israeli attaché in Brussels. Because Cypher had prohibited him from contacting the Mossad network, his options for obtaining a stash of weapons in Japan were limited. The Kidon operative was pleasantly surprised to hear that Colonel Amar was familiar with intelligence service methods and eager to help—no questions asked. Eytan, however, did have to promise that his actions wouldn't cause an international incident, considering the last time.

Elena and he agreed that flying out of Prague would be too risky. The likelihood that a victim of the camp siege could give even a vague description of the duo was slim, but it was possible, all the same.

They left before sunrise for a more than four-hour motorcycle ride to Frankfurt and hopped on a plane from there. Both takeoff and the long-distance flight were smooth sailing. Cypher had sprung for two seats in business class, and Eytan was getting a taste of the sweet life, with all the legroom a giant could ever wish for.

After eleven hours in the sky, most of which were dedicated to contemplating potential scenarios, they landed at Narita International Airport in Tokyo, a city where they had never before set foot. With their false passports in hand, the two agents breezed through customs. They loaded up on yens and took a taxi to Shibuya.

The sidewalks of the bustling urban shopping district were crammed with an eclectic mix of people. There were briefcase-wielding businessmen in form-fitting dark suits and girls in high school uniforms. Teenage boys sporting buzz cuts, razor cuts, and flattops stopped here and there to ogle young women in dresses so short, Eytan could almost see what wasn't underneath. Another woman in a gold silk kimono, a traditional bun atop her head, weaved her way against the current of pedestrian traffic. She looked like someone straight out of a James Clavell novel.

The pedestrians, walking alone and in groups, appeared largely indifferent to one another, yet the mass of humanity seemed to be in brilliant harmony. Live and let live, Eytan thought.

Like two kids entering Willy Wonka's chocolate factory, Eytan and Elena marveled at the huge billboard screens displaying advertisements of all sorts. Eytan had heard that there were digital billboards in Tokyo that could read a passerby's gender and age. Off the main thoroughfares sporting these technological wonders were ancient alleys bulging with tiny shops offering anything a tourist or Tokyo native could possibly want.

The taxi dropped them off at the Neko Café, the spot where Ehud Amar had arranged to have the promised materials delivered. The two agents were ushered to a small room, where a strange figure—a cross between a teenager and a manga doll—asked them to take off their shoes and wash their hands. While Elena obliged with no trouble at all, Eytan fumbled. He wasn't used

198 David Khara

to any ceremony of this sort and felt like a Barnum and Bailey clown. It took him a few moments, but once they were both barefooted and clean-handed, Eytan and Elena exchanged bows with their host and were allowed to go through the curtains leading to the restaurant.

Here they were presented with another rather un-ordinary sight.

The place was littered with cats. Felines pranced freely among the happy diners, who were sitting at tables and on large cushions on the floor.

The two agents found an inconspicuous spot in a corner of the room. Elena was grinning. She had teased Eytan that he would look even larger in Japan, and, indeed, young women all around were throwing glances at her colleague. The Israeli agent was usually able to adapt to any situation, but this was totally out of his comfort zone. Nonetheless, he sat quietly in his chair, his hands in his lap, even when two cats jumped up and began strutting across the table, their tails in the air.

Instead of a traditional menu, the waiter brought them a touch-screen tablet that displayed the food and drink selections—in English, to the agents' relief. Their orders were sent to the kitchen with the press of a button. Distracted by the whole atmosphere of the restaurant, Eytan and Elena had almost forgotten their reason for coming.

Two minutes later, bowls of soup and meat arrived at the table. One of the cats, a Chartreux, glided over to Elena's bowl of meat and started purring. Elena looked at it for a minute, then put a bit of meat in her palm and presented it to their furry guest. It delicately nibbled the gift and looked to her for more. The other cat sidled over to Eytan and did the same. He offered

THE SHIRO PROJECT 199

this cat some meat. The sensation of its small, coarse tongue licking his fingers clean put a smile on his face. It wasn't long before Eytan and Elena had given most of their food to the creatures. In exchange, the cats allowed the pair to stroke them.

"What geniuses came up with the idea for this place?" Elena wondered aloud as she gently pulled on her cat's ear.

"People in Tokyo are always working. They're never home enough to have pets. So they need a place like this."

He stopped talking when he realized a small black briefcase had been placed at his feet. Either the person sent from the embassy was extremely stealthy, or this eccentric restaurant had robbed him of his usual alertness.

"My elite secret-agent senses have been neutralized by a horde of harmless four-legged felines," he said, with a grumble. "An embarrassing episode like this could ruin my reputation."

He picked up the briefcase. "It breaks my heart to interrupt such an adorable scene, but we have to go."

"Okay," Elena replied without taking her gaze off the coiled ball of fur in her lap. She was rubbing its shoulder blades as it purred and looked ready to doze off.

Eytan rolled his eyes. "All right, let's go!" he ordered.

She groaned but sneaked in several more seconds under the guise of finishing her drink. Eytan was about to tell her again when his phone rang. It was Avi Lafner, his doctor friend at the clinic.

"What does he want now?" the giant growled as he indicated to Elena that he'd be waiting outside. She nodded and turned back to the felines.

Once on the sidewalk, Eytan, answered the call. He opened the conversation with a dry and unwelcoming, "What do you want?"

"Wow, is that your standard greeting?" Lafner asked.

"Sorry, Avi, but I'm in a hurry."

"You're always on the go. I just need two minutes of your time. I have the exam results on your stubborn little prisoner."

"I'm listening. Lay it on me."

"With you, I thought I had seen everything. But boy, was I wrong."

CHAPTER 29

No longer in any rush to see Elena emerge from the restaurant, Eytan paced the sidewalk as he listened to Avi Lafner's analysis of the exams performed on the unconscious woman after the struggle at the clinic. The doctor concluded with his diagnosis.

"You're sure about these results?" the agent asked.

The question was rhetorical. The physician enjoyed a good joke, but he took his job seriously.

"A hundred percent. So why didn't you tell me about the woman's condition? Did you really think I wouldn't be able to make the connection between the two of you?"

"You know exactly why I didn't say anything."

"By now you should know I'm not some Frankenstein wannabe like that demented scientist. One day that fact will make it through your thick skull. In any event, her affliction is spreading quickly. I don't think she has much time left."

"What about my serum? Could it work on her?"

"I already thought about that. The answer is no. She wouldn't survive. The gene mutation in your body makes your metabolism move faster at certain times. Basically, you heat up, and the serum cools you down. Her metabolism, on the other hand, is in a constant state of above-normal activity, like a pot of water on simmer. The serum wouldn't do anything for her. And

I don't know of any cure. At least, none in my area of medicine."

"So what should I expect now?"

"Ah, I take it you're still with her?"

"If I told you, I'd have to kill you."

"You're such a jerk. Well, it's hard to predict the progression in a patient like Elena. But it could start with a loss of consciousness, followed by vision problems, headaches, and mood swings. Nothing fun about it."

"So how much time does she have?"

"Most people with Elena's condition die within two to five years of diagnosis. But like you, she is far from the average patient. And since I'm unable to observe her more closely, I'd need a crystal ball to give you any more insight."

Eytan saw Elena coming out of the coffeehouse. She had a smile on her face.

"Thanks, Avi. I have to go. I'll keep you updated." The agent ended the call and put the phone back in his pocket.

"Any updates?" she asked cheerfully.

"No," he replied in a tone that was much more distracted than he intended.

"Oh, come on. What's with the dagger eyes? I was only a couple of minutes late."

"I wasn't making a face."

"It looked to me like you were."

There was a moment of awkward silence.

"Guess we're not going to quibble like an old married couple, are we," Elena said.

Eytan held up the small briefcase and changed the subject.

"This time we'll be traveling light. We'll have to be deft."

THE SHIRO PROJECT 203

Two hours later, they were cruising north, toward Utsunomiya, in a rented car. Their destination was the delivery address Elena had retrieved. According to the GPS, the trip would take about two hours. Eytan drove while his partner divvied up the modest weaponry provided by Ehud Amar. They had two Beretta pistols with silencers, the giant's weapon of choice, along with a round of magazines for each gun, and a knife with a serrated blade.

"Yep, we're definitely traveling light," she quipped.

Eytan was too absorbed by his thoughts and too focused on the road to respond.

They arrived on the outskirts of Utsunomiya in the early afternoon. They veered off the main route and drove through a suburban-looking area where tall apartment buildings were interspersed among single-story homes.

Eytan spotted a large sign, parked on the side of the road, and hurried out to examine it. Below the undecipherable Japanese characters was a short passage in English: "The Shinje Foundation Children's Summer Camp."

"I'm only asking this as a formality, but are you sure of the address?"

"Without a shadow of a doubt," Elena replied. "It's a perfect hideout for a secret industrial complex, don't you think?" She winked at Eytan.

Eytan conveyed his agreement as he massaged his shoulder, injured at the Consortium's BCI research center in Belgium. That place had been well hidden under an abandoned racetrack.

In a heavily wooded park at the foot of a mountain, the campsite extended as far as the eye could see. A simple fence marked the perimeter. A gate and a small booth occupied by two guards appeared to be

204 DAVID KHARA

the facility's only defense. Eytan and Elena did a quick tour of the surroundings. They detected no other security measures, not even a surveillance camera.

"This just gets better and better," Eytan said. "A few days ago we were raiding a Czech army camp. Now we're invading a children's camp. This isn't a mission. It's a circus show."

"Stop complaining. At least now we know that our terrorist hypothesis is correct. Using kids as a cover, perhaps even worse, as human shields—that says a lot about our man, don't you think?"

Eytan nodded. "All right, I've had enough. No more procrastinating. Let's go in." He started toward the gate.

"And what's your plan?" Elena asked, chasing after him.

Ignoring the question, Eytan approached the door of the little guardhouse. The two Japanese men stood up simultaneously. They came out and bowed in unison. Eytan returned the courtesy.

The more muscular of the two barely cleared the giant's shoulders. The stranger's unusual size seemed to fascinate him and make him uncomfortable at the same time. But he wasn't able to take in the sight for more than a few seconds. His good-afternoon greeting, "konichiwa," morphed into a high-pitched cry as the hulk grabbed him by the neck and lifted him off the ground. Eytan then pummeled the puny guard in the head.

"Ouch," Elena said. She launched a right hook at the second dumbstruck guard, who was sent flying into the window of the booth.

"What a shame," she said, rubbing her fist. "They were so polite."

"I bowed back, didn't I?"

"Good point."

Eytan dragged the two comatose men by their feet into their cubicle, while Elena meticulously searched it. No video surveillance monitors. No weapons. She did find a roll of duct tape, which she handed to Eytan so he could restrain the still unconscious victims. In a small wall cabinet, she also discovered a dozen keys labeled in Japanese. She grabbed them and stuck them in a pocket of her leather jacket.

With the guards secured, Eytan studied a wall map of the campground. It depicted the topography and features with the help of many simple icons. Apparently the camp offered a full range of activities from sunup to bedtime. The facilities included a swimming pool, tennis courts, a gymnasium, and even a riding stable.

The amenities were in the part of the camp that seemed to be farthest from the mountain overlooking the site. Eytan was puzzled by three icons of children's faces affixed to buildings that looked like cabins.

"I'm not buying any of this," he muttered. "If you had to build a laboratory filled to the brim with lethal substances, where would you put it?"

Elena thought for a second as she studied the map.

"In this spot," she said, pointing to an "H" at the foot of the mountain. A heliport—perfect for a quick getaway. Plus, it's not close to the kids."

"I'll go check it out," Eytan declared in a tone meant to discourage any challenges.

"What do you mean I'll go? What about me? What's my job?"

"You'll stay here and warn me if you see or hear anything strange. And don't try any funny business."

"No funny business," she repeated. "So how am I supposed to warn you, boss?"

The giant squatted and turned over the tied-up guards. He unstrapped two walkie-talkies from their belts and handed one to Elena, who frowned as she took the device.

And with that, he left the booth.

"Morg, why are you leaving me behind?"

Elena's voice revealed more than confusion. Eytan heard disappointment and even sadness. Lafner's words had been spinning in his head ever since they had left Tokyo. He could not allow the woman to take any heedless risks. The Kidon operative respected her efforts, but she was off the mission. On top of that, he couldn't figure out how to tell Elena about her illness and inevitable death.

He stopped but couldn't bear turning around and seeing her face.

"It's not that I don't trust you. This is just best for the mission and best for you."

Eytan headed off at full speed. He knew there were many forms of combat, and it took just as much courage—perhaps even more—to fight a debilitating illness as it did to take on a human enemy. He repeated this in his head over and over.

CHAPTER 30

Eytan had set off with a plan to get to the heliport as quickly as possible, but he now found himself wandering along pathways that meandered through the wooded and picturesque grounds. The blocky seventies-style buildings stood out conspicuously in these natural surroundings.

Eytan was taking this route not because he was interested in the scenery, but because he wanted to confirm a hunch that was growing stronger with each step. At the moment, this camp was deserted. There were certainly no children, and it appeared that the grounds and buildings were being worked on. Many of the structures had scaffolding. It was the same for the sports facilities. Two tennis and basketball courts with freshly painted lines attested to some of the changes awaiting the camp's residents.

Eytan was sure of one thing: the person in charge of this place was going all out for the sake of the children. The whole thing just didn't add up.

Eytan continued to head north, toward the mountain. He walked past one last structure, probably a cafeteria, and came to a row of trees. Pushing aside the branches, he was confronted with a chain-link fence that was about twelve feet high. Eytan guessed that this was the heliport site. Through the fence, Eytan saw another seventies-looking building, but this one was much more run-down. He estimated that the structure, atop concrete pillars, was about three hundred by sixty feet. A set of metal stairs led to the front door, which was chained shut.

Eytan bent down and picked a few blades of grass. He chose the largest one and placed it against one of the wires and listened for crackling. He folded the blade in half to make it shorter and once again placed it against the wire. Still no shock. Confident, Eytan hoisted himself over the barrier. Once on the other side, he unhooked the walkie-talkie and called Elena.

"I'm at the heliport."

"You took your sweet time."

"I wanted to make sure the camp was empty. It is."

"Fabulous." Eytan could hear the sarcasm in Elena's voice. "We knocked out those two guys just so I could play gatekeeper. I love it."

"Look, I'm sorry I had to leave you behind. But I'll explain later. Right now I'm going to check out a building I found near the landing zone. I'm sure it's no coincidence it wasn't on the map."

"Wait for me. I'm bored to death back here."

"No, I'd rather have you as backup in case something happens. The place looks deserted, and it probably is. But it also looks like there's some work going on, and I don't want us to be around if any construction crews come back. Better safe than sorry."

"Got any other clichés up your sleeve?"

"That cliché has saved my life on more than one occasion. Gotta go. Keep me posted if anything suspicious happens."

"If anything happens," Elena said and snorted. Eytan could almost see the snarky face she was making at the walkie-talkie.

Eytan hooked the device back onto his belt and trotted across the heliport. At the foot of the stairs, he took a quick look around. He crouched and made his way up the steps. Once at the door, he lifted the chain and examined it. The metal links were secured with a padlock. It looked new. Interesting.

A well-targeted bullet jolted the lock off the chain, and a simple shoulder shove was all that it took to open the door.

Despite the boredom, Elena remained on the lookout. She was fixating on Eytan's words: "best for the mission and best for you." He wasn't the kind of guy who just said things for the hell of it. So what did he mean by "best for you"? She could have thought about it more clearly, but the throbbing in her skull was becoming a killer headache. Staying still was making her antsy. And she was definitely sick of being Officer Baldy's personal assistant. Two more days and he'd be asking her to schedule his appointments.

A distant noise in the sky caught her attention. It was a repetitive beating, and it was getting louder by the second.

"Shit," she cursed as she grabbed the handheld transceiver. "Morg? Can you hear me?"

All she got in return was static. She checked the device. It appeared to be working.

"Eytan, if you can hear me, get out of there fast. A helicopter is coming."

Again, the same crackling noise. Elena cursed the device and threw it on the floor. She picked up her gun and darted into the campground.

Eytan entered a bright rectangular room with large windows. Its modest furnishings consisted of white plastic tables and chairs. To his left, a long tiled hallway leading to a metal door was lined with rooms. Eytan

210 DAVID KHARA

explored them, one by one. He discovered an inactive cold-storage chamber, a library whose shelves were devoid of books, and a large space in which six black desks were stacked haphazardly on top of one another. Then came a video surveillance room equipped with five monitors, all turned off.

Another room was filled with glass and wire cages. From there, a door led to what looked like a dissecting room. Boxes filled with scalpels, pliers, and other surgical instruments were perched on stainless-steel tables. He saw electron microscopes on workstations pushed against the wall. How charming, he thought. A wretched odor of household products—a pungent mix of disinfectant and dust—permeated the space.

He no longer doubted Elena's findings. He was willing to bet a lot of money that this place was hiding the answers they were looking for. But he still needed to know if the lab's exploits belonged to the past, present, or future.

Eytan walked into a spacious room that felt less industrial than the others. The closed window blinds let only thin beams of light filter into the space. What must have been an office contained boxes marked with the letters S and W. The gray walls had lighter areas. Eytan figured pictures had hung in these spots. And, indeed, there was one still hanging on the wall. It was a yellowing photograph of a nice-looking woman in a white lab coat. Her blond hair was tied back in a bun, and her arms were crossed. In the background, Eytan could make out a sign with the American eagle and a partially covered inscription with the letters FO and CK.

He lingered on the image for a moment. He was convinced that the man or woman who owned this property was preparing to relocate. Therefore, the lab

THE SHIRO PROJECT 211

had served its purpose. All he needed to find now was the nerve center. Eytan left the office and headed toward the heavy metal door at the end of the hallway.

He peeked through the small window in the door. He was getting closer. He pulled on the handle and entered the rectangular space, which appeared to take up all the square footage on this side of the building. The door shut behind him. There was a phone on each wall and a camera in every corner. Taking up much of the area was a large rectangular unit planted in the middle of the floor. It was so big, the remainder of the space served as a corridor around all four sides.

Each side of the unit had a large observation window. The unit was divided into smaller rooms, most of which contained biosafety cabinets, incubators, motorized centrifuges, and other lab equipment. Eytan saw the yellow biohazard symbol. Now he knew for sure—this was a P4 laboratory. White protective suits hanging in a cloakroom underscored his conclusion.

Just as he was beginning to inspect the setup, the ceiling lights went on. He heard a dull click coming from the door he had just gone through. Eytan's hand went for his gun. Hugging the wall, he started edging toward a corner where he could crane his neck and get a better look at the door.

A man was watching him through the glass window. Eytan could make out only his piercing blue eyes. There was no use in playing cat-and-mouse. He stepped away from his hiding place.

Eytan could now see that the man was holding a phone up to the window. Eytan responded by picking up the receiver of a nearby wall phone.

"You're not Japanese," the man said in perfect English.

"Good call," Eytan responded, trying to get a better look at his phone partner.

"SVR? NATO?"

"Nope and nope."

"Ah! So you must be working for the lab we stole the viral strains from. Well, I'm sorry to disappoint you, but they aren't here." Above him, Eytan heard fans coming on. He knew they were extraction fans. "Sorry, I don't have time to chat," the man said. "If it's any consolation, it'll be a quick death."

The man hung up and left. Eytan was already finding it hard to breathe. Relying on his above-average lung capacity, he drew a deep breath, filling his body with as much oxygen as possible before a vacuum was created in the corridor.

Crouched against the fence separating her from the building Eytan had described, Elena watched the helicopter as its blades spun. Two Asian men, fighting the blast of air from the blades, were doing something to the concrete supports. After a few minutes, they rushed toward the heliport, as two other guys, one of whom was Caucasian and carried a briefcase, came hurtling down the stairs. All of them hopped on the aircraft and took off immediately.

She waited for the helicopter to drift far enough away before jumping the fence and sprinting toward the entrance to the building.

Holding his breath, Eytan emptied his supply of bullets against the window in the door, which was beginning to crack. He banged the butt of his gun against it as hard as he could. His lungs were burning. His vision was starting to blur, and his arms were cramping. Each new assault on the door had a little less force.

The glass wouldn't budge. If only he had his trusty shoe explosives.

Elena rushed up the steps, driven even faster by the newly discovered threat to the building's supports. The room she found herself in was empty and showed no signs of struggle. There wasn't any time to go exploring. A loud, repetitive pounding caught her attention, and without thinking, she dashed toward the dark corridor to her left. She ran down the hall and stopped cold in front of the obstacle separating her from Eytan. She was transfixed by the scene before her. Behind the glass window filled with spidery cracks, her partner was staring back at her with a contorted face.

She snapped out of her trance and furiously pulled on the door handle. It refused to budge. She looked around and spotted a boxlike fixture on the wall. It had two lights, one red and the other green. Naturally, the red light was blinking. She kickboxed it until it broke off the wall, revealing a weave of cables. She grabbed hold of them and ripped them out in a bundle of sparks. The door made a loud click, and she opened it immediately.

Eytan fell into her arms. It took all her strength not to topple backward under the weight of the massive man. She lowered him gently to the floor. The giant inhaled such a huge breath, she couldn't imagine where he could put all the air. His face flushed with color as he regained his senses.

"Come on. We have to get out of here, and fast!" she said, helping him to his feet. "They attached explosives to the pillars under the building. Hurry!"

"You go first!"

Elena ran through the hall, with Eytan hot on her heels. The first explosion went off behind them,

214 DAVID KHARA

followed by another. The building began caving in. Elena started running even faster, taking the Kidon agent by surprise. He doubled his efforts to catch up and escape the collapsing roof.

Without slowing, Elena grabbed her gun and emptied her bullets into the window at the end of the hall. The glass shattered. As she prepared to leap through the opening, she felt an arm wrap around her waist and a huge hand shield her head. Then a brusque shove lifted her off the ground and propelled her forward like a torpedo. As two more blasts finished off the building, Elena soared through the air, securely strapped to Eytan's chest. She had no idea how long they stayed suspended. The landing wasn't as bad as she anticipated. When she opened her eyes, she realized why.

Eytan lay sprawled under her. He had cushioned her fall and absorbed almost all of the shock of the landing. She glanced over her shoulder at the spot where the laboratory had stood. In its place was a heap of rubble. A cloud of gray dust was drifting into the air. She looked back at the giant and saw that he was wincing and holding his ribs. She rolled over to take her weight off him.

"You disobeyed my orders," Eytan grumbled.

"I'm the only one who's allowed to kill you."

Eytan laughed so hard, he was soon moaning and coughing. With great effort, he sat up and examined his jacket. The flying glass and metal had shredded the right side.

"Shit," he said.

Elena stood up and extended a hand to Eytan, who took it. She had to use all her strength to avoid toppling over as she helped him rise to his feet. Upright again, he rubbed his ribs under his T-shirt.

THE SHIRO PROJECT 215

"You're not banged up too badly are you?" she asked.

"Nothing that won't heal," he replied.

"I tried to warn you about the chopper, but my message wasn't getting through."

"What did you see?"

"There was a light-haired dude in a suit with three men who looked like bodyguards. They got into the helicopter and took off.

Breathing heavily, Eytan was walking a few steps behind her. "You should have kept them from leaving," he said.

"Need I remind you of my limited intel? How could I make that kind of decision? To be safe, I stuck with my partner. I may be a bitch, but I'm loyal."

"Thanks for getting me get out of there," he said. "But we're in a bad position. Our opponents know they're being followed, and we've lost their trail."

"I don't agree. By now they're assuming you're dead, and that's a huge plus for us."

"I think we might actually have another clue."

"Which is?"

"In one of the offices, I found boxes that had the letters S and W written on them. There was also a photograph of a Caucasian woman."

"Okay, a new lead. The S and W might be initials. We'll have to see if there's a Western-sounding name with those initials somewhere in the Shinje archives."

"It's a long shot, but I'll take anything at this point."

They crossed the campground at a slower pace than Elena would have liked. Eytan was breathing with difficulty, and he was keeping his right arm close to his chest. The landing outside the destroyed lab had taken a toll. Elena offered to inspect Eytan's wounds, but he waved her off.

216 DAVID KHARA

They left the campground and returned to their car. Wheezing, Eytan rested against the passenger-side door before getting in. Elena headed toward the driver's side, ready to slide behind the wheel.

"One second," he said. "I need to tell you something."

"Can't it wait until we're on the road?"

"No, it can't."

"Okay, what is it?"

"When you came out of the cat café, I wasn't mad that you had taken your time. I was preoccupied. I had just found out why you lost consciousness in Tel Aviv."

"Yeah, I was wondering why that happened. But why are you bringing it up now?"

"Because before I didn't know how to tell you. You have a brain tumor. According to Avi Lafner, it's because of your mutation. It's a side effect that's specific to the mutagen they gave you."

Elena felt like she had just been sucker punched. She turned around and leaned against the door with her eyes closed. The random blindness she had experienced in the Czech Republic, the headaches… Suddenly she was a child again, in that hospital bed. She replayed the conversation between her father and Professor Bleiberg and remembered how it had filled her with hope.

Then came the injection and nearly intolerable pain that had her practically knocking at death's door before finally offering her a new life. All these years she had believed that she was free of the physical constraints that bound everyone else to a normal life span and relatively limited capabilities. She had assumed she was above the laws of nature. Like Patient 302, she represented a turning point in human evolution. All that to learn that she would be spewing her guts after endless hours of chemotherapy and spending the rest of her days in a palliative care unit.

"That's why I wanted you to stay back earlier."

Fighting tears, she opened her eyes.

"You didn't want to be dragging a dead weight, is that it?"

"No. Even if you were half as good as you are now, I'd still want you to be my partner. I didn't want to... I mean... I'm sorry."

"How long do I have?"

"Not long."

Elena took a deep breath and wiped her cheeks.

"We'd better get to Tokyo, then. We shouldn't be wasting any time. You take the backseat. You'll be more comfortable."

Eytan started to get into the car, but Elena, who had come over to his side, stopped him.

"I don't want any pep talks, Morg. And no endless negotiating or banishing me to the sidelines. I'm finishing this mission with you. If I have to go down..."

Eytan didn't say anything. For people like them, this was the only way to go.

The only acceptable way.

CHAPTER 31

The mood in the car was dreary. Elena, unaccustomed to driving on the left side of the road, was uncomfortable behind the wheel. In the backseat, Eytan was holding his side and stewing. Between the disastrous turn of events at the lab and the news about Elena's health, he felt like everything was spiraling out of control. His worries had multiplied exponentially since the start of the mission. But his biggest concern was Eli, who was still being held captive. The only bright spot was the thought that his enemies believed he was dead. This would give him the element of surprise once he caught up to them. If he caught up to them.

No, things were definitely not unfolding the way he had hoped. He winced at the pain in his side.

Elena veered out of the fast lane and took an exit to a sleepy residential neighborhood outside Tokyo. She parked in a secluded alley, turned off the engine, and climbed into the backseat.

"Stop acting so macho, and raise your arms," she commanded.

Eytan obeyed, opting to avoid the woman's temper, as she clearly had no intentions of backing down. She took off his khaki T-shirt and discovered the extent of his injuries. A constellation of glass and metal debris studded the entire side of his body. He had to be in unbelievable pain, given the amount of shrapnel lodged

THE SHIRO PROJECT 219

in his flesh. She placed her fingers on his stomach and felt him shudder.

"We're going to patch you up before we do anything else."

"It's nothing," he lied.

"You won't get very far like that."

"We have no idea where we're going anyway."

"All the more reason to get you cleaned up before figuring out our next move. I saw a supermarket on the street we just passed. I'll walk over and get what we need. Don't move."

"That won't be a problem," he said, trying to keep his face from twisting into a grimace.

Elena slammed the door shut and headed toward the store. She examined the products in the pharmacy section and settled on a first-aid kit, hoping it would provide just about everything she needed. She also bought a set of tweezers.

At the register, she found herself stuck between a businessman in a black suit that was at least one size too small and two postpubescent boys who were listening to their MP3 players. Elena wasn't about to waste any effort trying to make sense of this strange world. The man in front of her was skimming the Tokyo Shimbun. Towering above the suit by a good half foot, she had no trouble reading over his shoulder. She just wished she understood Japanese.

She could still understand the pictures, though—at least one of them—and a second later, she snatched the paper from its owner's hands. Ignoring his indignant cries and the stares of the other customers, she ripped out a page.

"Shut up," she screamed. "Does anyone here speak English?"

220 DAVID KHARA

The store employees and customers looked at each other in confusion. The short businessman raised a timid finger. Elena held out the page for him to read. She pointed to the article accompanying the photo. "Translate," she said.

The Japanese man began reading the article.

"Hai. Boss Shinje Corp., Hirokazu Shinje, died, age ninety-three years. His assistant, Sean Woodridge, becomes boss Shinje Corp. Will attend opening of Shinje Conference Center in Shinjuku neighborhood tonight."

She pointed at her impromptu interpreter's watch.

"What time?"

He scanned the text for a moment and nodded when he found it.

"Nine o'clock."

Elena searched her memory for the right expression as she stood before her smiling new friend. She recalled a scene from a movie she had seen years earlier.

"Arigato," she said, bowing low with her hands on her thighs.

The man bowed in return, as did the half dozen other people still gathered around them. Before getting caught up in a nonstop ballet of bows, Elena threw a wad of yens on the counter and fled the store.

She rushed to the car. There, she found Eytan as white as a ghost. She had barely sat down before showing him the article from the paper.

"We caught a break!" she cried triumphantly.

He tried to skim the page but couldn't. Elena was waving it as though it were a freshly minted college diploma.

"If you say so," he said, leaning his head on the back of the seat.

"The guy in the photo. S.W. Sean Woodridge. That's who I saw leaving the lab and getting into the

THE SHIRO PROJECT 221

helicopter. And even better, I know where he's going to be tonight!"

"Excellent news," he mumbled in a shaky voice. "If it wouldn't be too much trouble, could you get this shit out of me? My fingers are too fat."

Elena moved the front seats up as far as they would go to give herself enough maneuvering room in the back to tend to Eytan. She opened the first-aid kit and took out a few cotton pads, some bandages, and antiseptic ointment. She unwrapped the tweezers, which she proceeded to disinfect.

"All right, Morg, strip down," she ordered.

Eytan looked like he was about to laugh, then winced in pain. He removed his T-shirt and lifted his right arm as high as he could to expose his wounded side. Elena slid her fingers across his abs toward the injured area. She felt him shiver.

She focused on extracting the numerous shards and bandaging the man. There was no better way to distract herself from the giant's smooth, hairless skin and his shallow breaths, which were blowing softly against her face. Perhaps this was the last flesh she'd ever have the chance to touch. She tightened her grip on the tweezers and concentrated on the task. Anything to keep from imagining herself lying naked next to this man.

"Do you always wear the same clothes?" she asked as she plucked out the first piece of glass.

"Yes. I mean not exactly the same. I have a bunch of duplicates," he said.

"How's that? You allergic to fashion? Can't find the right size?"

Her heartbeat was picking up, and she was breathing more quickly. Trying to extract a piece of metal, she pushed it in deeper.

222 DAVID KHARA

"Hey! Careful!" the giant protested.

"Sorry."

"I don't have anything against fashion. I try to stay practical for professional reasons. Plus, my clothes have sentimental value. It's a long story."

She stopped prying and continued her work. It took her another ten minutes or so.

"There, I'm finished," Elena announced proudly as she affixed one last adhesive strip to his side. "You'll be feeling better in no time."

She backed out of the car. A gust of cool air rushed in. Eytan attempted a few shoulder rolls.

"You're a miracle worker," he said, straightening himself. "Thanks."

Elena carefully closed the kit as she leaned against the car. "Does Mr. Macho have a weakness for nurses?"

She immediately regretted the comment. Eytan replied with a high-pitched laugh, which he was quick to suppress. He got out of the car and practiced flexing to check his muscle range. He walked to the back of the vehicle, opened the trunk, threw in his torn clothes, and took out his backpack, from which he retrieved a perfectly folded T-shirt and jacket—both identical to his previous outfit.

"The chameleon has recovered his skin?"

"Exactly," he replied as he adjusted the shoulders and sleeves.

Eytan glanced at the digital clock on the dashboard.

"Well, it's almost seven o'clock. I suggest we pay a little visit to the Shinje Conference Center for the nine o'clock dedication.

"That's where we'll be meeting our target?"

"Yep."

"Get behind the wheel. I'm going to count our remaining ammo supply." Now, if only her headache would go away.

CHAPTER 32

The last rays of sunlight reflected on the Shinje Convention Center's glass façade, making the enormous circular building sparkle like diamonds. The structure dominated the park, which had been redesigned in honor of the opening of the facility. All expenses on the Shinje Corporation's dime, as indicated in several languages on a conspicuous plaque. An island of tranquility in the midst of heavy workweek traffic, the park had a tea house, a restaurant, a greenhouse, several lakes, an English garden, and an elaborate French garden. The conference center was just off the main entrance.

The crowd was dense and indifferent. Eytan and Elena were skeptically reading the giant marquee on the shiny glass and steel edifice.

"No surprise here," Elena said. "The center's inaugural event is an international conference on virology."

"Between the fancy-pants specialists from around the world, all the government officials, and reporters who are here to cover the event, you've got everyone needed for a lovely bloodbath," Eytan replied.

He was already focused on three refrigerated trucks bearing the logo of a French celebrity chef. They were parked at the service entrance. Deliverymen were unloading carts with food trays and hauling them into the building as a few bored-looking security officers nodded them through the doors. No decent shindig

THE SHIRO PROJECT 225

would be complete without a caterer and inevitable finger foods, Eytan thought.

"If you were planning on taking out all these people in one spot with the help of a virus, how would you do it?" Elena said.

"Something simple, like circulating it through the ventilation system."

"Easy and effective."

"All we have to do now is find the HVAC equipment," Eytan said. He was feeling charged. He rubbed his hands together and continued. "Did you know that Tokyo has the most three-star Michelin restaurants in the world?"

"Oh yeah? Uh, no, I didn't know that. What the fuck does that have to do with anything? Pardon my French."

He grinned at Elena.

"So what do you have up your sleeve now?"

"You really have to start eating better," he whispered in her ear before starting down the sidewalk that led to the service entrance.

Eytan and Elena walked to the back of the third truck, a few steps behind a young delivery guy. The latter jumped in to collect the remaining food supply. Eytan hopped in behind the man. Elena partially closed the back doors to obscure the scene from any onlookers. A few seconds and some thumping sounds later, the agent's hand emerged. He was holding a mini mille-feuille, which she swiped from him, laughing.

Eytan and Elena loaded the two carts that were left and walked past the security officers, who ignored them as they entered the building. The glittery glass-walled lobby was already bustling with activity. A number of guests were making their way to two massive see-through staircases that led to a mezzanine floor.

An employee directed them away from the lobby and toward double doors concealed from public view. The two agents did as they were instructed and entered the kitchen, where waiters and waitresses were juggling trays and ice buckets. In the middle of the frenzy, Elena and Eytan dumped their load on a stainless-steel counter. Elena tapped a waiter's elbow and asked how to get to the basement. Distracted and anxious to get his food out to the guests, he nodded toward another door.

Elena gestured to Eytan to follow her, and they both vanished amid the general indifference.

The basement was a labyrinth of cramped hallways that rumbled with the sounds of machinery. A network of pipes ran along the walls and ceiling, forcing Eytan to crouch, which triggered a new round of pain.

"Since we each have only one bullet left, it'll be hand-to-hand combat," Eytan said as they entered what he presumed was the building's nerve center. "There's a good chance our opponents will be launching their attack as soon as all the guests have gathered for the speech. We'll wait for them here."

The building's electrical panels, as well as the heating, cooling, and ventilation systems, were in this space.

"I hope we're right about their plan," Elena said. "How are your injuries holding up?"

"Badly, but fortunately for us, it's our force of will that makes us indestructible," Eytan replied. He tried stretching his arm toward the ceiling and grimaced.

"Amen" Elena said.

Half an hour later, two men in jeans, T-shirts, and sneakers burst into the room, pushing a large cart loaded with metal barrels marked "chromium." The tall Asian men stopped in the middle of the room and started unloading the cargo.

THE SHIRO PROJECT 227

The duo became a trio with the arrival of a new member, who was stockier than his counterparts. They exchanged a few nervous words. An authoritative command from the hallway put an end to their discussion. The three henchmen stood straight in a military manner and saluted the last arrival, who was wearing a three-piece business suit. Elena recognized the Caucasian man with the harsh face and square jaw. He was Sean Woodridge, whose picture she had seen in the paper. Elena guessed he was in his early sixties, although he still had a full head of blond hair. The small wrinkles in the corners of his blue eyes accentuated the depth of his gaze. Over six feet tall, he radiated natural authority as he addressed his undeniably devoted troupe in perfect Japanese.

Eytan chose this moment to emerge from his hiding spot in an adjacent storage area stocked with brooms and cleaning supplies.

"Surprise!" he yelled with open arms. The four men glared at him as though he were a ghost. The shocked looks on their faces disappeared as Woodridge opened his mouth to speak.

"You should be dead," he said.

"I should be," Eytan confirmed, smiling.

"Only a minor setback."

Woodridge barked another order in Japanese. The three minions rushed toward the giant. Two of them had barely taken a step, when each received a strong kick to the head. Hanging from a well-secured cold-water pipe in the ceiling, Elena had been waiting for the right moment. She jumped to the ground, swayed a little, caught her balance, and advanced toward the two guys, groggy but very much in the fight.

Eytan's assailant, handicapped by his opponent's almost unfair height advantage, attempted a jab. It caught air, but a second later the man successfully landed a kick to Eytan's injured side. Despite the pain, the agent trapped the attacker's calf with his right arm, placed his right hand against his thigh, and swept him off the ground. Eytan released him, and the man went sailing into the electrical panel. One eliminated from the equation.

Out of breath, Eytan watched as Elena tried to dance around the two remaining henchmen, who had formed a barrier to block the way to their boss. He was now on the run.

"He's getting away!" Eytan yelled.

When she turned toward him, he could tell by her pale complexion and fatigued eyes that she was waning. She pulled out her gun and pointed it toward the runaway.

"Aim for his legs," Eytan ordered.

Elena lowered her weapon, but one of the men kicked it and threw her off-target.

Woodridge grabbed his back and slowed to a trot. Nevertheless, he continued down the hall and soon disappeared.

"Go get him," Elena said. "I'll take care of the others."

Her voice sounded shaky, but she managed to whack the two Japanese men with a series of swivel kicks and cleared the way for Eytan, who quickly darted through the opening.

CHAPTER 33

With great concentration, Elena had vanquished her adversaries. She had taken the first man out by kicking him in the stomach. The second one had required an additional flurry of punches and a devastating upper-cut, which had cracked his neck. With sweat dripping down her face, she relished this victory. But it was bittersweet. Was it because she had become aware of her own weakness? Because she dreaded ending her life stuck in a hospital bed? Illness and old age were agonizing prospects. Thanks to the miracles of science, she had escaped the first one, and she had hoped to avoid the second. Her current state, however, proved that nature would always win out. How ironic.

The pain bore into her skull. She felt nauseous and was having trouble navigating the basement hallways. Then she pictured her partner's scarred back, which she had glimpsed in their hotel room in Prague. As intense pain shot through her head, she grasped the meaning of Eytan's words. *It's our force of will that makes us indestructible.* She pressed on, placing one foot in front of the other and leaning against the walls to keep her balance. At last, she arrived at the door leading to the outside. She wanted to finish the job once and for all.

Eytan was running as fast as his injuries would al-low. He could feel the blood soaking his T-shirt, and it only increased his desire to destroy Woodridge. The latter had left the building and had scampered into the mazelike hedges in the park.

The Kidon agent disregarded the pain that hindered his breathing a little more with each stride. The narrow and convoluted walkways, however, soon caused him to slow down. He found it difficult, even impossible, to orient himself in the labyrinth of paths and plantings. Eytan doubted that Woodridge was doing any better. He decided to favor caution over speed, hoping he would find the way out before his opponent. And anyway, running too fast would only worsen his bleeding and render him even weaker.

Eytan finally came to a circular area about two hundred feet in diameter. A fountain set off by a double row of cheery trees was at the center. Water flowed from a tall piece of granite into a finely sculpted basin flanked by stone benches. The layout was perfectly symmetrical, giving the space a sense of timeless balance. The splashing of the water, coupled with the swooshing sound of wind flowing through the hedges, created a hypnotic musicality. The person who built this sanctuary was clearly a worshiper of nature, beauty, and peace. Woodridge was standing in front of the water feature, his back to Eytan, his arms dangling at his sides and his briefcase at his feet. He turned to face the agent, who was advancing slowly.

"Exquisite, isn't it?"

Eytan stopped a few feet from him.

"I don't think I've ever seen anything so soothing," replied the giant, the nose of his weapon pointing toward the ground.

"I'm surprised that a goon from a deadly secret-service organization would appreciate a place like this," Woodridge said, directing his own weapon toward

Eytan, who then raised his gun and pointed it at the man.

"And I'm just as shocked to see a terrorist marveling its beauty."

"I'm not a terrorist," Woodridge said. He was visibly offended.

The reaction underscored Eytan's theory about the man.

"And I'm no goon," the giant said.

"Have we gotten off on the wrong foot?"

"You tell me."

"Perhaps it's time for proper introductions? I'm Sean Woodridge, recently named president of the Shinje Corp. after the passing of Shinje-san. Before that unfortunate event, I was his second-in-command.

The man finished his sentence with a perfectly executed Japanese-style bow.

"Eytan Morg, Metsada agent, Nazi and war-criminal hunter, responsible for stopping your biochemical attacks."

His introduction was not accompanied with a bow, which brought a smile to Woodridge's face.

"Metsada?"

"Let's just say it's a special ops division of Mossad. But I'm actually here on a personal mission. It would take too long to explain."

Eytan sat down on one of the stone benches. He opened his jacket to reveal the blood smeared across the right side of his polo. In a similar fashion, Sean exposed the wound inflicted by Elena's gunshot and sat down on the opposite bench.

"To be honest, I didn't think your intentions were purely terrorist in nature," Eytan said.

"The Children of Shiro is anything but a terrorist group."

"I figured as much after searching your office."

"And what brought you here?"

"The black-and-white photo taken at Fort Detrick. Did you know you look exactly like your mother?"

"My father told me that all the time," the man said.

"And he was right," Eytan concluded. He stretched out his legs and allowed himself to relax a bit.

"So tell me, Sean. What or whom are you seeking revenge for?"

CHAPTER 34

HARBIN, UNIT 731, AUGUST 1945

The bitter taste of defeat and dishonor was mixed with the unbearable smell of burning flesh, as corpses were heaved into the device named "the barbecue." The attack on Manchuria by the soviets, combined with the atomic bombing of Hiroshima and Nagasaki, had spread fear throughout the military ranks and provoked panic among the leaders of Unit 731.

Although Hirokazu Shinje welcomed the end of the war and consequently all activities at Shiro Ishii's research center, he hoped to flee the grounds before it fell into the hands of the communists.

A chaotic frenzy had ruled the complex since Mr. Ishii's announcement of the Japanese surrender. They had been ordered to destroy all evidence of experiments conducted in the previous nine years. Documents were being systematically incinerated, along with the remaining test subjects.

With his arms folded across his chest, Hirokazu watched pensively as the rusty furnace consumed the last of his papers. He had no regrets about the scientific work he had accomplished. His studies had paved the way for numerous vaccines against tropical diseases and would most certainly resonate favorably within medical communities around the world in the looming postwar era. And anyway, unlike his colleagues, who got drunk at night and slept with enslaved prostitutes in the unit's whorehouses, he had dedicated his evenings to designing prosthetic limbs for the mutilated guinea pigs.

Hirokazu had lost his haughtiness. He was no longer a self-assured, arrogant graduate. He had lost any desire to compete with his fellow researchers, who had the fanatic desire to please his majesty, Lieutenant General Shiro Ishii. Their absorption had pushed them to commit extreme acts that were more barbaric than scientific, all the while stabbing their colleagues in the back.

When the medical team was ordered to gather on the main square across from the executive-staff offices, rumors of an Ishii-mandated collective suicide began to circulate. Those who knew him well, especially Hirokazu Shinje, understood how little this immoral man cared about the code of bushido. Ishii's priority had always been his own advancement and glory. Not in a million years would he choose to die for the sake of honor.

And as Hirokazu expected, suicide was never mentioned during the impassioned speech delivered to the troupes.

As the explosive blasts started reducing Unit 731 to a pile of rubble, everyone on the square promised to stay silent about the tests and the tactics. No matter the circumstance. No matter the price.

The future would prove to Hirokazu that it was easier laying down the law than abiding by it.

TOKYO, 1946

Hirokazu's highly anticipated homecoming was traumatic. Radio propaganda, the only source of information for troops occupying China, had not relayed the extent of Japan's bleak condition.

Napalm bombs had ravaged the wooden houses in the old city of Tokyo, demolishing most of them. It was reported that more than one hundred thousand people had perished in the flames of a single air raid.

On January 1, 1946, the newspapers had published a message from Emperor Hirohito. He was renouncing his divine status. His nationalist generals had thrown the country into a senseless war. Faced with the humiliating reality that the country was not destined for world domination, all of Japan was paying the price.

After a short stay with his parents upon his return home, Hirokazu started working at a hospital in Tokyo. The facility welcomed the esteemed physician like a godsend. It was drowning in a flood of sick and wounded patients—victims of mutilations, burnings, and malnutrition. He was never short of work and spent his days and many nights consulting with and operating on patients.

The fatigue and long hours were nothing compared with his experience in Unit 731. Memories of it haunted him in his sleep. As time went on, however, Hirokazu started to heal and make amends. He began to enjoy the true purpose of medicine. Little by little, his unease subsided, although it never disappeared.

In the spring, he started seeing a beautiful nurse at the hospital, Iyona. Their relationship blossomed quickly and seemed to have all the right ingredients for marriage. He loved the woman with all his heart. She was petite yet brave and had the most adorable

236 DAVID KHARA

little nose. But Hirokazu never brought up the subject of marriage. And as he stalled, much bigger events intervened.

Over the course of the year, newspapers, which were now controlled by the Americans, had reported incessantly on war crimes committed under General Tōjō Hideki's authority. The papers followed all events leading to the trials of regime dignitaries. Some men of honor had killed themselves before they could be arrested. Others collaborated, shifting blame to their subordinates. This cowardly behavior rattled Hirokazu.

Then one day, he came across an article that referred to the atrocities committed by Unit 731 in Manchuria. According to the report, everyone who had worked under Shiro Ishii was considered a criminal. The truth flashed before the eyes of the doctor, who felt years older than his age: Unit 731 had tarnished the entire human race. It was decided. If he had to go on trial, he would confess and accept the judges' verdict.

What was the point of marrying Iyona and condemning her to premature widowhood?

NEW YORK, 1983

The seminar was taking place in a four-hundred-seat lecture hall, but no more than two dozen people were scattered throughout the room. They listened in horror to the fate brought upon the people of Harbin. In a shaky voice, Hirokazu detailed how plague-infested fleas had been released over whole villages. With his notes in hand, he recited the number of deaths caused by these experiments and others. By the end of the war, the final tally was estimated at three hundred thousand to five hundred thousand. Hirokazu proceeded to recount how human beings were frozen for frostbite experiments, how they were cut open while still alive, how their unborn children were mutilated in the name of science. Determined to atone for his crimes, he spared nothing as he outlined the details of Unit 731 to the courageous few who were spending two hours with him, plunged deep into the last circle of hell.

Three critical events over the course of thirty years had pushed Hirokazu to go on a worldwide tour to expose the realities of Unit 731. First was Ishii's clandestine sale of Unit 731's medical discoveries to the US intelligence service in a successful attempt to save his own skin. Money, immunity, and obscurity—the perfect recipe for absolution.

Next came the revelation of this agreement by US government officials during a taking-out-the-garbage mission designed to unmask the wrongdoings of previous administrations. They were doing this under the guise of starting fresh.

The final event was Iyona's death. She had succumbed to pneumonia in the winter of 1982, thirty-four years after Hirokazu and she had married. Hirokazu had never been brought to trial or even charged. During their marriage, the couple had tried to become parents, but Iyona could never carry a baby to term. Eventually, the physical and emotional trauma led them to abandon the idea altogether.

The year they were married, Hirokazu started a company that manufactured orthopedic prosthetics. Initially, he marketed his products in Japan. But his company soon took off, and it wasn't long before he was distributing his prosthetics around the world.

During their thirty-six years together, Hirokazu had never told Iyona about his past in Manchuria. He

238 David Khara

didn't want to return to that dark place, and he was scared that Iyona would stop loving him.

So now, as a widower, he was testifying out in the open for the whole world to hear. He assumed that his status as the founder of a global company and an example of a modern Japan whose corporate frenzy had swept away all militant and—even worse—nationalist leanings would draw hoards of spectators and reporters. But in this Cold War era, few seemed to care about what he had to say. More often than not, he found the lecture hall practically empty. The press didn't seem interested either.

The New York conference marked the end of his tour, but he planned to lead other campaigns, as his road to redemption was a long one.

At the end of his speech, he opened up the floor to the audience. It was really a formality, as he hardly ever received any questions. As he expected, his offer was met with silence, and the lecture hall emptied. One young man, however, remained. Not only did he stay, he also stepped up to the stage. The fellow towered over Hirokazu. He had a natural poise, underscored by broad shoulders and the confident manner in which he held his head. But these characteristics were less striking than his blond hair, which seemed to shine brighter than the summer sun. He didn't appear to be any older than thirty. And now he was doing a timid but promising ojigi.

"Mr. Shinje," he said with just the right amount of respect. "Thank you for delivering such a fascinating lecture."

"Thank you for coming to hear it," Hirokazu replied, bowing in turn. "I'm surprised to see someone as young as yourself interested in this subject."

"It affects me on a personal level."

THE SHIRO PROJECT 239

"How so?"

"My mother worked at Fort Detrick in the late fifties. She was killed under circumstances classified as top secret for reasons of national security. The incident was exposed in published documents detailing the biological experimentation program led by the US from 1950 to 1970. At the same time, the American government made public its collaboration with Unit 731's most prominent scientists. My mother was killed by a biological weapon in the building where she and her team worked. Rumor has it that the researchers at Fort Detrick were following up on Shiro Ishii's work. I'm convinced that..."

"I see," Hirokazu said.

"According to my father, she would sometimes meet with German and Japanese scientists for the purpose of her mission."

Hirokazu froze. The full responsibility he and his brother scientists bore had materialized in front of him, in this young man, the living proof that all actions had consequences, even long after those acts were committed. The sharp pain of guilt clawed at the Japanese man's soul.

"And what's your career plan?"

"I recently graduated from law school, sir, where I specialized in commercial law. I speak several languages. I'm working on my Japanese."

It would take a long time for the boy to master all the nuances of the culture, but he certainly knew the Japanese way of making a request without flat-out asking. His desire was obvious.

"Perhaps you are curious enough about my country to try your hand at a professional experience there?" Hirokazu asked.

240 DAVID KHARA

"Certainly, sir. I would like to immerse myself in both the Japanese language and the Japanese culture."

Nice response, Hirokazu thought.

"Wonderful. I should be able to find a place for you. I'm looking forward to seeing what you can do."

"Thank you, sir," the young man replied. He gave his future employer a perfect bow.

"I don't believe I caught your name."

"I never gave it to you, sir. My name is Woodridge. Sean Woodridge."

A PARK NEAR HIROKAZU SHINJE'S RESIDENCE, NORTH OF TOKYO

Only a small portion of his day was dedicated to business. At most, he would look over a few proposals from his board of directors. The years had flown by, leaving Hirokazu with a head of white hair, a deeply wrinkled face, and some brown liver spots. He used a wheelchair, but he considered himself quite healthy for his many years on earth. He had a youthful mind and a resilient body, and he had never been sick a day, even though his lack of sleep should have weakened his immune system. His business, meanwhile, was still quite successful, and he was married again—to a wonderful woman who was fifteen years his junior. It was enough to make any man happy. On this particular summer evening, he was gazing at the setting sun's reflection on one of his estate's tranquil ponds.

Why had he been blessed this way? Indeed, why had his former Unit 731 colleagues, also successful businessmen and government officials, been similarly blessed? Numerous companies—mostly pharmaceuticals—had benefited substantially from the research conducted at Harbin.

Hirokazu was proud of just one of his accomplishments: his foundation. Under the masterful management of his assistant, the foundation was making charitable contributions to organizations around the world that helped young victims of armed conflict. These organizations gave children the medical and educational assistance they desperately needed. As he waited by the pond, Hirokazu looked forward to meeting with his right-hand man to go over the final touches on his plans for their biggest project to date.

"Lovely evening, wouldn't you say, Mr. Shinje?" It was a familiar voice that Hirokazu was always glad to hear.

"Indeed. I'm trying to appreciate my remaining few."

"Don't say things like that. You're as solid as an oak tree," Sean Woodridge replied as he turned the old man's wheelchair around.

He sat down on the ground across from Hirokazu with no concern about getting grass stains on his well-tailored suit. He held a thick stack of papers that were threatening to fly away.

"How are the plans coming?" Hirokazu asked eagerly.

"It's all here, sir. Construction is almost finished. By the end of summer, our research center near Utsunomiya will be Shinje's summer camp and will welcome more than one hundred children. I've brought you maps and photos to give you an idea. We'll have a dedication ceremony together."

"I'm looking forward to it. I've moved up the dedication of our new conference center in Tokyo in order to be at the camp for the opening."

242 David Khara

"I'm sure the children and the staff will be delighted to see you. However, I'm afraid I have some bad news."

Hirokazu nodded and waited for his second-in-command to continue.

"One of our security people has informed me of a laboratory developing a genetically modified virus to be used for military purposes. I've taken care of it, sir."

Hirokazu sighed and looked at Sean with fondness.

"Are you sure that's the only solution?"

"Sir, you've traveled the globe, alerted the press, and faced criticism from your own people. You've done everything in your power to tell the world. But your bravery has been met with silence and contempt. If we don't act, who will?"

"I don't mean to contradict you, but are you really sure there is no other…"

Hirokazu's face was twisted in a grimace. The elderly man clutched his right arm. "My chest…" He tried to get up but fell forward instead.

Sean leaped up to catch his mentor and shouted for help. His male nurse, who had been sitting on a nearby bench, came running at full speed. By the time he arrived, Sean was holding the dead man in his arms and running his fingers through his hair. Hirokazu's eyes were locked on Sean's.

Sean picked up the dossier and slipped it under Hirokazu's wrinkled hands. He reread the title on the folder: "The Children of Shinje Summer Camp."

Sean let the tears wash over him.

The Children of Shinje was Hirokazu Shinje's legacy.

For his part, Sean Woodridge would give the world the Children of Shiro.

CHAPTER 35

Tokyo, 2010

Eytan listened closely to Sean Woodridge's story. Each and every word shone with respect and admiration for the person whom Sean called Shinje-san.

The two wounded men were calmly staring at each other. Eytan searched his pocket for his cigar case. He took it out, selected a smoke, and stuck it between his teeth.

"It could have been a beautiful story," he said as he lit a match.

"Yes, it could have been." Woodridge pointed at the Cuban. "Is this the appropriate place for that?"

"I can't think of a more appropriate place or occasion."

He held out the case to Woodridge, who accepted. A few seconds later, they were taking in the sweet vanilla aroma.

"Japan's surrender marked the end of World War II and the immediate transition into the Cold War," Sean said. "As a Mossad agent, you must be familiar with Operation Paperclip."

Eytan nodded. "Yeah. A bunch of German scientist were given jobs in the US after the war."

"The same thing happened here, around one man in particular."

244 David Khara

"Shiro Ishii, the boss of Unit 731," Eytan said.

"Exactly. Seeing as you've heard of the man, I'll skip over his long list of wrongdoings. Once the soviets arrived in Manchuria, all activity at the center was terminated, and shortly thereafter, Unit 731 was blown up by its own people. Ishii and his crew sold their research to the US. The Americans had become obsessed with the idea that the Soviets could get their hands on the research and use it to develop biological and chemical weapons."

"The two allies turned on each other as early as the Yalta Conference. Just two years prior, the Americans were sending Stalin supplies and raw materials. The Americans and the British even called him Uncle Joe."

"Yes, it's absurd. Ishii was a greedy crook and used the superpowers' mutual distrust to full advantage. Thanks to his deal with the Americans, he and his collaborators got off with a nice chunk of change and immunity. The US held up its end of the bargain, keeping the sensitive information secret until the nineteen eighties."

"I remember that. But all the same, the revelations didn't cause much of a stir."

"No, despite Shinje-san's best efforts. So I vowed to do everything in my power to keep such horrors from happening again. Whatever it took. In order to keep that promise, I created the Children of Shiro, an organization for those who had been abused by various governments in the past half century. The Shinje Foundation generously donated the money needed to train our organization's members. They were then assigned to problematic labs around the globe. They served as private watchdogs. Their mission was to alert us of any significant changes in the status quo."

"Which is what happened."

THE SHIRO PROJECT 245

"Exactly."

"So why the need to create your own labs and steal those strains?"

"We take weapons from evil people and use their own arms against them. The Russian authorities conducted nuclear tests on their own soldiers, while the Czechs were developing poisons and psychoactive drugs. Thanks to our intervention, they're now off their stride, focused on when and where the next disaster will occur. If it weren't for you, tonight would have marked the pinnacle of our activities. Alas..."

"So why these specific activities, as you call them, to achieve your goals?"

"You still don't get it, do you?" Woodridge studied Eytan's blue eyes. "And yet it's so obvious. We live in an image-crazed society. Men like you who are ready to throw a punch or draw a gun—you're living in the past. Fighting an enemy with metal and ammo isn't enough anymore. Nowadays, you need the power of the camera, as well. Nothing beats a media-friendly massacre covered incessantly by every single news outlet. So, in that respect, the Internet deserves a medal as one of the deadliest weapons out there. Know why? Because if you toss a victim to the wolves, the masses will lap it up. Toss hundreds of victims to the wolves, and they'll lap it up even more greedily. They'll devour any ludicrous piece of garbage, as long as they get pleasure out of it. Never once getting their hands dirty. These days, our conversations are filled with this kind of crap. And those who aren't interested, those who are more restrained, they're social outcasts. Reason is collapsing under the weight of emotion. Well, if people are begging for sensationalism, we're more than happy to give it to them."

246 David Khara

"And thus finish the failed mission Shinje set out for himself in the nineteen eighties. I see," Eytan muttered. He sighed and asked, "Did you think you could pull this off with no consequences? Were you willing to risk your own mentor's life? He was planning to be here for the dedication."

"I would have gotten him out in time. But it didn't matter in the end, because he died before we could open the center. To answer your first question, yes, I was prepared to do anything necessary to force the world powers to admit their crimes. The martyrs in Moscow and Pardubice are a testament to our determination. I wanted to ignite a global awakening, even if it meant taking innocent lives. This was my fate. And man must accept his fate. Trying to avoid it is delusional."

"Fate, the ultimate excuse. But it won't exonerate your sins. We're all responsible for our actions.'"

"I wasn't expecting you to understand."

"Ah, but Sean, I'm the one person who could actually understand you."

Eytan slowly removed his jacket and dropped it to the ground. He rolled up the right sleeve of his shirt to reveal the serial number tattooed on his forearm.

"Who are you?" Sean Woodridge asked, horrified.

"I'm what remains of a boy who was deported to Poland in 1940 by the Nazis. The very pseudo scientists you condemn conducted experiments on Jewish kids for over a year in hopes of perfecting the Aryan race. I'm living proof of their success and also their failure."

"What do you mean?"

"I survived. I ran away and joined the Polish resistance. Since then, I've devoted my life to hunting down Nazi criminals and bringing them to justice or, if I have no choice, taking them out myself. I'm their own weapon of destruction turned against them."

Sean was silent for a moment. Having delved into the dark depths of such horrors himself, he was not surprised by the story.

"So you and I are exactly the same," he said. Eytan could hear the note of vindication in his voice.

"We couldn't be more different. You sacrifice lives, while I try to save them. I don't let anger determine my actions. The ends don't always justify the means. If they did, we'd be no better than our opponents."

"It's not always that black and white. Do you know what MacArthur said in his speech after Japan surrendered?"

"What's that?"

"I know his words by heart. They disgust me. 'It is my earnest hope and, indeed, the hope of all mankind that from this solemn occasion a better world shall emerge out of the blood and carnage of the past—a world dedicated to the dignity of man and the fulfillment of his most cherished wish for freedom, tolerance, and justice.' Two years later, he approved Shiro Ishii's immunity."

"Enlightening."

"There you have it. I sought to condemn the cynical behavior of a few men so that the smallest number of people would suffer from their wrongdoings."

"I don't approve of your methods, Sean, as much as your motivations speak to me."

Sean Woodridge closed his eyes. The evening wind ruffled his blond hair. "This is a beautiful place to leave this life," he said softly. He was smiling wistfully.

"I've seen worse," Eytan replied. "But no one has to die today. Hand me your gun, Sean, and let's leave it at that."

Woodridge opened his eyes again.

"Don't worry about the barrels in the conference center. The virus has a short life span. In a few hours, it will be harmless. Inside my briefcase you'll find a set of envelopes. They hold all the information about the actions we've taken. It's up to you to decide what to do with it. Congratulations, Eytan Morg, you've completed your mission."

Before Eytan could react, Sean brought the gun to his temple and pulled the trigger.

Elena, now freed of her head pain, heard the gunshot in the park. She ran toward the sound and stopped when she spotted Eytan leaving the grounds. He was carrying a briefcase in his right hand. His left hand was tucked inside his jacket. He was holding his side and walking with great difficulty.

She ran up to him, offering to help. He declined.

"It's over," he said gravely.

"I took care of the guys in the equipment room. Did you kill Woodridge?"

"No. He accepted the consequences of his own failure," Eytan said.

"That guy was crazy, wasn't he?"

"Madness leads to desperation. Desperation leads to madness. And the victims become the executioners. We're living proof, wouldn't you agree? If only he had used a different method."

"'If only' could apply to us too," Elena said. She put her hand on the giant's arm. "At least we succeeded."

Silence fell on the park. Eytan inhaled deeply. Had they actually succeeded?

Desperation did lead to madness. It had happened to Sean. The Kidon agent saw the value in each life

THE SHIRO PROJECT 249

he took. Trying war criminals made sense because it brought awareness to the general public, Eichmann's trial was the most glaring illustration of this. But Woodridge was right about one thing. The fundamental values of community, solidarity, and equality were becoming lost in the world. People were focused on their jobs, the latest films, and their sports teams. Yes, they made a hue and cry over one particular outrage or another, but they quickly moved on. In reality, they believed in nothing. It made Eytan look like an idealist in comparison.

"Now what?" Elena asked.

"We need to make a choice."

The woman stared into the giant's eyes.

"Mine's already been made."

CHAPTER 36

NORTH OF SAN FRANCISCO, THREE DAYS LATER

Large black clouds hanging low in the sky meant a storm was imminent. A wet-smelling electricity filled the air. Eytan was leaning against the hood of his pickup truck, parked along the bank of a turbulent waterfall that plunged deep into a valley. The hillside was covered with trees that stretched as far as the eye could see and kept the spot safely out sight.

The agent's phone was glued to his ear as he fed the directions to Cypher's men. An hour earlier, he had sent them meandering over San Francisco's hilly streets to keep them off balance. Every so often, he glanced at incoming texts. Eytan had set up checkpoints along the way and was now getting updates from the band of informants he had recruited with a few greenbacks bearing the image of Benjamin Franklin. Formed that very morning, his team was composed of bums, store cashiers, a garbage man, and even a random driver whose car had broken down near the Golden Gate Bridge.

The last checkpoint message finally appeared. The text read: "Black Jeep Wrangler arrived."

"I told you Cypher would come through," said Elena, who had been waiting silently by his side.

Eytan covered the speaker on his phone.

THE SHIRO PROJECT 251

"Better safe..."

"...than sorry. Thanks, I've heard that one before."

Eytan gave her a snide smile and continued his guided tour. At last, they heard the sound of a fast-approaching vehicle. The four-wheel-drive SUV came into sight and parked on the other side of the river. A bridge spanning the river, which was about a hundred feet away, separated Eytan from Eli. Cypher, a mere messenger until this point, spoke up.

"Well, Mr. Morg. As promised, my men will be returning your friend safe and sound. I'm thrilled that our collaboration was such a success."

"I, for one, am happy it's over," Eytan said. "Is this the part where you ask me to come work for you?"

Cypher burst out laughing. "Exactly, Mr. Morg. Your intellect never ceases to amaze me."

"You already know my answer."

"Unfortunately."

"Don't be so greedy. Taking me on would be a double win for you. Not only would you be getting back your star agent, Elena, but more important..."

"More important?" Cypher asked. Eytan could hear the curiosity and excitement in his voice.

"Am I correct to assume that you used to run the Consortium's operations, making you responsible for security?"

"No secret there," Cypher replied. Now he sounded suspicious.

"That means keeping the lab strains secure was your responsibility. Your little playmates wouldn't have been very happy about such a serious breach. From what I know about the Consortium's methods, mistakes can cost a pretty penny. So you had to resort to extreme measures to fix the problem as discreetly as possible. Otherwise, it would have been bye-bye. True or false?"

252 DAVID KHARA

"Incredible, simply incredible. Well, you certainly helped me out of a jam. And that's the only reason I'm letting you have Eli Karman back."

With that, the SUV's doors opened, and two men in ties, black suits, and white button-down shirts emerged. Their getup made Eytan smirk. In this setting, the suits were entirely too conspicuous. And it would certainly be hard to fight in those things. This would work to his advantage if the situation came to that.

Surrounded by the watchdogs, Eli appeared from behind the car. He looked tired, and tense, but Eytan didn't see any bruises or other signs of trauma. He seemed to be okay.

Eytan grabbed a sniper rifle from the pickup's passenger seat.

"Go ahead," he whispered to Elena. "But no funny business. I'm watching you."

She stared at him with her head slightly tilted. A single bead of sweat rolled down her cheek and landed on her pale lips.

"I'm happy your friend is free," she said.

"He's not free yet. Now go!" He nodded toward the SUV.

Elena gave him a smile he couldn't quite comprehend. He didn't have time for that anyway. Eli was walking toward him from the other side of the bridge.

Eytan was locked in shooting position, staring at the black suits through his sniper scope. The same went for the shooter stationed next to the SUV. Eytan celebrated each slow step that Eli made toward him. No gunfire. No explosions. His friend's shoulders were hunched, and Eytan saw the fear in his eyes. Elena's nimble catlike walk, on the other hand, was surprisingly relaxed. The two captives crossed paths without exchanging even a glance.

THE SHIRO PROJECT 253

When Eli reached the pickup without a single hiccup, he grinned and went to hug Eytan, but the giant didn't budge.

"Get in the truck! Driver's side. Start the engine. Whatever happens, don't get out."

The giant's tone allowed for no questions. Eli slid behind the wheel of the pickup.

Elena stared into the face of each man. She had no idea who any of them were.

"Miss, get in. We're leaving."

"Did you bring me a weapon?" she asked.

"It's in the glove compartment."

She leaned into the passenger side of the SUV and opened the glove box. As she was taking out the gun, a man with dark shades and a buzz cut handed her a cell phone. Cypher wanted to talk to her. Signaling the sniper to lower his weapon, she walked away from the vehicle to take the call. He obeyed but stayed on guard.

"Elena, my dear. So happy to hear you've been released."

"Thank you, sir, for doing what had to be done."

"Of course, you know how much I value your talents. Those men will be driving you back to me. I'm anxious to hear the information you've gathered on our Patient 302."

Elena held the phone between her ear and shoulder, freeing her hands to check her weapon's bullet count.

"I'd like permission to do away with Eytan Morg, sir."

"Negative. I have other plans for you."

"In that case, I have some news."

"Is it important?" Cypher asked, intrigued.

"Yes, it's very important. I fucking quit, sir."

She threw the phone to the ground and fired a bullet into the thigh of the man standing closest to her. Then she snagged the sniper in both shoulders. Before the driver had the chance to draw his weapon, a bullet had been lodged in his arm.

Elena walked over to each victim and collected the weapons and ammo, which she tossed into the river.

Eytan had been watching the whole scene through his sniper scope. He opened the passenger-side door of the pickup and put his rifle and phone on the seat.

"Can we go now?" Eli asked restlessly.

"I have one more thing to settle," the agent replied as he shut the door.

He started toward the bridge. Halfway across, he stopped.

Elena had been checking the SUV for any remaining weapons. Assured that there were none, she walked to her side of the bridge, leaving the three wounded men behind.

"Coming back so soon?" Eytan shouted.

"I've been waiting for this moment for a long time," Elena yelled back. "I wouldn't miss it for the world."

She tightened her grip on her weapon.

Eytan opened his vest and took out a small handgun.

"Are you sure about this? We have options," he said.

Elena looked around. The treetops on the surrounding hills almost reached the clouds racing across the sky. Thunder rumbled in the distance. Most likely, the heavens were unleashing their wrath over San Francisco. Surging water was splashing against the bridge supports and misting the air.

"No, people like us don't have options," she said and sighed. "We both knew how this story would end."

He stared at her with unyielding eyes.

THE SHIRO PROJECT 255

"If you say so."

She lifted her weapon and pointed it at Eytan. But before she could steady her aim, she heard the crack of a gunshot. She brought a hand to her chest, stunned by her opponent's speed. A splotch of blood on her shirt swelled between her breasts.

A second shot caused her to lose hold of her gun and threw her against the steel guardrail. The giant watched Elena topple over the barrier into the vast unknown. He caught the sound of her body hitting the water.

Eytan put his gun back in its holster and returned to the pickup. He got in and told Eli to step on the gas. Just then, his phone began to vibrate. Eytan answered and heard Cypher breathing on the other end.

"She made her choice," the Kidon operative said. "I tried to stop her. No dice."

"I've lost a great deal in this affair." Eytan could hear the rage in the Consortium master's voice. The man's civil façade was quickly falling apart. "However, I won't be the only one to suffer. I didn't want it to come to this, Mr. Morg, but I'm going to make sure your life becomes a living, inescapable hell."

"I've escaped from hell before. I'll do it again. So you want to try and make me suffer? Be my guest. But you should know that I'm going to spend every day of my life hunting you down. And once I find you, I'm going to lodge a bullet between your eyes."

A long silence fell before Cypher replied.

"You went behind the back of your own intelligence service and assaulted agents from a NATO-member country. I hope you've enjoyed living in the shadows, because you're about to step into the spotlight. Tracking me will be the least of your worries."

256 DAVID KHARA

And with that, he ended the call. Frowning, Eytan put the phone down. The next time he'd speak to that man, he'd be the one putting an end to their conversation. Once and for all.

Eytan's jaw was locked tight, but his eyes were moist.

"I'm happy to have you back in one piece," Eytan said, looking straight ahead. He swallowed, trying to get rid of the lump in his throat.

"Yes, thanks for everything," his friend replied. The muscles in his face were beginning to relax. "We have a lot of catching up to do."

"You'd have done the same for me," the giant said.

"Well, with my arthritis and weak lungs, I doubt I'd have gotten the same results."

Eytan relaxed his shoulders, picked up his phone, and punched in a number.

"Is it just me, or do you spend more time making calls than a telemarketer?" Eli asked.

"Just two more. Both for good causes. But for the rest of the summer, I don't want to be anywhere near this thing." Eytan touched his friend's arm to put their conversation on hold as the person on the other end picked up.

"Branislav?"

"Hey, Eytan! How'd it go?"

"Perfectly. Please thank your wife and her friend from the special effects studio in LA. He did an excellent job. Even I believed it."

"I take it Elena really hammed it up," the journalist said.

"She didn't go too overboard. Her performance was actually pretty convincing."

"I know you're speaking from experience. Do you think you'll ever see her again?"

THE SHIRO PROJECT 257

"No, she wants to live on her own for the little time she has left. I understand."

"All right, Eytan. So see you soon?"

"See ya never, Bran. Good luck with everything."

Eytan ended the call. This time he was grinning.

"Can you tell me what's going on? I'm completely lost."

"You just had a front-row ticket to a staged showdown. We arranged the whole thing so the feisty Consortium member could leave her organization."

Eli smiled playfully. "I don't believe it. Eytan Morg, an accomplice to an elaborate lie?"

"Men lie, Eli. Women lie too. But guns always tell the truth."

He gazed at the horizon.

"More or less…"

As the wind started to blow harder, and the rain began to fall, Eytan gave Eli a cheeky wink.

The agent leaned forward, reached beneath his seat, and pulled out a leather briefcase engraved with the initials S.W. He placed it on his lap, opened it, and took out a dozen large manila envelopes.

"Do you mind stopping at the first post office we come across?" he asked. "There are some things I need to mail. But before we do that, we need to make that second call. I think Rose should have some news for us, Grandpa."

EPILOGUE

LANGLEY, VIRGINIA, SIX MONTHS LATER

The office looked like a junkyard cluttered with soda cans, sandwich wrappers, and copies of Variety, Entertainment Weekly, and Game Informer. A custodian's nightmare. They all avoided Ryan Martin's workspace like the plague. The Goliath-sized computer engineer was almost six feet five and weighed close to three hundred pounds. He figured his skills, which surpassed those of his coworkers, gave him the right to overindulge. Denied a secret agent's license to kill, he settled for a license to fill—meaning his space. And it had started out to be a nice one, much better than the cubicles in the communal area reserved for most of the CIA's computer and network surveillance department.

Ryan had been discovered by the agency five years earlier, while, as an MIT student, he was attending a seminar organized by a software and operating systems company. During a lecture on security breaching delivered by some bigwig, Ryan had fired off brilliant arguments that put the speaker to shame. His valid points were met with huge rounds of applause, and it wasn't long before corporate vultures were swooping in with job offers. Ultimately, however, he couldn't resist the lure of working for a covert government agency.

THE SHIRO PROJECT 259

In a mere six months, he had pointed out in highly detailed memos every single weakness in the internal information system, which he deemed "ancient, inefficient, and overcomplicated." He had been authorized to give all his attention to the development of new protocols. The IT department, often dumbfounded by his genius initiatives, was just happy to follow his lead and reap the rewards.

Ryan was living the dream. He had a fat salary, highly tolerant supervisors, and almost total job control. In addition, his job gave him lots of free time to tinker with his favorite hobby—actually his only hobby—testing new software programs.

Today's trial wasn't particularly exciting. It was part of a long-term big data analysis overhaul. Working on the theory that automation could always maximize task efficiency, he was running a program on all image files stored in CIA-agent cell phones. The software identified the places, documents, and people who appeared in the photos and moved them into the designated databases in order to streamline the classification and cross-referencing systems. To test it out, he went into the agency's recent unresolved cases and pulled up an image taken from the cell phone of former agent Bernard Dean, who had been executed by a bullet to the neck. The image—which happened to be sent by agent Jacqueline Walls from Switzerland—showed a three-quarter view of a man from behind. Without paying any more attention to the content of the image, Ryan had launched his search.

Over the course of several hours, tens of thousands of pictures, millions maybe, flooded the screen as the search attempted to find a match with the photo.

Just as Ryan was sinking his teeth into a panini sandwich dripping with melted cheese and Italian ham, the computer started playing the theme music from The Simpsons. Ryan was a fan of vintage television, and this was one of his many personalized settings.

Ryan wiped his greasy hands on a crumpled napkin and put his fingers on the keyboard.

The software had pulled up an image from the internal database. He enlarged the photo. It had been taken from a slightly elevated position in a gymnasium and showed the African American agent from behind. He was wearing a pair of tight shorts and a T-shirt embellished with an American eagle. It appeared that he was talking with a bald man in shorts and a long-sleeved polo. The scene itself looked harmless. The file's origins, however, less so. It was from a hodgepodge archive that contained documents from the early nineteen seventies. Ryan had installed the archive a few months earlier—a huge pain in the ass.

The file's caption read: "US Air Force Academy, Colorado Springs. Intergovernmental training program, US-ISRAEL. In photo: trainee Bernard Dean with instructor Eytan Morgenstern. June 1975."

Ryan assumed that the software had selected the image because of Dean. But the computer specialist soon realized that the program wasn't establishing a link with the young Dean but rather with the large fellow, Morgenstern, who was with him. His curiosity piqued to the max, Ryan got to work. He launched every single image-processing program at his disposal. Then he proceeded to spend the next half hour typing away with a grace and finesse that were quite unexpected for a man of his size. At last, displayed on his ginormous screens were the two photos, side by side.

Faced with the unbelievable results, he leaned back in his chair, his fingers knitted behind his head, and heaved a sigh so heavy, a pastry wrapper went flying off his desk. The display before him was simply astonishing. It most certainly explained why certain segments of agency intelligence had been kept off-limits to him.

"The truth really is out there," he thought to himself as he picked up his phone.

In memory of Edith and Valérie.

Thank you for reading The Shiro Project.

We invite you to share your thoughts and reactions on Goodreads and your favorite social media and retail platforms.

We appreciate your support.

About the Author

David Khara studied law, worked as a reporter for Agence France Press, was a top-level athlete, and ran his own business for a number of years. Now he is a full-time writer. Khara wrote his first novel—a vampire thriller—in 2010, before starting his Consortium thriller series. The first in the series, *The Bleiberg Project*, became an immediate bestseller in France, catapulting Khara into the ranks of the country's top thriller writers.

About the Translator

Sophie Weiner is a freelance translator and book publishing assistant from Baltimore, Maryland. After earning degrees in French from Bucknell University and New York University, Sophie went on to complete a master's in literary translation from the Sorbonne, where she focused her thesis on translating wordplay in works by Oulipo authors. She has translated and written for web-based companies dedicated to art, cinema, and fashion as well as for nonprofit organizations. Growing up with Babar, Madeline, and The Little Prince, Sophie was bitten by the Francophile bug at an early age, and is fortunate enough to have lived in Paris, Lille, and the Loire Valley.

About Le French Book

Le French Book is a New York-based publisher specializing in great reads from France. It was founded in December 2011 because, as founder Anne Trager says, "I couldn't stand it anymore. There are just too many good books not reaching a broader audience. There is a very vibrant, creative culture in France, and we want to get them out to more readers."

www.lefrenchbook.com

Discover more books from

Le French Book

Paris Homicide Mysteries by Frédérique Molay
An edge-of-your-seat mysteries set in Paris, where
Chief of Police Nico Sirsky and his crack team fight
crime in the French capital.
www.parishomicide.com

The Paris Lawyer by Sylvie Granotier
A psychological thriller set between the sophisticated
corridors of Paris and a small backwater in central
France, where rolling hills and quiet country life hide
dark secrets.
www.theparislawyer.com

The Greenland Breach by Bernard Besson
The Arctic ice caps are breaking up. Europe and
the East Coast of the United States brace for a tidal
wave. A team of freelance spies face a merciless war
for control of discoveries that will change the future
of humanity.
www.thegreenlandbreach.com

The Winemaker Detective Series
by Jean-Pierre Alaux and Noël Balen
A total Epicurean immersion in French countryside
and gourmet attitude with two expert winemakers
turned amateur sleuths gumshoeing around wine
country. Already translated: *Treachery in Bordeaux,*
Grand Cru Heist and *Nightmare in Burgundy.*
www.thewinemakerdetective.com

CPSIA information can be obtained at www.ICGtesting.com
Printed in the USA
BVOW09*0102090115

381778BV00003B/4/P